Every Day Doughnuts

Every Day Doughnuts

A Novel by

Patrice Adcroft

St. Martin's Press

EVERY DAY DOUGHNUTS. Copyright © 1992 by Patrice Adcroft. All rights reserved. Printed in the United States of America. No part of this book may be used or reproduced in any manner whatsoever without written permission except in the case of brief quotations embodied in critical articles or reviews. For information, address St. Martin's Press, 175 Fifth Avenue, New York, N.Y. 10010.

Grateful acknowledgment is given to the publishers for permission to reprint lyrics from the following: "Girls Just Want to Have Fun," by Robert Hazard. Copyright © 1979 Sony Tunes, Inc. All rights administered by Sony Music Publishing, 8 Music Sq. W., Nashville, TN 37203. Reprinted by permission.

Design by Judith Christensen

Library of Congress Cataloging-in-Publication Data

Adcroft, Patrice G.
    Every day doughnuts / Patrice Adcroft.
        p.   cm.
    "A Thomas Dunne book."
    ISBN 0-312-08139-1
    I. Title.
PS3551.D3974B3   1992
813'.54—dc20   92-25851
                                                              CIP

First Edition: November 1992

10 9 8 7 6 5 4 3 2 1

For my father and mother,
and all who were part of 1101 Wyoming Avenue

Contents

Every Day Doughnuts

T hings rise here. That's the purpose of this place, called Every Day Doughnuts. An eighteen-stool, five coffee-pot shop in Scranton, Pennsylvania. Not the prettiest stop in the greater Northeast, fancy taking a back seat to function. You can't always make a good doughnut and still look good. The process has its price.

In the shop's back, out of the customers' reach (but not out of sight) the doughnuts are made, three times a day. Four or five times if there's a sale. A baker begins the beguine with a brew, stirred up hours before the customers arrive, a potion concocted from water, yeast, and yeast food—the stuff yeast feeds on. Funny to think that yeast has an appetite, a yearning to be satisfied if the outcome's to be prize dough. Once, on a dare, the baker's helper drank down a cup filled with the liquid. Poor Wade Lowbar felt hungry and too-full at once, unable to choose between lunch table and bathroom. The baker had to send him home.

Four hours after the brew sets, the baker pours it into a bowl large enough to hide a small child comfortably. He adds more water and the doughnut mix (flour, eggs, milk, shortening, salt included). The liquid goes in first, followed by the solids, so that no single ingredient sticks to the vat. Instead, everything comes together. Oh yes. Here the baker adds more yeast. The early-morning waitresses get to witness this act while they're setting up, checking the napkin holders and the cash register.

Everything generally goes smoothly to this point. People can be taught to measure things out carefully, if that behavior doesn't come natural-like, and there's a clipboard on a barrel that holds a checklist with exact proportions. But after the first step, the temptation to slack off a bit, or to hurry the process, can strike. Over-mixing the ingredients, or using the wrong-size paddle weakens the gluten, the strength of the dough. An enthusiastic baker, or one distracted by his own dreams, is more likely to produce a faulty dough—a dough whose fibers are nicked or broken.

Usually the baker, his concentration regained, will discover the cracks while rolling out the dough or while cutting it up; but other times this weakness doesn't show up until much later, after the doughnut's been iced, or filled, or dusted with sugar. There are consequences: the doughnut's shelf life will be shortened. A passing waitress might spot the flaws for the baker, and save herself the customers' complaints. ("These don't taste fresh. Take them off the bill. I'm not made of money.") Evelyn Caine, an Every Day veteran, once claimed the dough was cracked, and stuck a spatula into the cutting table for emphasis. She caused such a ruckus that Mr. Raymond, the owner, darted out of his office to see for himself. The owner, once a baker (on the night shift, circa 1960), can always tell the quality of a dough.

After the dough is cut into uniform circles (really octagons, but the heat smooths out those rough edges), the flat, plain rings go into a proofer. First-time visitors always peer into this glass, airtight box, as do the delivery men and the doughnut packers. If tours of the shop were given (they aren't), this is where the schoolchildren would stop and point. No one can resist the box's steamy magic, the dance of heat and moisture and the unseen yeast.

If the temperature's too warm inside the box, the doughnuts swell quickly, squeezing the hole shut. That's called balling up. It may seem, appearances being what they are, that these doughnuts, puffed and proud, are superior. They do have a presence. But ideally, a doughnut should slip over your baby finger, sitting there like a fat ring. Pretty enough to bite into. Without the hole, the relief of air, the doughnut's flavor will suffer. And a customer will hesitate before ordering a second helping, pushing his coffee cup aside prematurely.

If the proofer's too cold, even by a few degrees, the dough oozes into the proofer's trays until the circles become all hole. Wrung out. A customer could jump through them, or so the joke goes. Workers call the misfits hula hoops, necklaces, fan belts. Hoops won't survive the fryer, the next leg of the journey. They don't have it in them to take the heat, to cook. Or if they survive, they'll stand out from the rest, thin attempts at making do. Along the way these doughy fan belts may end up on the floor, crushed by the bakers' boots, the packer's rubber soles, or the truckers' sneakers. More mess for the janitor. Doreen Raymond, the owner's daughter, home from the late shift and alone on her parents' porch, has tried scraping these stubborn ribbons from her plump nurse's shoes. There's no hope of it. In too deep.

When the proofing is finished, the rings are ready for the fryer. The temperature of the grease is 375 degrees, hot enough to cause a third-degree burn. That's happened a whole lot less than you would expect. Most people respect a flame, or fear it enough to pay attention. In the fryer, the doughnut's water evaporates, and the shortening is absorbed (vegetable, not animal). The customers eating fresh doughnuts, and the lady who buys the stales to feed her pigs, both appreciate this distinction; vegetable shortening, they claim, being the healthier.

Despite the intense heat, yeast doughnuts seldom burn. At worst they brown a little, the skin becoming a bit wrinkled. Weary-looking, but easily covered with icing. Around dusk, the shop has that same worn feeling. The waitresses do what they can to brighten it. On holidays, Marie Eden hangs banners, American flags, paper witches, plastic fruit. A girl from the school across the way paints snow scenes on the windows at Christmastime. Like an older woman decked out for a party, Every Day's age is still evident beneath the geegaws.

All in all, Every Day's a rather benevolent place. And the events there are small, insignificant, though not necessarily forgettable. In the back, the baker drops his doughs into the fiery bath, frys them, then pushes the screen filled with fresh baked doughnuts to the surface.

Things rise here.

Staying

Marie

Evelyn Caine started in. First she made the joke about a shotgun wedding. Marie failed to get it—she merely replied that her fiancé was not in the military. Then the boys from the Buick shop began teasing Marie about her fiancé's car. "You and that car have the same body," they said.

Marie Eden and her fiancé, Lester, were the talk of the doughnut shop, their names tossed across the green-speckled counter several times a day. People had said months ago that Lester fancied Marie—he'd boast that no one had her way with the Ring King, the machine that spat out hot cake doughnuts. Marie was especially adept at taking a wooden stick and flipping the doughnuts manually when the motor gave out at the end of the shift. Lester also lauded Marie's skill for placing a doughnut in the dead center of a wax napkin when serving a customer, making the presentation all the more memorable. But Marie, whose sole male companion for the whole of her forty-six years had been her father, believed that Lester was just plain talkative.

"I think he wants a lot more than talk," Evelyn had sniped.

What he wanted was nothing short of marriage, a concept that Marie had shaken from her brain at the age of eleven when the doctor advised the family that her foot—twisted since birth—would never be "normal." Despite the brace and the steel-plated shoe, it would always appear that she was at once coming and going.

Marie never dwelled on the foot, never read it as some kind of punishment, as her mother did. Her father, who had worked as the janitor at the school catercorner from the shop, said her affliction made her special, all the more dear. Marie couldn't see that, either. The foot was just there, something that had grown of its own accord, without regard for order. The less you asked from it, the better off you were. In a way it reminded her of the ornery Evelyn Caine.

The couple's first date went well enough: after Marie got off work she changed into an orangey-colored skirt with a matching vest and an ecru blouse. The collar on the blouse could be pulled into a big, flat bow or a tie, and Marie, in a moment of inspiration, twisted one end around the other like a long crueller, then anchored it with a pin in the shape of a poodle. The poodle, originally one of a pair, was gold, wore cat-eye sunglasses and hadn't seen the light of day since Marie's eighth-grade graduation. Though she had bathed the night before, the greasy sweetness that rose from the Ring King covered Marie's hair like a scented veil. Sniffing a curl's end, she reached for the baby powder and sprinkled it liberally on her head—the way the teenage girls who worked weekends would do before leaving the shop. Marie then combed the powder through gently, careful to preserve the waves she had pinned in last evening. When Lester cranked the bell, she was just dusting her cheeks with some Angel Face powder, another favorite of the girls. For Christmas Terri Kudja, who worked a split shift, had given her a small bottle of a cologne called Heaven Scent, and Marie tucked the clear vial into her bag, figuring she could dab some on during the movie.

Marie answered her door the way she believed her father would have, somewhat somberly asking Lester to please come inside. Since her father's death four years ago Marie had lived alone in half of the two-family house. She liked the way Lester never presumed to sit. He just waited politely and quipped, "You sure look attractive out of uniform." And when Marie put a light on in the living room before closing the door to leave, Lester simply said, "Now that's what I call smart."

While walking down the aisle in the movie house the heel of Marie's corrective shoe caught on an errant carpet thread. She didn't drop a single kernel of popcorn but Lester had seen her jerk forward slightly and then catch herself. Ushering her to the nearest empty seat, Lester glanced down at the foot long enough to prompt Marie to say, jokingly, "Oh my gosh. It was perfect earlier this evening!" Months later Lester would tell Marie that she won his heart with that remark.

Just once during the movie he took her hand. It felt as though she had slipped her fingers into a damp rubber glove, one that had dropped into the doughnut shop sink by mistake. Lester held her hand for a good ten seconds before letting it fall back into her lap. When he left to get a box of chocolate goobers she groped through her pocketbook for the Heaven Scent, then thought again.

Driving Marie home, Lester talked about the automobile club where he worked, putting together Triptiks for club members. He himself had been only to Florida, and had taken a plane, but he knew all of the southern interstates by number and the locations of the quality motels. Modestly, he confessed that he had a real gift for telephone talk.

"If you ever need any of that information—or if any of your girlfriends do—I'd be happy to help out," he offered as he pulled up in front of the small house. Before saying good-night he asked if she'd go out again. She nodded and turned toward the lighted window, feeling comforted, as though her father were waiting up.

The next day, when Lester came in the shop for his regular coffee and honey-dipped doughnut he winked at Marie, who was running a cleaning rag down the length of the coffee counter. She lifted each sugar bowl and napkin holder as she went so she wouldn't miss a spot. Marie returned Lester's wink, then sensed the sting of a blush rising from her neck into her cheeks which she'd once again blotted with Angel Face.

"What's with you?" Evelyn asked, plunging a bottle scrubber

into the bowl of a coffee pot, then giving the pot a second rinse. "You getting hot flashes?"

Marie turned on the heel of her good foot and went through the swinging door to the back of the shop and the Ring King, which Evelyn never had gotten the hang of.

On their fourth date Lester stayed until 1:57 A.M., according to the clock radio that sat on Marie's mantle. Marie hadn't been up that late talking to anyone since the night of her father's funeral. They'd gone to Gus Genetti's for the $5.95 special, lobster tail stuffed with crabmeat. Lester offered to let her keep the complimentary book of matches and she slipped the pack into her sweatercoat pocket to please him. Why on earth did people save matches from restaurants—even the fancy places? she wondered. Evelyn boasted of a collection she kept in an oversize brandy snifter displayed on her coffee table, explaining to Marie that it was a conversation piece. Marie's father had bought her mother an electric stove years ago, so Marie never had a reason to strike a light. She lit candles at church occasionally but even then always took the flame from another votive.

Holding the house door open behind her, she asked Lester if he would like some hot chocolate. He bit his lower lip as if chewing the answer over once or twice before letting it fall from his mouth. "I think that would be just fine," he told her.

"You make yourself comfortable—Les," she said, hesitating a little before shortening his name. "I'll heat up the milk. Bosco OK by you?"

He looked toward the TV set, a late-1950s model higher than it was wide, admiring how she valued older things, and then glanced back up at Marie. "Real good. Real fine," he answered, his hands riding his kneecaps.

Lester had made a mental list of the things he wanted to ask her, personal-like. Her birthday, for one; her favorite color, for another. "I keep up on those magazine quizzes," he explained with some confidence. "A color choice can tell you a lot about compatibility."

Marie placed the cocoa tray on the coffee table and seated herself just a few inches from Lester. "What does it mean," she asked, allowing Lester to take both her hands into his, "if you don't have one?" Then, seeing that her remark had somehow hurt his pride, she added gently, "I guess I don't go in much for what they say in magazines. It always seems they tell you exactly what they think you want to hear."

Lester struck the rest of the list from his head. For the remainder of the night, encouraged by Marie's affection, the way she had now taken his hands and cradled them in her own, he talked about his boyhood. He pointed to a quarter-moon of a scar that rose above his right eye. Marie had the urge to run her finger over it, lightly, but stopped herself.

"No need to say how cruel kids can be, I suppose," he began, pulling his eye away from her bad foot. "This happened in a snowball fight. One of the neighborhood kids dressed a stone up as a snowball and took aim." It had stunned Lester so, he explained, that he couldn't hold back the tears and the other boys let loose, pelting him with snow and ice. Then they fell to the ground, laughing.

"There was a little girl, playing in the yard, making a snow family. She yelled out to them, 'Don't you dare laugh. He's hurt.' For some reason, Marie, you remind me of that little girl."

The story moved her so that she drew Lester even closer. Six weeks later they were engaged. The ring had come from Steve Pronko, the Diamond Czar, on the boulevard in Dickson City. It was cut into the shape of a heart, and the salesman discussed for a full ten minutes which way the ring should rest on Marie's finger—with the bottom of the heart pointing toward Lester or toward herself. After Marie tried it on she warned Lester against making the purchase, but she was secretly delighted when "he sprung it on me, smack in the middle of dinner at Genetti's," she told the other waitresses. That night it was she who remembered to take the matches.

On the way home Marie asked that they stop at the lookout, a stone balcony at the top of Moosic Street that allowed a view of the entire city. Mostly kids used it for necking but occasionally an older couple would drive in, leave their car, and rest their arms on the granite shelf that surrounded the overlook.

"Nearly pretty as a picture—like one of those velvet ones with the lights," Lester commented. He pointed out Venus, then the Dipper. "I'd like to pin them on a wall for you to have, Marie."

Marie closed her hand over his index finger, cool from the night air. "Les," she said, laughing, "put your hand where it belongs." She drew it toward her blouse. It lingered there, motionless, much the way a tissue tucked into the bodice of her uniform would have. A breeze stirred and she caught the smell of Heaven Scent, though she couldn't tell for sure whether it had come from her or from one of the teenage girls parked behind them.

She asked Lester to stay the night. Neither had work the next day and they had planned to talk about the wedding details. Lester hesitated over his Bosco, letting the sweet steam rise up over his glasses like an evening mist. His shoes suddenly seemed too small for him.

"I want you to know," he began, working his finger against the rim of the cup, "how much I respect you, Marie. I don't know if you'd feel right if we didn't wait. And I don't want you doing something just because you think it'd please me."

The suggestion hung above them like a new moon, unsure of its place in the sky. Marie gathered her sweater around her and then lightly touched Lester's knee. Outside, a cluster of kids carrying a boom box sang along to Cyndy Lauper's "Girls Just Want to Have Fun." Marie stood up to hear the words more clearly:

> Oh mother dear we're not the fortunate ones
> Girls just want to have fun

She looked at Lester to see his response to the serenaders. He was struggling to stay awake, his head wobbling on his shoulders.

> Oh daddy dear you know you're still number one
> But girls they want to have fun.

The words dangled like a necklace in Marie's head and she smiled and said softly, "I wasn't asking just to please you. I was hoping it would please me."

She lifted the cocoa tray from the table and walked to the kitchen. For fifteen minutes she let her hands soak in the warm dishwater. Then she painstakingly dried the cups, saucers, and pot. When she called out, "Les," only the sound of a car passing by reached her. Lester had removed his jacket and, using it as a pillow, had carefully laid himself out on the couch. He shivered in his sleep. His tie, which he'd loosened a tad, hung toward the floor like the pendulum on a human clock. Marie had never noticed how gray his skin was, particularly the skin on his face, and as she thought to herself, he's old, the taste of her own heart filled her mouth. But instead of putting out the light and going up to her room, she wedged herself into the space between his feet and the end of the sofa.

The position was damned uncomfortable, even before he kicked her. The sofa's metal innards nipped at the small of her back and her bad foot started to go numb. She had jiggled it, trying to free the foot from the brown weighted shoe, when Lester, disturbed by the movement, whacked her in the stomach with the heel of his Hush Puppy.

"Lester," she whispered, catching hold of the offending foot and rubbing his ankle between her hands. "Honey, you're here with me."

He fell back into his stupor without uttering a sound. She sat with his feet anchored in her lap for three full hours, reasoning that he might awake. His lips and nose quivered now and again and more than once he swiped at his face. The noises from the kitchen—a burp from the sink, the grating buzz of the fridge—helped her mark the time. When she could bear the discomfort no longer, she pushed his feet forward as if she were passing through the turnstile at Food Fair and got up. Here was Les, in her house, asleep on the sofa, unaware of her, the night, the way the light cast its own gray glow on the carpet and walls. He somehow had managed to draw a circle of life around himself, one she couldn't enter. Marie felt end-of-the-world lonely, a human fragment made all the more invisible by the presence of another.

* * *

9

Marie liked the sex part. Funny, considering that she'd rarely thought about it since adolescence, when a seventy-eight-year-old great uncle offered to "take care of her" (meaning her virginity) one night as she was on her way to the bathroom. She had slept in the tub with the door locked. Marie always ignored Evelyn Caine's descriptions in "living color" (Evelyn's words) of the scenes from the romance books or the occasional X-rated movie shown on cable.

Lester was shy, but his body was as comfortable as an old pillow that has given itself to its owner's shape. Not for an instant did she think that the act was sinful or that they were wrong not to wait until after the wedding. Marie saw each night together as something whole in and of itself, a pleasant surprise that you were half expecting, like presents on your birthday.

Conscious of appearances, Lester handled the affair with an awkwardness he mistook for savvy. He'd park his car around the corner, in front of the school yard, and then creep back through the alley so that no one from the automobile club—or from the doughnut shop, he'd say to Marie—could talk.

"You and I may think it's only natural, given our feelings, but you just can't count on other folks' understanding," he told her.

The shop front, which was long and narrow with floor-to-ceiling windows, sometimes got difficult for Marie. If she had to travel from one end, where the doughnuts were showcased and sold by the box, to the other, where the coffee-bar sat, trying to quickly serve customers on either end, she was likely to trip over the bad foot as it swung wildly, propelled by her extra effort. Once she had ended up flat on her face and told the customers as she slid along the waxed floor, doughnuts in hand—a mighty save—that she was thinking about a career in baseball. Immediately afterward, though, she sought out the Ring King, which only the customers who planted themselves in the corner, next to the cigarette machine, could view.

That same day, Lester brought a few AAA buddies into the shop to meet Marie. With much apology he asked the people sitting in the corner if they would move, so he could wave to his fiancée. The three men settled their back ends on the stools and ordered coffee and cream-filled doughnuts from Terri Kudja, who brought them a "new" doughnut to sample (Terri was forever reinventing the doughnut), and the trio watched Marie standing over the bath of hot oil. She urged the rings of dough along, keeping their formation perfect. Finally looking up, to stretch her neck a bit, she spied Lester waving, gesturing to his pals. Terri was pouring refills, which meant, Marie deduced, that they'd been observing her for five to ten minutes. She found it a strain to smile.

A month before the wedding date the waitresses threw Marie a bridal shower. Evelyn insisted on hosting the party, her attempt at taking charge, and she even dragged home the cardboard from which she fashioned a wishing well. Each guest was to buy a different herb or spice—cinnamon, sage, thyme, curry—wrap the tin, and drop it into the well for Marie to take home. For party favors Evelyn got her cousin who sold Avon door to door to donate two dozen cologne samples—tiny glass vials with tips nearly as thin as a needle. Each of the guests was also to bring a dish, her specialty. The only thing Evelyn asked: that all of the food be white.

Marie hadn't been to Evelyn's apartment previously and guessed that something was afoot when Evelyn "de-manded" that Marie stop off one Saturday after she'd worked a half shift. Evelyn had a chime instead of a bell (she had saved up) and Marie could hear it trill merrily in the cool autumn air even though Evelyn lived on the second floor of the yellow stucco house. The porch furniture had been removed except for one chair. Here sat a scarecrow—a hat, plaid shirt, and pair of old pants stuffed with the leaves from the chestnut tree that sheltered the front yard.

"It's open," Evelyn called from the top of the staircase. "Hurry up."

The girls had decorated the small, rectangular living room with paper bells and bows. Perched on one arm of the loveseat was Doreen Raymond, the daughter of the doughnut shop owner; Evelyn hovered above her. The night-shift waitresses were cross-legged on the floor. Two of the teenage waitresses stood by the

11

kitchen door and a favorite customer was on the couch. The others waited in folding chairs, knees pressed together. A small pyramid of gifts had been built on the coffee table, just behind the wishing well. Marie scraped a bubble of chocolate icing from the skirt of her white uniform as her coworkers clapped.

"I see I'm color coordinated," she said, motioning toward the white plastic tablecloth and the spread of cauliflower crudités, chicken strips, marshmallow salad, and angel food cake.

The women played two games. For the first, called How Well Do You Know the Bride? they all answered a set of questions the way they believed Marie would answer. During the second, Alphabet Dream House, each guest received five letters and had to furnish the rooms with items whose names began with those letters.

"Bedrooms first," said Evelyn, arranging the letters *C, H, V, M,* and *T* in front of them. "Canopy bed, hope chest, vanity"—here the girls all said 'oooh'—"mahogany desk, and Tiffany lamp."

Terri Kudja, next in line, made the best of her lot. "H, P, R, I, F. Hmm. Hamper, photograph, r-rag rug, ivory coverlet," she announced.

"F," said one of the teenagers. Terri gave a triumphant hoot. "Futon."

"What?" came the reply from a half dozen.

"Futon. A Japanese mattress," she explained, frustrated.

"Now girls," said Evelyn, "that's why we have our dictionary. Look it up, Terri. Find it for us."

Marie distracted them for a moment. "How about this," she said. "W—waterbed."

Terri closed the book. "Futon's not in there," she said. "But they exist."

Again Marie intervened. "As a matter of fact, Lester and I considered one," she lied.

At the end of the game the women voted on the best dream house—and the one most likely to resemble Marie and Lester's. Evelyn Caine came in second both times. ("I wasn't even trying," she told Doreen.) In between they all sipped Dixie Cups full of sparkling wine.

Only the waitresses from the night shift drank heartily, though Marie was doing a fair job of keeping up.

"I think Lester's really—cute," said Doreen, who had spent one semester away at a junior college and returned after a tragic breakup with the food service director. "And he really honest-to-God cares about you, Marie. He's not just in there for the short haul."

Marie nodded in agreement and lifted a series of measuring cups from its box. Evelyn asked for the name of the donor—she was making a list of who gave what. It was then that Marie felt the wine taking effect.

"I wish," she said, bending over, trying to keep the words safe between them, "that you wouldn't."

"All the etiquette books recommend that the hostess record each of the gifts and the giver. It's a courtesy to the bride-to-be," Evelyn announced, continuing with her rightful duty. "It's so you can mention the item in the thank-you card. It's the proper way."

Clapping her hand over Evelyn's, Marie said, "Don't."

Evelyn put the pad and pencil aside.

The things in the closet didn't bother Marie at first. After all, Lester stayed over several nights a week and it was easier for him to leave a few sets of clothes at her house than to drive home each time he wanted to change his shirt. She tried putting his belongings in a hall closet but Lester insisted on having them in the bedroom. The brown slacks, tan shirts, and yellow ties (Lester's favorite color) hung beside Marie's uniforms, inching them toward the back of the closet.

Then he left two pairs of shoes, one for dress, the other for relaxing, on the closet floor. And a half dozen hankies, the plaid kind, with two pairs of boxer shorts, placed on the shelf where Marie stored her scarves and a wool hat that had been her mother's. Lester remarked how good it made him feel to look in and see his things next to Marie's. Marie just thought it looked crowded.

His kitchen gadgets were another story. He liked making Marie freshly squeezed orange juice and her cut glass squeezer didn't have a seed separator. So he surprised her one day by bringing his over, setting it on the counter and tucking Marie's into the bottom kitchen drawer, where the squeezer could double as a rubber band holder, he explained. She never said a thing.

On a Saturday morning at 7:00 A.M., two weeks before the wedding, Lester drove to Sofanelli's fruit market to buy a dozen oranges—the Sunkist kind. When Marie awoke a jelly glass filled with pulpy liquid sat on the bedstand. Lester was grinning beside it.

"You're beautiful in the morning, you know that, Marie?" he said, reaching beneath the covers for her hand. "Oh, so beautiful."

Lester had opened the curtains and an arrow of sunlight glanced his shoulder. The trees in the backyard had gone mad with color and Marie thought she had never seen so perfect a day. Leaving her for an instant, Lester lumbered to the closet and pulled a hanky from the shelf. While crossing the room he blew his nose, then reclaimed his place on the edge of the bed. She heard some of her belongings fall from the shelf. Lester smiled and handed her the juice glass. Gazing out over the yard Marie took the tumbler from her fiancé and poured the juice over his head.

The liquid ran through his hair and down his face, slowed some by the furrows in his forehead and cheeks. With the corner of the sheet Lester blotted his head and face.

"You're upset," he said, so slowly and earnestly that Marie shook with anger. "About the closet, I mean. And my clothes being here."

The words startled her.

"I think you should go, Les," she said, smoothing the blankets. Her words had a will of their own. "Maybe it's for the better."

Making a bridge of his fingers, Lester lifted his hands to his face. "Marie."

But she was already out of the bed, pulling on her robe. "You don't have to take everything now; I can box things up and leave them on the porch," she added.

He knew that she wouldn't give in. Lifting himself from the bed and following her through the bedroom door required all of Lester's strength.

14

"I don't regret any of it—really, Lester. I thank you for it," she continued, working her way through the hall and then down the stairs. The stairs hindered her—her bad foot bumped along and Lester was reminded of a child dragging a small brown bear. She caught her breath at the landing. "And I will always feel love for you Lester, that much I can promise. But it's time to go. You should just go."

She waited by the front door for Lester to gather his coat and hat. Bits of orange-and-white pulp shone in his hair like confetti. His collar and shirt were streaked with juice and when he hugged her she felt the dampness against her skin. Returning the hug was impossible. Instead, when he said "Please," she broke from him, gently.

The gifts proved problematic. The thank-you notes had gone out a good ten days before and she had no way of remembering who gave what. There was no list from the shower (yes, for once Evelyn had been right). The etiquette book, which Marie had now decided to defer to, said presents must be returned immediately. She called everyone who'd been invited to the wedding, explaining that it was called off and saying that she hoped they could make other plans for the day.

Each of the waitresses responded differently to the news. Doreen Raymond, the shopowner's daughter, cried when she saw Marie. Taking a hanky (a real one, the cloth kind with flowers embroidered on it and a lace hem) from her pocket, Doreen poked at the corners of her eyes, strangely yet bravely oblivious to the mascara shadows her tears were casting. Terri Kudja brought her a bouquet of balloons that said LET YOUR SPIRITS SOAR. Evelyn clicked her tongue in disgust and wondered aloud if Lester was dating yet. The other waitresses walked around Marie as if she were ice and one abrupt movement—or even one word—would cause her to crack. The customers suggested that Marie take time off.

Instead Marie began putting in extra hours, at least two each day, for which she refused additional pay. Always diligent, she now became more productive than anyone else in the shop. She devised a new system for rotating the coffee pots so that all of the coffee was used, not just the freshest. When the customers were settled, instead of staying to chat or tidy up the front, she retreated to the back. She learned to work the jelly machine, a metal basin filled with raspberry goo that shot through two sharp metal pipes and into the empty doughnuts, while also keeping watch on the Ring King.

"It's like she's grown eyes in the back of her head," commented the baker.

"Maybe there's an eye in that foot," said Evelyn.

The owner, seizing opportunity, promoted Marie to morning supervisor (at which point Evelyn asked to be put on nights but was told no). Now Marie arrived even earlier each morning to arrange schedules, do special training (one of her goals was to have several waitresses comfortable with the Ring King), and, once a week, take inventory of the paper cups, bags, sugar packets, stirrers, coffee packets and filters, napkins (wax and paper), cola syrups, tea bags, cream cartons, and a dozen other significant items. For these efforts she received a raise of $1.50 an hour. People started treating her differently (better?). The Buick boys had stopped harassing her and no one, including Marie, joked about her deformity.

Her house seemed more pleasant than she ever remembered. Calling to one of the neighborhood paperboys, Wade Lowbar, she asked if he'd like to earn a ten-dollar bill helping her rearrange some furniture. The sixteen-year-old proved to have a knack for this and when they were finished the living room looked quite pretty. The next Saturday Marie sorted through her top bureau drawer and threw out the half-full bottle of Heaven Scent, a tube of lipstick named Nearly Pink, and the Angel Face pressed powder. Boarding a bus to downtown Scranton, she got off at the Globe Store, headed straight for the cosmetics counter, asked to be "made over," and ended up buying twenty dollars worth of glosses and gels, all in colors of *her* choosing.

Of course there were times when Marie missed Lester—the companionship, the dinners out. When he phoned she was civil, even polite. But she wouldn't see him, despite the love letters—

notes, really, left every day for a month in her mailbox. In fact, she couldn't even bring herself to walk by the automobile club. Nor could she sleep at night for the first few months.

Lester, from a distance, made sure she was safe at night, either driving by her house just around the time she'd turn off the living room light or calling to "check up." For him the Every Day Doughnut Shop was off limits; he bought his morning crueller and coffee from the "vendeteria" in the AAA's basement.

The phone conversation with Evelyn—*she* called Lester—worried him most. Evelyn prefaced the talk by saying that she really didn't much like either one of them.

"But something has to be done," Evelyn explained. "Marie's throwing her heart, soul, and foot into her work and it isn't healthy. And she's wearing eyeliner."

Before hanging up, though, Evelyn told Lester that she wished him well and that if he ever felt the need for a home-cooked meal to give her a ring.

So Lester started keeping a closer watch on Marie, trailing her for two whole weekends. Some days he told himself it was just enough to see her, waiting on the corner of Market and Sanderson for the bus to work. Once he got dangerously close and worried that he wouldn't be able to stop himself from at least saying hello and holding her hand. He tried distracting himself by making containers of freshly squeezed juices and giving them to his friends and doing volunteer work at the public library. But the barnacle called hope clung to him through all the tides of his emotions.

Marie decided to throw herself a party celebrating "the best year of my life." The guest list consisted of a few neighbors, most of the waitresses—Evelyn included—the deaf baker who worked early mornings, Wade, the paperboy, two women from the pocketbook factory, and all of the Buick boys. Nobody brought up Lester's name—he and Marie had seldom spoken over the last three months and Marie saw no reason to invite him. Marie borrowed a tape player from Terri and Doreen Raymond was to choose the music. Le Mans, Terri's boyfriend, and the other Buick boys chipped in for a keg.

At the grocery store Marie purchased four kinds of dip and, to make things more festive, tortilla chips. She debated about the large sheet cake, then decided against it, since somebody might put two and two together and realize it was her birthday. Instead she picked up a small boxed cake decorated with roses. The tray of cold cuts, salami, turkey, ham, and American cheese surrounded by pickles came from the deli counter.

No one arrived on time and Marie found herself at 7:30 arranging the rolls once again. Evelyn appeared, solo, at 7:45 and she and Marie sat at the opposite corners of the couch like bookends for about twenty minutes, making shop talk. Finally, a little after 8:00, there were a series of thuds on the porch and a dozen people drifted into the living room, more than had ever been inside the small house.

Doreen slipped a reggae cassette into the player and the boys set the keg in an aluminum tub. The music wasn't Marie's taste and the beer was sure to ruin the kitchen linoleum, but the waitress felt a sense of accomplishment, glad for the clatter people's voices made, the colors that filled the rooms.

"Thanks for coming," Marie said to Terri and then went to welcome her other guests. "Boys," she said waving at a group of the Buick mechanics, "you enjoy yourselves now."

The talk at first was random, little more than hellos and how are you's. But slowly an order came about—Terri and Le Mans nestled in a corner, speaking in soft tones; Doreen and Wade danced in the kitchen; Evelyn and the ladies from the purse factory picked the chives from the chives and sour cream dip. The Buick boys had turned on the television and hunkered over the set, looking for the play-offs. Once in awhile someone would change position, speaking with someone new on their way to the kitchen. There were spilled drinks which Marie ignored, food crushed into the carpeting but no major incidents, only the business of people losing themselves to the moment, using up the night with talk and music.

Marie didn't do much talking—she saw the role of a hostess as insuring everybody else's good time, so she refilled bowls, fixed sandwiches on request, mastered the tape deck. Once, watching Wade and Doreen gyrating, she thought about dancing. Instead, sitting alongside the factory ladies, she listened politely to their talk, adding phrases like "Yes, that's very true, isn't it?"

It wasn't that the women ignored Marie; they simply kept on with their own thoughts. Later she tried telling a joke she'd heard to one of the Buick crew. He laughed at the wrong part. When she offered Terri some cold cuts Terri rubbed Marie's arm and pushed her in the direction of the kitchen.

"I think I'll cut the cake," she said to the room and thought, maybe I will tell them it's my birthday. But the cake had already been carved up by a zealous coworker. Finally Marie searched the room for Evelyn, who had left without saying good-bye. Her friends—her guests—liked her fine, that Marie knew. It was something else that was bothering her. The house had taken on a life of its own, apart from her.

Her white cardigan hung inside the hall closet. She reached for it and, without anyone noticing, she headed for the porch. Though it was early September the air was already beginning to chill. The first part of the walk she hurried, pushed along by self-anger; then, as her foot started to ache, she slowed her steps. For a few minutes she lost her bearings; gazing up at the night sky she tried picking out the North Star. There was Venus and that cluster that Lester knew and a wealth of other heavenly bodies he could call by name. She told herself she would turn around, go home, and stop this nonsense, this childishness. It was just a question of getting back to where she was meant to be. Her place in the world.

Then she remembered her father's game. It came to her from some cold pond deep within her brain, a pond that the evening had somehow disturbed. When Marie was about five she and her father played Secret Wish. Before he tucked her into bed, father and daughter pored over a large picture book, filled with drawings of famous places—Buckingham Palace, Mount Rushmore, the coliseum, the pyramids. Inside the back cover her father had pasted a photograph of their home.

He'd close the book and say, "Think of a place, Marie. And let me guess it."

Every night he guessed right. For months he claimed it was magic. But on her seventh birthday, pressed for an answer, he told her how he'd managed it: he *knew* her. She recalled his face as he said the words, kind of sad, hurt-looking.

"Maybe one, two people really know you your whole life. If you're very lucky." Then, probably sensing her confusion and the gravity of his message, he added, "I bet we're two of the luckiest people ever put on the earth."

Lester knew her. Not so good that he'd predict her every thought—sometimes he'd be flat, dead-away wrong. But there were things that she had never explained, never talked out that Lester, well, understood.

He came to the door after the second ring. She watched him peer through the glass oval and then listened as the lock turned over and the chain slid off. Lester was wearing one of his wide yellow ties. Pulling on the screen door she stood just outside the threshold, her foot a doorjamb. Inside, on the dining room table was a birthday cake, candles unlit. Worrying his bottom lip, Lester held himself back a bit. Marie nodded her head and said, "Now."

Terri

erri Kudja, the morning-shift waitress who moonlighted as a belly dancer, was lost in North Scranton. She got directions over the phone, but with the light in the phone booth burned out she had to write the instructions in the dark. Back in the car, she couldn't read what she'd written. None of the gas stations stayed open after eight and she wasn't stopping by a convenient mart dressed like a genie. She had to draw the line somewhere.

After driving around for an hour in search of the client's house, she finally gave up and headed home. As part of her dancing routine she also delivered a dozen balloons, which she now dragged out of the backseat. She was convinced that the balloon and belly-dancing combination was unbeatable, the appeal much broader than just one or the other. Being innovative was how people made it.

Terri would have to reimburse her supplier at the balloon store, but what the heck—she handed the bouquet to her two oldest kids as she walked in the door and called to her sister, who was rocking the baby. The baby was mulatto, her oldest child, black, the middle, a redhead. The neighbors at the project called Terri Miss United Nations.

21

"I'm here, everybody," she said, cuddling her children. "The sleep genie's here to tuck you in." Then she said to her sister, after she'd bathed the kids and kissed them good night, "It was a bust. I'll have to get better organized. There's no reason why I can't manage a waitress job *and* the belly dancing and balloon deliveries. There's people who do more than that."

"Like who?" her sister asked.

Terri had learned "the exotic and useful art" of belly dancing (the catalog's description) at the YWCA. Her girlfriend dropped out after the second lesson but Terri completed the six-week course, convinced that she could work days at the doughnut shop and hire out to party services at night. She bought the dancing clothes from her teacher, a blue-and-green gauze two-piece with sequins on the cuffs of the blouse and pants and bordering the V-neckline. The instructor threw in the three sets of silver finger-taps. Terri looked a little skinny in the outfit but not unattractive. The balloons she carried helped fill her out.

"It's an investment in the future," she had told her boyfriend Le Mans when he asked the price of her lessons and gear. She'd borrowed fifty dollars from Marie, the morning manager, to take the course.

"Just don't walk around the projects like that or people will start saying 'There goes the neighborhood,' " Le Mans joked.

The trouble with the neighbors began after Terri's new couch and the Big Wheel bicycle arrived. The floral sofa sat on the project's front lawn while Terri and her oldest, Mandy, moved all of the living room furniture against one wall. Being a good neighbor, Terri let the project kids jump on the couch (it had a plastic sheet) for fifteen minutes before telling them to scoot. By then the mothers and aunts had assembled out front and wanted to know just where she had gotten the money.

"I've been saving," Terri said, shooing her own kids into the apartment. Not one of the crowd offered to help Terri drag the sofa inside.

"This isn't the kind of stuff you get with double coupons," observed Lila, whose own four-year-old had already claimed the Big Wheel.

"My part-time work is adding up," Terri explained, reining in her hair with a rubber band. "You could do it, too. It just takes planning."

"Next thing you know," Lila said to the others, "she'll be leaving the projects altogether. Sending those children to tennis lessons."

Terri let go a little breath, half exasperation, half determination, and got ready to move the couch herself.

"Jealousy's a terrible thing," explained Terri's mother. She stretched the words over her Vaseline-coated lips for emphasis. "A terrible thing."

She picked the lint from a pair of Terri's fishnet stockings, then inspected her own legs, heavily traveled by a network of varicose veins. "I remember when I could wear these," she said, easing the stocking over her hand and then up her arm, intent on finding a snag. None appeared.

Outside, the Big Wheel crunched over the broken walkway on its way into the house. Two weeks old now, it was missing part of a handlebar and the plastic seat had a mean crack. Terri swung the screen door open for the middle child, Daniel, and the two of them pulled the bike into the living room. Though late in the afternoon, Terri still wore her doughnut shop uniform. Daniel dug his hand into a front pocket, hoping to unearth some forgotten tip. He came up empty.

"Eh-eh-eh," Terri said, pushing him in the direction of the bathroom. "Wash up for dinner."

Daniel pointed to his mother's jelly-stained skirt. "You, too, Mom," he said.

Taking a set of finger cymbals from atop the refrigerator, Terri coaxed her mother, Flo, to join her. "Come on, Mama. It will do you good. I want to show you this new step."

Flo shifted her generous weight to another section of what she'd dubbed "the never-ending sofa." The cushions gave willingly.

"Teresa, I didn't move that much when I gave birth," she said, following Terri's hips with her eyes.

Reaching for her mother's hands, Terri pulled the woman into the middle of the room and began spinning around her, a human top. "Just go with it, Mama, go with it," Terri urged.

The kids, hearing the taps, raced into the room and clutched at their grandmother's ample hips. Flo felt like the flying swings at Rocky Glen Amusement Park. After three minutes of rocking and reeling she fell to the couch, exhausted.

"Something about it bothers me, Teresa," said Flo, gesturing for the children to sit. "It just doesn't seem Christian to be rotating yourself like that."

Terri, grabbing a brush from a shelf, furiously began to braid her daughter's hair. "What's not Christian about it, anyway? It's part of the Hindu culture and Hinduism shares many of the same principles as Christianity," Terri offered, paraphrasing the *World Book Encyclopedia*. "Really, it's fascinating, Mama. I've been reading a lot about India."

"That's not gonna get you made a manager at the shop, honey," her mother reprimanded. "That's not gonna feed your children."

"It's feeding me. It's feeding me some spiritual food," Terri replied.

"You're talking blasphemy, now, Teresa. Just like your cousin Artis," her mother warned.

Terri grabbed a fishnet stocking and pulled it down over her own smooth face. It flattened her nose, distorted her eyes, mashed her hair, transforming her into the survivor of a nuclear accident.

"And if I'm not a good Christian, I'll end up just like that poor soul—punished by her own thoughts in a grease fire," she mocked.

The kids loved it when their mom got crazy. They yanked stockings over their own heads, surrounded their grandmother, and became gnomes, yelping and screeching, hopping around, adding to the bedlam.

When the neighbors saw Flo slam the door in disgust and then hurry across the lawn without bidding any of the stoop sitters good-bye, they began the talk about Terri turning on her own mama.

Not even the cruelest neighbors envied Terri her shift at the doughnut shop. She split it—4:30 A.M. till 6:30 A.M., when she'd return to get the kids off to school and day care—and then 9:00 until 3:00. It was hard getting up, but once she did, Terri relished the early morning hours. The older man, Russell, who packed the deliveries for the doughnut truckers, worked out of a back room and kept to himself. The deaf baker wasn't given to long conversations, and the second baker, Branley Orbis, a ministry student, didn't come in until 7:00. So Terri had a good two hours of silence, time she used to fill the morning's doughnuts with cream, or blackberry, raspberry, or apple jelly, and then ice them, stack them on trays, and listen to her own thoughts until opening the shop's front door at 6:00. Lately Terri had tried meditating while preparing the pastries, but she'd become so distracted by the chant of her own soul that twice now she'd put apple icing on berry doughnuts.

The baker signaled for some coffee, forming a mug with his hand and tipping the invisible brew into his mouth. Store policy said employees paid for their drinks, but he never offered to, so Terri usually ended up putting the baker's share in the till. Pushing the swinging door to the store's front, she started a pot of coffee and noticed the Hare Krishna crossing the street. The rope belt that hung from his robe marked his stride. He clutched a candle in his right hand, a white taper whose flame, protected by the wall of his left palm, exposed his face in the pre-dawn light.

"Vishnu," Terri called, knowing that no one could hear her, although she could swear that he nodded as he followed the bridge to the town's university. Before she fully realized what she'd done, the waitress had a sack of doughnuts clutched in her fist and was running down the street, calling after him, her apron slipping from her hips.

He waved the gift away. "But they're fresh, they're fresh," she offered by way of explanation. Heading back toward the shop, she left them on a cement bench at the bus shelter, for the first rider, and hoped her karma would change.

That night Terri got a fifty-dollar tip on her belly-dancing balloon delivery. The order, phoned into the balloon company by the local Humane Society, was sent to an E. A. Crane on North Washington Avenue, the toniest block in the city. The card read, "With thanks for your numerous donations and adoptions." When E. answered the door Terri knew her delivery had been switched with the lollipop clown—E. stood four eleven, had probably been presented to society in the twenties, and she was trailed by at least one hundred cats. Calicos, Persians, tigers, and toms sat on the staircase, along the window sills, perched on the couch backs (four once-velveteen couches), the top of the breakfront. A tabby climbed the drapes. The stench was overwhelming and Terri had to force herself not to gag. Two Siamese kittens sat in their owner's arms. Terri thought of calling the balloon store and telling them there'd been a mix-up, but E. insisted that Terri join her in the living room.

At E.'s request, Terri began her dance, moving about more slowly than usual, trying to lower her oxygen intake. Trying to act like a yogi. The cats loved it. They stretched out around the dancer, purring and yawning, a few mixed breeds batting at the hem of her harem pants. The sequins held. Halfway through her performance the felines broke into a chorus, mewing in unison. Terri smiled graciously at E. and noticed that the elderly woman was conducting this choir, her arms, the texture of crepe paper, flapping by her sides. And the lady's mouth was open. Terri, curious, circled closer to find out if E. was actually meowing.

Terri ended her dance with the clatter of finger cymbals, holding her arms in a circle at her waist and bowing her head. E. applauded vigorously and, placing two fingers in her mouth, whistled like a sailor. When E. handed her the fifty-dollar bill, Terri thanked her but explained that the balloons and entertainment were presents, gifts from the Humane Society.

"I know. But this is for you," said E. in a human cat voice. "The past two years they've sent that damn lollipop clown. Who could enjoy that?"

For three months straight Terri earned between twenty-five and one hundred dollars per delivery, in tips alone. The belly dancer–balloon combination was taking off. The three kids got new sneakers and Flo five pairs of support hose—which Terri had to mail because her mother's anger continued—and Terri bought herself a day-long course on Indian cooking. The neighbors harped about the smell and called the kids the Raghead family.

At five one morning, Terri convinced the baker to put a sprinkling of curry into half a dozen doughnuts, "just to experiment." She bribed him, saying she'd buy his cigarettes for the next week if he'd do it this once. Last month Terri had invented a peanut butter and jelly doughnut, making a trayful for the customers to sample. She ended up buying them herself and giving the hybrids to the project kids. Even so, her enthusiasm persuaded the baker to fry her latest concoction in the Ring King, away from the other doughnuts, in case the curry smell lingered. From the outside the doughnuts appeared to be no different than any of the others.

"The dirty half-dozen," the baker said, plopping them into a wax bag. "Happy eating."

Terri broke off a small piece of the fried dough and offered the man a nibble.

"Never touch them," he said.

Terri's boyfriend, Le Mans, tried the doughnuts that evening, after the kids had bedded down. "They're OK," he said, finishing up number three and still guessing at the mystery ingredient. "They taste like you dunked them in onion dip mix."

"Think they'll sell?" Terri asked and relayed the story of convincing the baker to add a dash of curry. Then she brought up the subject of leaving the projects. She'd take on a third job—making Indian food for parties—and move to a real apartment, perhaps even half a double house like her friend Marie's.

"I wish I could help you out, Terri, I really do," Le Mans interrupted. But Terri knew his situation—an ailing mother whom he lived with, along with his little sister and her four kids—and told him no way.

"I can do it myself. I know I can. My kids need a change, anyway. It will do us all a world of good," she said.

Opening a kitchen drawer, she waved a composition book at Le Mans and turned to the first page, where she'd printed the word GOALS in capital letters. After each project was a time frame— four weeks, four months, a year.

"Visit a tope? What the hell is a tope?" Le Mans asked, confused but good-natured.

"That's number ten, Le Mans. I have to get to all of these other things first," she stressed, more determined than ever. And when they kissed good night Terri knew it was their last. Moving forward was the name of the game.

Of all the people who hung out in the projects, Le Mans was probably the best liked. Terri had met him at the doughnut shop— he was one of the Buick boys, mechanics at the dealership who took their coffee break at 2:30, right before Terri got off. The first time he came by the projects he stopped to talk to Lila, the kids, and all of the stoop sitters before knocking on Terri's door. He made it a point to learn the names of every child and old lady in the project and greeted them accordingly. So Terri wasn't the only one who missed having him around, though she complained about it a lot less than the others. He was a nice guy with very little money or motivation who took on mythic proportions after the breakup.

"The best father figure a kid could have," taunted Lila. "You know what those school ladies say about our kids needing daddies."

"How many chances you think you got, girl?" her mother asked. "Seems to me he's about the last one. If I had a last chance, I wouldn't squander it."

The decision to break up was a mutual one and Terri felt good about the way it ended—no tantrums, no threats, the promise to stay friends. She was happy with her life. She had catered two parties out of town and the tips from her belly dancing were coming in strong.

She had written in the tablet "Leave the projects: 12 months." Three months before her deadline she found half of a double house in West Side, five blocks from the public school. It had a climbing tree in front, a plot of land big enough for a swing set, and a small garden out back. Terri had asked three of her neighbors to come look with her and two just plain refused. The third, Lila, mocked, "Why don't you ask Le Mans?" As Terri was about to go by herself, Flo showed up, dressed in her "wake suit," topped by a black straw boater with veil. And when they arrived they saw the deaf baker and Marie standing on the porch.

"We thought you could use a little moral support," they said as Terri led her coworkers and Flo through the rooms.

Every space was an adventure waiting to happen; the house had two dormers where the kids could play at being Rapunzel, a pantry for Terri's cache of spices, and a tiny dressing room off the master bedroom with a built-in vanity. Opening her purse, Terri lifted out a small four-armed goddess, which she'd wrapped in tissue, and placed it on the vanity. "We're home, girl," she said.

The kids had a hard time adjusting. The oldest, Mandy, kept asking to move back to the projects, or to be adopted by one of her friends' families. Daniel reminded her that they'd been called the Raghead family, but Mandy pointed out that that was " 'cause of Mom. No one really believes we're into that stuff."

When Mandy decorated the "god thing" with smurf stickers, Terri sat down with her daughter and asked her if she'd help out at work for a couple of mornings. Letting Mandy take the two days off from school, Terri got her up at 4:00, dressed her daughter all in white, wrapped an apron around her, and plopped a baker's hat on her head. For the time she put in Mandy would receive $2.75 an hour—half of Terri's wage.

The baker signed the word *hello*, then spoke it aloud, and Mandy's fingers spelled *hi* in return, quick to pick up the game. Handing her a clump of dough, he told her to make whatever shape she wanted, and he'd fry it up. She poked out an *M*, then pummeled it, and played at forming a cat, but the ears and tail wouldn't hold together.

"Just one piece," tutored the baker, glancing over at Mandy and her mother.

Mandy rolled a skinny snake, doubled it, and formed a question mark, pinching the handle a little from the bottom so it had the appearance of a period.

"How great," Terri said, and gave her daughter the task of

dunking the cake doughnuts in a swirling vat of warm chocolate. Most of it ended up on Mandy, so Terri demonstrated with a twist of the wrist how to evenly coat just the top of the doughnut.

"I got it, Mom," she said, holding up one like a prize. The baker gave her a thumbs up.

Across from the jelly and icing machines sat large bowls of powdered sugar, cinnamon sugar, shredded coconut, and crushed peanuts.

"Take your pick, honey," Terri said, and Mandy grabbed for the cinnamon sugar. Terri dropped a dozen warm doughnuts into the container. "It's a big people's sandbox. Just make sure they're all nice and tan," she explained, and watched as Mandy tossed the doughnuts until they each wore a cinnamon sugar coat.

Mother and daughter placed the doughnuts side by side on a tray and Terri whisked them out front for the morning's customers.

"How do you like that new house?" the baker asked Mandy when Terri left to arrange the trays and put on the coffee. The baker always sounded as though he were speaking underwater. Mandy wiggled her shoulders indifferently, a bit of a snot.

"Your Mom's a little weird—you know that, don't you? But so am I. So are a lot of people," he added, lifting the fried question mark high into the air with a wooden stick.

"I'm not," Mandy mouthed, and the baker read her lips.

"Then how come you didn't just make a doughnut, like everybody else?"

Terri's activities left little time for meeting her neighbors—that's why they hadn't come around, she told herself. The elderly couple who owned Terri's house lived next door and twice a week she took home fresh doughnuts for their breakfast. Their forty-three-year-old son Gene, who spent his days selling pharmaceuticals, caught a glimpse of Terri leaving for a delivery in her genie suit one evening and stayed with the kids until she returned. He asked her to a block barbecue the following Saturday.

Terri wore her only matching summer outfit, a black-and-white striped cotton top with shorts that Lila had called Terri's jailbird suit. The other women were in pastels, either shorts that came to their knees or slacks. No one volunteered introductions, though everyone acted polite. Pointing to the nearly empty tray of fried vegetables and poori, one of her best dishes, Terri finally interrupted the hostess to say she was glad she'd brought along some Indian food.

"That was Indian—Indian food?" the hostess asked, biting into each of her words. "We thought it was some southwestern cuisine. Excuse me," she said, breaking away and hurrying the tray and its remains into the house. She glared at Gene, saying from the side of her mouth, "I hope we aren't all sick. I hope we don't get something."

She returned with the tray cleaned, handed it to Gene, and nodded at Terri. "Help yourself to the meat," the hostess told them, attending to her other guests.

The couple sat at the end of a picnic table eating while the neighbors broke into small groups. Terri left Gene's side several times and tried to talk kids with some of the mothers. They seemed to ignore her. Finally she said to a circle of women who'd steered the conversation away from her, "This is so different from my old neighborhood."

"It is really a wonderful place, isn't it," announced one of the younger moms. "We all get along."

When Terri catered her next party she made a dozen extra plates, one for each of the people who'd attended the barbecue. Wrapping them in plastic, she topped them off with her personalized sticker: "Terri's Tastees." The houses where the back door was open, she left the treats on the kitchen table; otherwise she placed them just inside the screen door, with the door left far enough ajar so that the kids wouldn't trample them. No one thanked Terri themselves, but they did send their children around to let her know they'd received the plates and would contact her if they wanted any more. She told herself that for now, that was good enough.

The school became a haven for Terri and her children; Mandy and Daniel signed up for every club, and by the end of the year Mandy had been voted most popular girl. The preschool sat adjacent to the elementary building, so dropping off all three youngsters was a cinch.

Terri got so caught up in the school fairs, her dancing, and redoing the bathroom that she didn't even realize that they'd been settled for a full year. Le Mans mentioned it to her one day at the shop—he still dropped by on his coffee break and was always anxious to hear Terri's stories. As she poured fifteen coffees to go for a construction crew ("lots of sugar, Sugar," the foreman shouted), Terri told Le Mans about the kids locking their grandmother in the bathroom during the renovations.

"Flo was in there, cleaning, telling the kids that if they didn't clear away the water toys she'd pitch them straight out the window. So while she was scrubbing the sink, Daniel put the floats in a straight line heading for the door and locked her in from the outside. When she went to turn the knob it fell off in her hand and she was bellowing from the window, 'Teresa, your children are possessed,' for the benefit of the neighborhood. We had to take the door off its hinges," Terri finished, laughing, handing the construction worker his order. "But the bathroom turned out great," she added.

"You make any good friends since the move?" Le Mans asked. "That's a whole different place than the projects."

Terri wagged her head a bit, putting him off. "The people seem nice enough," she explained. "I really haven't had any free time."

He gave her a questioning look, knowing her too well.

"Now Le Mans," she lectured. "I'm sure if there was a problem, they'd all be very helpful," Terri observed.

It was the second Saturday in October when the man from the Internal Revenue Service came to the door. At first Terri took him for an insurance salesman, the way he studied his briefcase as he climbed the steps to the porch. He spoke to her so politely she thought he must also be a neighbor, finally bidding her welcome.

"Nice to see you," she said, clearing two chairs on the porch.

Nodding, he pulled out his picture ID, with the word *Agent* in front of his name.

"Unreported earnings, Miss Kudja," he explained, taking a manila folder from his case, his manner controlled and businesslike. "Failure to report earnings from free-lance activities violates the law. This letter apprises you that taxes must be paid on those monies that went unreported over the past three years. In the event that you want to contest—"

Terri interrupted his monologue. "There's no contesting it, Mr. . . . er . . . Wise," she said, reading his name from the ID. "But I don't have the money to pay back taxes. I'm a single parent who's barely squeaking by." She drew a deep breath, to calm herself, to give herself some strength, and looked him right in the eye.

Here Mr. Wise relaxed a bit. "Look. We don't usually make house calls—but I live right around the corner and your case was brought to my attention. I have two kids myself, weekend visiting rights." He seemed to glance wistfully at the skateboard on the porch.

Terri's arms were rigid, as if they were holding up all around her. She didn't care about his kids.

"You know," he said in a more intimate tone, "you have been pretty obvious."

"Is that the problem?" Terri asked. "That I've been obvious?" Her voice betrayed her hurt.

"Listen," he said, seductively gentle, "with just your day job you still qualify for the projects. You can probably go back. It may just be a matter of paying a fine and giving up the house." He leaned forward confidentially. "Hey now. All we guys think you're pretty hot. Cheer up."

Terri wanted to spit at him. She wanted to scream something like "Talk to my lawyer" but realized how ridiculous it would sound. So she stood up, said good-bye, and listened as he told her that she'd receive another notice with further details on the charge.

Along with the sound of doughnut screens dropping into the fryer Terri could hear a language, words falling over one another for minutes on end. She'd slept so little this last week that she might have been imagining the occasional "Lord Jesus" and "Amen, amen, amen," the only discernible phrases. The deaf baker was sick and Branley Orbis, the apprentice preacher, was filling in, slowly turning out the morning's doughnuts. Terri knew that she should help him, should urge him on, but she was having a hard time summoning up the energy.

"Need some coffee?" she called to him, but he couldn't hear her voice over his own.

"Coffee, Branley?" she repeated, irritated. She walked over to the fryer and stationed herself at the far end. *"Coffee?"*

He finally looked up, embarrassed that she'd witnessed his recitation, his practice.

"I'd like to hear it," said Terri, her anger dissipating at the sight of his pained expression. "I could use some inspiration. I might be—" She hesitated. "It might be good for both of us."

Branley carefully inspected the fried doughnuts before setting them aside. Terri had dragged over a stack of empty trays. Menacingly, she dangled a tray over the fryer.

"I'm not ready," he answered, a bit horrified.

"Anything. Just repeat what you were saying," she insisted. "Please."

He stood, shaking his head. "Spreading the word takes time."

For once Terri stifled the impulse to console another. The tray fell to the floor.

When Terri finally explained the predicament to Le Mans, he promised he'd get to the bottom of it and would make "the informer pay." That evening he headed for the projects. Lila had just left her apartment and tried to duck back in when he nabbed her. Le Mans gripped Lila's arm. "It was you, wasn't it," he insisted, watching her wince from the anticipated pain.

"I swear, no. I swear on my new dinette set," Lila returned.

He dropped her arm in disgust. "Who was it, then?"

Lila massaged her arm as the tears fell down her cheeks. "Nobody from the projects. When those guys came round here, they already had her. We wouldn't even give them the satisfaction of agreeing with them—we all said she was too damn lazy to be working on the side."

He trembled from the anger and kicked up the edges of the small lawn lining the concrete as he walked away. Lila started for her apartment and then yelled for him.

"Le Mans," she cried, half-choking on his name. "Her new neighbors. Maybe the neighbors," she said and closed the door.

One week before the family was due to move, Flo stood on the porch, castigating her daughter. Terri had called her twice that week, to mind the kids while she inquired about loans. "You wanted too much, girl," Flo said. "You just can't want too much in life."

The kids were crouched on the window seat, lips fluttering, holding back what they could.

"You watch, Mama," Terri said, grabbing her purse and hurrying across the porch like she'd caught fire. "I want even more. And I'm going to get more. Keep an eye on the kids." Under her arm was the goal book—she flipped through the pages looking for the map she'd placed there. She wasn't entirely sure of the address of her destination, but once in the car she realized that if she got to the general vicinity, someone in the area could point out the building.

The road changed direction so quickly and she was driving so fast that she nearly hit a man walking along the shoulder.

"Hey, you," she said, nearly breathless, watching his hand leave the cord on his robe and travel upward in a tender greeting. Leaning over to the passenger side, Terri opened the door and gestured for the Hare Krishna to get in. Every motion seemed so deliberate that when he clapped his hand over the seat-back Terri knew that he would understand.

"First," she said, pointing to the page in the book, "we visit your temple—that tope place. Second, I find someone to loan me enough to pay my taxes so my kids can stay put. I can do it. It's just a matter of thinking it out clearly."

The Hare Krishna's gaze was fixed on the road ahead, a path that led directly to his dwelling. "Do you see the second tree?" he asked, and she replied no, she couldn't.

"What tree?" she insisted, frantic. "What tree?"

She started, for the first time in years, to cry. He helped Terri steer the car to the shoulder and held her hand, allowing her to weep. Even as she sobbed she was conscious of his breathing, slow and calming, as rhythmic as an ancient sea.

"You cannot see the second tree," he said, "because we have yet to pass the first."

Branley

Branley Orbis practiced his preaching over the fryer. He used to imagine that the heat was coming from those souls headed for hell, souls he could snatch from eternal damnation, from fire and pain, men, women, and children he could save by standing perilously close to the inferno. "Rise up," he'd command, pressing the foot pedal that either freed the doughnuts from the bubbling grease or plunged them into the depths. Inspecting the doughnuts' browned skins and the band of white around their middle, the baker would grab the ends of the doughnut screen with gloved hands, hold it above the trough of scalding liquid, set it on the cooling rack, and cry, "Go and sin no more."

Within minutes he'd collect a new congregation, wresting their limp and pallid spirits from the proof box, the glass cabinet where the yeast worked its miracle, and he would begin anew. "The face of the Lord is turned upon you, his path shall be made clear unto you"—once again the foot would reach for the lever, dropping the screen into the oil. "And that path is strewn with temptation, with the corruption of the flesh, the disruption of the mind, the destruction of the soul. We," Branley would stress, glancing at the minute hand on the wall clock, "must fix our gaze on the face of the Lord, each moment of our earthly journey."

Occasionally he lost one. A deviant ring would slip off the side of the rack and into the pit of despair, only to be charred and shrunken when it finally was retrieved. "Those who fall from grace and cry out not for the faith that is Jesus, the hope that is Jesus, the love that is Jesus," he'd explain, tossing the blackened remains into a garbage pail, "shall never enter the pearly gates."

The pearly gates lay just steps away, in the form of the pool of white glaze in which he dipped the doughnuts. Now the foot would reach for a pedal that dropped the baked goods into the sugary river. "Be born again in the goodness of the Lord," he'd continue, baptizing by the dozens those prepared for immersion. "Jesus our Savior will make the blackest sheep white, will purify thine every thought, word, and deed."

The other workers on the shift took his banter in stride, preferring the preacher's rants to the complaints—arthritic fingers, fallen arches, aching back—of the deaf baker who also worked mornings. Branley kept his contact with the deaf baker to a minimum, not knowing what might be expected of him in their relationship. In fact, Branley spoke best when no one was around, when he had only his own congregation to please.

"The only problem is," said Evelyn Caine, "he's preaching to the converted."

Baptist Bible College was exactly twenty-three minutes from the shop. In bad weather the commute could swell to forty-two, even forty-five minutes. One snowy night Branley made it three-quarters of the way to the school and then had to pull over at the Bluebird Diner until the salt trucks came on duty. He thought of Lot and his rebellious wife, of Sodom, and the passage in Luke: "Remember Lot's wife." The trucks cut a path for him up the hill to the college, never turning back. When he arrived only five minutes of class time remained.

Branley had hoped that the teacher would admonish him with a passage from the Bible, and on his way into the classroom the student thumbed the index to find an appropriate quotation. Instead the teacher merely said, "Bad weather, isn't it." Sometimes

Branley worried that the faculty didn't take things seriously enough.

The night courses were filled with people with a calling, the chosen who'd received a message to minister. Branley's vocation had been particularly strong. He received it five years ago while watching television at his cousin Leola's house. A western was playing. He reached over, turned off the set, and said to Leola, out of nowhere, in a voice reminiscent of his dead father's, "Ask and it shall be given."

"I'll have vanilla ice cream," she answered.

Ignoring her, he walked out of the house, climbed into his car, and the next morning enrolled in the night school at Baptist Bible. His faith was shaken for just one moment, when he said to a secretary, "How long before you'll call me Reverend?"

"When hell freezes over," she replied, laughing, and then, seeing his horror at the remark, added, "Hey—I'm just a temp. And I'm Catholic, padre."

Branley hadn't expected to be tested so quickly. But the trials were what made his calling so interesting.

All of the bakers complained about the grease-drenched floor, the risk of slipping and falling in front of the fryer. The deaf baker, hurrying to finish his work, had twice caught himself in mid-fall; Branley walked carefully around the fryer to prevent any mishaps. The men laid down sheets of brown paper which they peeled up and discarded after each shift, but the solution was a mediocre one, since the paper, too, skidded along the floor after awhile. Then Branley came up with the idea of using a pallet to prevent them, he said, from "backsliding." The shortening dripped down between the slats, which easily could be wiped off, and the platform was removed and the floor cleaned just once a day. The janitor hinged two pallets together, folding them up at night while the floor dried. Along the seam underneath the platform Branley painted the words *Jesus wept*.

The deaf baker stood on the boards and they held his weight, but Branley was the first to use the stage, ascending it like Jacob's ladder, taking in his heaven and earth. The three extra inches allowed him a view of the top flights of the proof box and the dough he had cut into uniform circles, one indistinguishable from the next. In the box, temperature, air, and pressure were controlled with little chance of error. As long as Branley had blended the ingredients—flour, water, yeast, and a packaged doughnut mix—correctly, the ivory circles would begin to puff up, identical Christian soldiers.

The baker began experimenting with the length of time the doughnuts stayed in the box, adding two, four, then ten seconds, long enough to race through the Twenty-third Psalm. At the "though I walk through the valley of the shadow" he'd drop the pressure a notch, so the doughnuts wouldn't get so swollen they'd pop.

Just a few months after taking the job, Branley was producing the lightest, tastiest doughnuts in town. He also had the least amount of waste, losing perhaps one doughnut in the fryer to every five the other bakers lost. The owner, Mr. Raymond, made a point of praising his work, saying, "You make a better doughnut than anyone—but me." And the customers who sat counterside upped their order from their usual two honey-dipped to three. The only shortcoming: Branley's shift, made longer by the extraordinary care he took, occasionally spilled into the next one. Even the simplest of actions—sponging off the slats on the pallet—was accompanied by great ritual and preaching. Bowing down to reach the wooden ties, he'd cry, "The Lord will wipe away the tears from all faces."

"Amen, and move it," Evelyn would reply. She could make out only a few of Branley's ravings. "We don't have seven days to get these doughnuts out. Ask the Lord Jesus to put some pep in your step."

Branley reminded himself that the Lord moved in mysterious ways, and Evelyn Caine was surely among them.

The small group assembled every Sunday afternoon on the corner of Wyoming and Poplar, across from the doughnut shop, some setting up their music on the ends of their instruments, others opening their texts. One cadet would take charge of distributing tracts.

"Here come the Sallies," Evelyn said, and the customers would swivel their stools and peer through the shop's glass front, enjoying the show. Horns lifted, tambourines at chest level, the Salvation Army Band waited for a signal from their leader. He gave a nod and the tinny sound of "Onward Christian Soldiers" reached the ears of the unfaithful.

"He's an officer," Evelyn explained.

One young woman, perhaps eighteen, tugged at her navy blue skirt while the officer conducted. Her black tie shoes had tan soles that curled up over the shoes' edges. Both the men and the women wore hats. At the end of the third verse, while studying the officer, the young woman smoothed her skirt and opened her mouth in anticipation of the next hymn.

"My money says she's only in it to get her man," Evelyn's commentary continued.

"Dollars to doughnuts?" a customer yucked.

A neighborhood kid loitered on the corner, his dog by his side. The custodian at AAA crossed the street, a three-legged stool tucked beneath his arm. A van filled with a mother, father, and four kids slowed down to hear the officer speak.

"Getting their usual crowd, I see," chided Evelyn.

Since the December day was mild, the waitress walked over to the shop's front door and swung it open, wedging a piece of wood underneath the frame to let in the air and the voice of the lieutenant. The cadets stood at attention.

"Psalm Sixty-six, verses one through four, brothers and sisters. Make a joyful noise unto God, all ye lands: Sing forth the honour of his name: make his praise glorious. Say unto God, How terrible art thou in thy works! through the greatness of thy power shall thine enemies submit themselves unto thee. All the earth shall worship thee, and shall sing unto thee; they shall sing to thy name."

The singing commenced once more, and Evelyn pulled the door closed.

"Hey, I was listening," protested one of the customers.

Evelyn was in the packing room, her hands on the deaf baker's shoulders, guiding him through a dance step. She was attending her twenty-fifth high school reunion and needed someone to practice with her. Branley happened upon them while digging for an extra box of sugar.

"Hey, Branley," Evelyn said, twirling at the end of the baker's arm, "why don't you cut in?"

Her partner stopped short. "The Baptists frown on this, don't they?" the baker asked. "No dancing, card playing, smoking, drinking, moviegoing?"

Branley, shielding his eyes with his forearm, moved away from them.

"Didn't mean to offend," said the baker. "You can really blast us if it helps."

Not a single passage came to Branley's mind.

The shipment of doughnut mix was lost in Virginia, so the bakers had to cut back on their production. "Just until we can get another load up here," said Mr. Raymond. The deaf baker, who had far more experience than Branley, showed him how to reduce all of the measurements in proportion. The kindness made Branley so uneasy that he had difficulty starting his morning preaching.

Branley poured half the amount he normally used into the pail, lowered the stainless steel beater into the brew, and turned on the electric mixer. His eyes, bright blue beads, rolled back a bit and the heat from the nearby fryer made him a little light-headed. He'd been up late studying his scripture. "Be fruitful and multiply," he commanded. He scraped the pail, easing the rubbery dough onto a table, and ran a rolling pin over its surface, stretching it into a sheet twice the length of his arm. Dividing the sheet in half, he took one portion and massaged it with the rolling pin again. "Make thineself supple unto the Lord's will. As the wind would bend the willow, so, too, would Christ Jesus work through you. Through you, with you, and in you." The thin blanket of dough had doubled in length and he halved it, placing one portion aside. Now there were three pieces, each one flatter than the next.

Dusting the table with flour, he reclaimed one of the original pieces and then sprinkled it, too, with a pinch of flour, to prevent the dough from sticking to the pin. He twisted the sheet into a knot, kneaded it with his fingers, pulled at the edges as if the dough were taffy, and started the rolling process once again. The blisters of sweat that had formed on his forehead now burst and he lifted his forearm upward to wipe away the moisture. Using a metal spatula, he cut the length in three this time—Branley's fingers began to cramp around the ends of the pin, but he pushed on. He bowed his head to curb the dizziness and remembered the exodus of the Israelites, their hunger in the wilderness, and the manna that lay on the ground that had rained from heaven. A cloud seemed to form around him as he kneaded the batter, flattened it with the pin, and divided the fruits of his labor again and again and again, forming two where there had been one. At one point he rolled the pin over his hand, thinking it was the tablet of dough.

"Branley. Hello, Branley," Mr. Raymond shouted, though he was standing just a few inches from the baker. "Orbis. You measure your ingredients?" The owner checked the log to make sure the proportions were correct.

Laid out on the cutting table, like pieces of linen, were a dozen—actually, a baker's dozen—lengths of dough. Trembling a bit from his effort, Branley asked, humbler than usual, "Is there enough here for the Sabbath?"

"I should make you cut them, fry them, and eat them yourself," said his boss, folding over six of the sheets and plopping them into a large bowl. "Put these in the refrigerator. Less work for the next shift." And then he added in a stage whisper, "Nobody's ever gotten that kind of yield from those measurements. You watch your calculations, you hear?"

Three students in a row, now, had failed to answer the professor's question about Revelations. Most nights Branley's hand would slice the air, his foot counting out the time it took another disciple to answer. Instead he was noticeably quiet, tracing a chain of circles on his desk with his finger. "The Great Tribulation, Branley," said the teacher. "Why so called?"

"He is a chosen vessel unto me," Branley muttered. "I am the chosen vessel."

"Mr. Orbis. Speak up. Project that strong voice unto the Lord," the professor urged and Branley let loose.

"If a man therefore purge himself from these, he shall be a vessel unto honour, sanctified, and meet for the master's use."

The teacher shook his head and walked toward Branley. "Very nice. Timothy Two. The book I am addressing is Revelation, for those remaining classmembers who are interested in the ministry."

Branley excused himself and left the class early.

Totally disoriented, the would-be preacher almost overlooked his gas gauge registering *E.* He had a vague recollection of a service station, with three pumps, about a mile north; when he reached it the attendant was putting out the lights. Branley fairly coasted into the lot. The ruggedness of the body made Branley assume the worker was a man, but when the attendant turned around, Branley saw a woman's face, soft and fleshy, yellow hair tucked into a cap. He opened his window.

"You're out, aren't you?" she asked, annoyed by the delay, her manner bullish. "You have to wait while I go in and get the key. It's a miracle I'm still here."

Getting out of the car, Branley followed behind her. "Why do you say a miracle?" he pressed her. "Can you define a miracle?"

The woman ran her eyes over Branley's frame, searching for a weapon. She stood close enough to sniff his breath. It smelled remarkably sweet, but with no trace of alcohol. He had the most irritating expression, like his mind had been dulled by a blow he himself had inflicted.

"OK," she said, "it's a miracle I'm willing to do this. It's a miracle I don't just leave you stranded. It's a miracle you've got a license. Are you a divinity student? This area is lousy with your type." She filled the gas tank, her solid hips rubbing against Branley's car.

"What you're saying is that miracles can happen to the unworthy. That the spirit can penetrate even those who are not ready?" Branley hung on, desperate for some understanding.

44

"You want a sermon you're gonna have to pay more than that," she answered, pointing to the $13.30 on the pump.

He pulled two tens from his wallet. She stashed the money in the back pocket of her jeans and said, as she locked up again, "You can make it further on fumes than you think."

Branley's slumber was heavy and troubled, a sleep that seemed to roll over on itself, endlessly. When he finally awoke, the late afternoon sun was spending itself on the porch of the house across from his apartment. He had missed the entire day. He got up, made note of the time, walked to the kitchen, where he drank three glasses of water, ate the crust on a piece of white bread (the center he placed in the bag, along with a half dozen other centers), and returned to his room. Then, after reprimanding himself severely for his sloth, Branley bent over to straighten the covers and instead fell into a peaceful sleep. Outside, like some arrogant schoolchild, the night wind kicked up the dirt around the foundation of the house, scattering the grass seed the landlord had planted that March morning.

Branley had never stopped by the doughnut shop on a Sunday. His pattern was to attend nine o'clock services, do some homework, drive over to his cousin Leola's for a Sunday dinner with Le and her mother, Branley's Aunt Maisie. Every week they ate the same: roast chicken with gravy made from a can of cream of chicken soup. Le insisted on carrots for her eyes—still twenty-twenty at the age of thirty-six—and Branley always brought a dessert he'd made the day before. Only today he came without.

Leola worked at Sear's, in the shoe department. She'd seen the sorriest-looking feet in America. "Some of these people would sooner buy a new pair of shoes than cut their toenails," she said, passing the carrots.

"I'll be needing a pair of sandals," said Branley, and then, under his breath, quoted, " 'and your feet shod with the preparation of the gospel of peace.' "

Aunt Maisie apologized for not making peas.

"They won't be out for another couple months," said Leola, and then, seeing her mother's puzzled expression explained, "Sandals, Mama. The sandals."

He took them to the shop for dessert—his way of apologizing for the fact that he hadn't baked anything. Entering through the back door, he prepared to give the grand tour, to describe the process in lay terms, as it were. The deaf baker was wrapping things up early, so the frying was nearly complete. After showing off the mixing bowls, rolling board, and cutting table, Branley flipped open a window on the proof box to indicate where the doughnuts rose. The preaching baker heard the voice, faint but distinctive, telling him to commence his ministry.

"Le?" he asked.

"Yes?"

"Something you want to know?"

"Oh—you'd like me to ask questions, is that it?" she said, attempting to humor him. "OK, how long do the dough rings stay in this thing?"

He leaned in toward the proof box a second time and listened. The voice spoke again. Branley nervously glanced around the room. The deaf baker introduced himself to Branley's relatives and asked if they were enjoying the tour.

"*Oh, yes,*" shouted Le. "*Thank you, yes.*" Then, to make doubly sure he understood, she took a notepad and pencil from a table and wrote "Thanks—wonderful."

The three stepped up on the pallet ("Careful," warned Branley) and stared down into the fryer. Branley seemed to be counting the bits of debris.

"Well, will you look at that," puffed Maisie, seeing absolutely nothing extraordinary. She'd have preferred to be home watching wrestling. "Uh-huh."

Le, hoping to quicken their pace, headed for the glazer. "Something I've always wanted to do," she explained, dipping her finger into the liquid and coating it with the sugary icing, then popping the finger into her mouth.

"Don't hold back, honey," said Evelyn Caine, slamming an empty tray onto a table. "Nobody else does."

Before she could do it again, Branley pulled her away and said, "You've tainted the waters." Feeling the spirit welling up inside him, he grabbed hold of his Aunt Maisie with his free hand and said, "We'd better leave. I'm not feeling well."

Both Maisie and Le began fussing, shuffling their feet like kids yanked from a candy store and asking Branley why he had brought them there if they weren't going to have a treat. Dashing into the back room filled with doughnuts packed for delivery, Branley lifted a box of glazed from a shelf and thrust them toward Le.

The tiny band's music was barely audible from where he stood. Evelyn was making a derisive remark about a young woman "punched up next to the officer." Le handed the doughnuts back to Branley and pushed her way through the swinging door to the shop front. "Le," he cried, anger inhabiting his voice, lowering the tone. "Don't. We're leaving. We're out of here."

She stopped for a moment to take in the scene across the way. "Isn't that sweet," Leola said and beckoned for Branley and Maisie to join her.

The Salvation Army Band had just finished their second song, "There Is a Balm in Gilead." Standing adjacent to the bandleader was the girl from the previous week. She held the lieutenant's horn as he began his preaching. All of the customers, Maisie and Le included, sat at attention, waiting for the homily to begin.

"See that pap at the end there—the old guy with a horn?" asked one of mechanics from the Buick garage. "He used to be a drinking buddy. Every Sunday afternoon for a good fifteen years we commiserated at Cruddy Ruddy's Bar. I bet he can still belt them down."

"She's going to get herself in trouble, wait and see," Evelyn said, nodding her head and motioning toward the young woman in blue with her elbow. To punctuate her statement she tilted her pelvis a bit to the side, the seam of her white uniform straining with the movement. Under her right arm the material was split a bit. "She'll nab him one way or another."

"Mama," sighed Le, eager to make a contribution, "isn't that Furball Ferell's youngest brother?"

Maisie swiveled her stool around. "I will not acknowledge

47

anyone from that family. My lord, that boy would lick the fur off a kitten before he drowned it."

Branley couldn't bear to hear another word. "Hypocrites," he said, and then louder, "hypocrites, hypocrites, hypocrites. For the congregation of hypocrites shall be desolate, and fire shall consume the tabernacles of bribery." Using a box of yeast as a step, he climbed onto the counter, stumbled, and then straightened up, his arms outstretched, reaching toward the spirit.

"There is no need, Branley," cried Maisie, trying to pull him down. "No need of dessert today. We can do without."

The band had paused a moment to watch the spectacle across from them—a man, maybe thirty, of slender build and with wispy blond hair walking on top of the counter, the customers getting up off their stools and standing with their backs to the windows, a congregation alert to the power of their leader. The band offered a prayer, not for themselves, but for their brethern nearby, a prayer of forgiveness and redemption. And for one moment there was quiet, quiet that conquered time and action, a stillness that crept from the inside out of each one of them, Le and Maisie and the Buick boys, the couple leaning against the cigarette machine, all of the pilgrims with the Salvation Army, and the deaf baker who came out to help, and even Evelyn Caine, who, as Branley delivered his message in a voice free and melodic as a songbird's, swore that she had heard God.

Mr. Raymond

The Greeks broke ground for their "donut" shop just two blocks west of Every Day's location. That April morning Mr. Raymond, Every Day's owner, stood in his competitor's lot. He walked alongside the construction crew and proclaimed, "Competition's good. Keeps you on your toes." He lifted up on his ten toes for emphasis.

"Morning," he said to the foreman and handed him a pencil stamped with the slogan "We Make a POINT of Making the Best Doughnuts—Every Day." Then he marched back to his own business and asked his daughter, Doreen, why his neon sign wasn't lit.

"Could be it's burned out," she said, tossing a washrag over the chocolate crueller she'd been sneaking. "I could go check."

"Do it myself," he said, biting down on his back teeth, and then, seeing a customer, he forced a smile and added, "Have a pencil. It's on the house."

Mr. Raymond spent the next two hours figuring out why the sign wouldn't light. Checking the switch, the wiring, and a separate fuse box, he finally climbed a narrow stairway to the roof. While there, he looked to see how far the building crew had progressed, leaning up against the sign to get a better view. They appeared to be taking a break.

"It's tough, real tough," Mr. Raymond said to the sign. "I give them one year at best."

Pacing the flat roof, he found three stray baseballs, all belonging to the kid janitor, and he waved to the mechanics crossing the street to his shop.

"Good morning," he shouted.

The sign flashed on. The owner jumped once and it went out, hopped again and it came to life. The words EVERY DAY danced above a neon sunrise. Mr. Raymond had received the sign in lieu of a $2,500 cash debt five years ago. He still intended to add the word DOUGHNUTS in the space between the letters and the sun's rays.

"Ah, well," he said, satisfied that the sign would now stay lit.

Back inside, he paused to listen to Branley say a few words over the fryer. Mr. Raymond pursed his lips, attempting to swallow the preacher's message. It seemed to go down the wrong pipe. A wash of acid bubbled in his throat.

"Let them try to find help," Mr. Raymond muttered. "They can't imagine what's out there."

Taking a doughnut from the rack, he poked it, sniffed it, broke it in half to see if it was baked through, and gave the baker a thumbs up. Once in the small paneled office he turned on the radio, switching stations to find a weather report.

"And a chance of showers tomorrow with rain continuing through the week," the announced read.

"Aha!" cried Mr. Raymond, thinking of his competitor's construction. In a tablet he wrote the date and sketched the ground-breaking scene with an Every Day pencil. At the office door lingered two waitresses, arguing over their schedules.

"Who's out front with the customers?" he asked.

"We've got it under control, Mr. R.," whined the skinnier woman, her long brown-blond hair piled high on her head. She wore a ring on each of her eight fingers. "I need to change my hours two days next week. She won't trade with me."

"Twice this month already," complained Evelyn Caine. "You can't make me."

"No, she can't," advised Mr. Raymond. Shaking his bald head

at them both, he said, "Cooperation is key. It's basic to success." He had learned this from a Dale Carnegie course, and knew it in his heart to be true. "I'm interested in your success, she's interested in the shop's success, you're interested in her success. It all adds up to the same thing," he stressed, in a fatherly tone. "Think about that and see Marie," he added, referring them to the morning manager. Through the years, he also had learned when to delegate.

The weather, cloudless for two weeks straight, allowed the build-ing to progress on schedule. On the way home each evening Mr. Raymond drove around the block twice to assess the day's work. Sitting beside him, Doreen asked if he was all right.

"They seem to have an awfully good spot; right at that major intersection," she said. "And that huge lot. Are you worried?"

"About what?" he said with a patronizing air, making her sound a little bit crazy.

At 6:30 A.M., however, Mr. Raymond camped in his car across from the Greek's store and measured the traffic with a hand-held counter. Stretching behind the wheel, shifting one leg and then the other, he watched as the new shop's owner pulled up in a Cadillac. For the first time that Mr. Raymond knew of, the Greek was inspecting the work, which was nearing completion. The man, dressed in a dark suit with a blue-and-white striped shirt, said nothing to the construction gang. Two younger men carried hot pink menu boards and a hot pink countertop. The shop's interior had begun to take shape and Mr. Raymond had to force himself to keep his eyes on the passing cars.

"Was that three cars just now or four?" he asked the windshield. "Damn."

He stuck to this task for two full hours. Arriving at his own store, he pointed to coffee stains on the turquoise counter and told Evelyn to hand him a sponge.

"If you've got time to lean, it's time to clean," he joked with her, his voice straining.

Tapping a customer on the shoulder, Mr. Raymond said pleas-antly, "Let me get that for you," and wiped up the sticky spots. "Here, a little present," he said to the Buick boy eating a peanut doughnut and handed him an Every Day calendar shaped like a doughnut truck that he'd pulled from his breast pocket. Good public relations never hurt.

"Got any more of those?" asked the middle-aged woman who'd ordered three glasses of water and one plain doughnut. "I'm always in here."

"Over here," said the city clerk, just walking in for his regular order of a dozen glazed. "And one for my secretary."

"Hold on," Mr. Raymond said, winking at the two who were asking. He waved his hand, genuinely pleased by his popularity. "Have to check in the back." The Greeks wouldn't have this kind of following. Business was built, in part, on personality, he remembered, the Dale Carnegie legend shining in his mind.

The baker and former paperboy Wade Lowbar, who'd just been hired as a helper, were staring into the industrial-size mixing bowl filled with newly made dough. Both seemed caught in a game of freeze tag. Suddenly the baker grabbed both sides of the tub and uttered a prayer. Wade appeared to be on the verge of tears.

"Let's go, let's go," said Mr. Raymond enthusiastically. "This isn't a Sunday service. Come on, Branley."

Wade lifted his index finger into the air.

"Look," he said to his boss.

"So you've got a scratch," Mr. Raymond said. "I've got twenty. Do you want to file for disability?" he mocked.

The preacher began dragging the hundred pounds of dough toward the cutting table, reciting a psalm. Wade waved his finger in Mr. Raymond's face.

"Mr. R., would you look?" he insisted, and Mr. Raymond grabbed the boy's finger and examined the digit, the skin white and blanched around the scabbed cut. Gathering all of his nerve, Wade, watching Mr. Raymond's shaking jowls, confessed, "I lost my Band-aid. In the mix. I was turning the dough in the bowl and it must have come off."

"It's one hundred pounds, this morning's run," explained the baker.

"I am aware," said Mr. Raymond softly, the muscles in his neck popping, his brow glowing a bright pink.

52

Evelyn Caine chose that moment to push on the swinging door, popping her head in the backroom. "How soon for hot glazed?" she yelled. Out front, the customer was saying, "Ask him about my calendar. I've been standing here——"

"*OK*," shouted Mr. Raymond, and Evelyn released the door. He stomped over to the vat and ordered, resolutely, "Throw it out. *Throw it all out.*"

Wade and the baker now scrambled to lift the great mound of protean dough from its container. They poured it onto the floor and dragged the rubbery lump to a large garbage can while Mr. Raymond, a human scribble, raced to gather the ingredients for a new run. The baker rolled the giant mixing bowl toward him and hurried the garbage to the dumpster behind the shop. Mr. Raymond grabbed the vat, locked it in place, and motioned for Wade to draw a pail of water. The baker returned and, composed now, said he'd pay for the loss. "Thank you, Mr. Raymond," he added, handing the owner the huge paddle that beat the dough. "May the Lord bless you. Bless you and reward you."

Mr. Raymond thrust the paddle toward his employee with a glare, almost ramming it through his belly. Evelyn, now a spectator, had removed her apron and folded it in half. She watched Mr. Raymond's rubber-soled foot coming toward her.

"What's that?" she asked.

"What's *what?*" he barked, wanting only to get on with things.

"On your shoe—hanging from the bottom of your shoe?" she said, bending over and pointing toward his toe.

Displaying the shoe's underside to his employee, the boss man crooked his leg to see for himself.

"Oh," said Evelyn. "Oops. Sorry. It's just a Band-aid."

He peeled it from the gummy surface and shook it vigorously at the baker and Wade.

"Look," he spit out. "You look."

At home that night he sat in the vibrating chair his wife had bought him, a turquoise leatherette lounger with various controls built into the armrest. It had never worked properly. He turned on the heating mode and a slight buzz began competing with the TV's static. His wife called out from the kitchen.

"I'm fine," he assured her. "It's fine."

"It's supposed to do that," she shouted. "That's the relaxing part."

He got out of the chair, squeezed himself behind it, leaned over, and pulled the cord from the socket. Sometimes he wondered if his wife, good intentioned as she was, was trying to kill him.

"Is the flag in?" he asked her, and she mumbled. "Why, no."

"All right. OK," he replied, authoritatively, going to his front porch and pulling on the flag line. Every house in the neighborhood wore a Stars and Stripes, but his was the largest. Tucking the cloth under his arm, he strutted up and down the block, waiting to see who took theirs in next.

The sign for Daisy Donuts was installed at eight o'clock and the new store opened by nine. The Greek, Mr. Andropolus, again dressed impeccably, released fifty balloons into the air (one for each donut flavor), turned the key in the door, held it for the first ten customers, got in his Caddy, and drove off. The waitresses, who looked to be college age, wore pink-and-white baseball caps, white jeans with pink smocks, white sneakers (no nurses' shoes), and big plastic buttons with their names and the day's special. One waitress stood in the parking lot that surrounded the building on three sides and offered free samples to passersby. Seeing Mr. Raymond stationed in his car across the street, pretending to read a newspaper, the waitress strolled over and knocked on the window, which was rolled halfway up.

"Fresh as a Daisy," she said, sticking the small pink tray in the car window.

Her hands and nails were immaculate and she had all of her teeth, blinding white rectangles with pink healthy gums that had never seen refined sugar, let alone a doughnut.

"I'm waiting for my wife," Mr. Raymond said, pointing to the outpatient mental health clinic.

"Maybe she'd like one," the waitress, percolating with cheer, replied.

What was she making an hour? Mr. Raymond wondered. How much did the hats cost? How many girls to a shift? How many filled donuts? How many plain?

"You look like you need a little Daisy break," the girl continued, her tone insipid.

"Got to give them away, huh?" Mr. Raymond laughed and, reaching for two different kinds, explained, "For the wife."

Placing them on the car seat, he picked the donuts up, one at a time. They were smaller than his, smaller and worse—heavier. Little rings of lead. The first donut's icing already had cracked. The outdoor waitress had a small crowd now and each stool in the shop was taken. A foreman from the book bindery held the door for two old ladies.

"It's the novelty," Mr. Raymond told the steering column wearily. "All that pink."

His own shop had two customers, one who'd ordered only a glass of water. The waitress, quickly stamping out her cigarette when she heard Mr. Raymond's footfall, wore a long baker's apron over her polyester uniform.

"I hear they have real nice outfits at Daisy," she jibed.

"I'm sure they do," said Mr. Raymond, indulging her.

"With little pink baseball caps," she pushed, touching the paper crown on her own head. A grease stain glistened in the corner of the hat.

"Mmm-hmm," said Mr. Raymond, watching the front for customers. The smell of the newly dipped glazed reached him and he smiled as the heat from the fryers took the chill off his day.

"They wear sneakers," she said in parting, and he called after, "They'll wear out faster. They're not made for the long haul."

Ripping a piece of paper from a notepad, he wrote a message to the morning manager that read, "Put Jeane Merckle on notice." Then he printed in all capital letters on the employee bulletin board, "WE WILL NOT BE SLAVES TO FASHION."

Each morning Daisy seemed to be drawing more and more "donut" lovers. Mr. Raymond counted six extra bags of stales a night, and the brats who usually dropped by just before closing to beg for leftovers had moved their hungry stomachs westward. All of this put more pressure on his salesmen, who delivered to the supermarkets, restaurants, and schools. Mr. Raymond had just hired a new salesman, a kid who'd spent the last year sleeping beneath a bridge. Marcus Tucker's life experience helped to place everything else in perspective. When the others groused about the mandate to add one new account Mr. Raymond countered, "It could be worse. You could be living under a bridge." Generally that stopped the conversation.

Mr. Raymond decided to conduct a spy mission to Daisy. Marcus, too grateful to betray a trust, would be an ideal candidate, one sure to keep the secret between them. Mr. Raymond called him into the office and told Marcus he had a big responsibility for him. Marcus's eyelid started doing the jitterbug and then his shoulder began to jerk, as if taxed by this additional weight. Even if he did make it into Daisy unnoticed, the tic in Marcus's eye would prevent him from seeing what was going on. Mr. Raymond abandoned the plan and merely asked Marcus to take charge of washing the trucks. Marcus wanted to kiss him.

That night Mr. Raymond and his wife went to the midnight madness sale at the Eynon Drug Department Store. Their kitchen linoleum was badly worn, a hand-me-down from the doughnut shop. Mrs. Raymond searched through the sample sheets and the discontinued colors for the best buy. She had her heart set on pink. Her husband tried steering her toward a brick red, then an orange.

"Pink," he said, looking nauseated, intent on disuading her. "The color of that medicine for the runs."

Always willing to compromise, she pressed her nose to a coral-colored square.

"Well, I'm the one that has to look at it up close," she explained.

He left her to make her selection and threaded his way through the crowds to the lawn section. A red, white, and blue cast iron cannon, "an authentic replica," exclaimed the tag, sat among the flamingos and jockeys. Before Mrs. Raymond had made her choice, her husband had paid for the cannon and asked the help to wheel it to his car.

* * *

At the shop, in a storage room next to the men's and women's toilets, sat the lost and found, three boxes filled with customers' leavings. Rifling through the sweaters, scarves, gloves, glasses, caps, and lighters, Mr. Raymond retrieved a long black cape and a squashed fedora, swung the great coat into the air, and, realizing that it would only draw attention, tossed it back in the bin. The wrap-around sunglasses would work; so would the cap with the John Deere emblem. The pair of mustard-colored driving gloves were a little tight, so he'd leave them unsnapped. He set these items aside and went to his office to find the Cuban cigar he'd received when waitress Terri Kudja had her third baby.

Gathering up his costume, he ducked into the men's room and bolted the door. In the pocked square mirror above the little sink was a face he didn't recognize. "How do you do," he said, and then congratulated himself on his resourcefulness.

Mr. Raymond removed the disguise, folded the goods under his arm, and checked the employees' closet for a suitable coat. When his search proved fruitless he resigned himself to a quick visit to the Goodwill store down the road. On the first rack he found an old hunter's quilted vest, with zip-in sleeves, size extra large. Over the left breast was a hole the size of an acorn, charred around the edges, which accounted for the vest's price—$2.50. He plunked down his money, sorting through his change for an extra thirty-five cents for an Uncle Sam patch to cover the hole.

From a phone booth he called the shop to say he was running a few errands and would return in an hour. Pulling into a church parking lot, Mr. Raymond grabbed his apparel and, using the parish's van as a screen, dressed for his performance. He found the whole charade a little thrilling. Unable to resist his own image, he twisted the van's sideview mirror toward him. Yes, from all appearances he seemed a new man, entirely.

Cutting through an alley, he noticed that his shoes were leaving a trail of flour. An occupational hazard, one sure to betray him. Placing a hand on a vacant warehouse for support, he removed the one shoe, turned it over, then scraped the bottom on a nearby rock. With his handkerchief and a bubble of spit he shined the shoe, picking at a clump of dried dough with his nail. He repeated the ritual with the second shoe and exhaled deeply—it had been a close call.

To further obscure his identity Mr. Raymond affected a limp—a hunting wound, he'd tell the waitress. "Now I only stalk sweet things," he'd add cleverly.

Six cars sat in Daisy's lot and eleven customers at the counter. Mr. Raymond recognized two of Every Day's regulars at the shop's far end. One he had just given a calendar. Every Day's owner had considered bringing a notebook but dismissed it as too risky. From his back pocket he drew a newspaper, not the local journal but a *New York Times*, a stroke of brilliance. As he pulled on the door that said PUSH ME, PLEASE he remembered to limp and wondered if he'd done so while crossing the street.

"Push," the waitress was shouting from the inside. "Just give it a itty-bitty shove. Here," she said, coming from around the counter and holding the door for Mr. Raymond.

"It's a hunting injury," he explained, and then, recognizing his own voice, his heart flopped. Recovering, he cleared his throat and continued an octave lower, "I'm here to hunt sweet things."

He hobbled over to a stool in the middle, where two large beauticians, their hair engineering feats of wonder, would block him from the customers he'd recognized. More comfortable with his role, Mr. Raymond dragged his leg for the last three steps, then used his hands to swing the limb forward once he was seated. Now he had the attention of at least three-quarters of the customers.

"Good morning," he said to the women beside him, and again he had to correct his voice. He growled a bit to prepare his tone, and then boomed, "Nice day."

The waitress stood over him, smiling, her scrubbed nails resting on the counter. "May I help you?" she asked, and before he could answer, she recited, "How about our special—juice, coffee, and a cinnamon doughnut?"

To throw her off a bit he merely nodded yes. The man knew he should be checking out the brand of coffee maker, the depth of the refrigerator, the donut setups, and the machinery in the back, clearly visible through the glass partition, but he was fascinated by the beautician's hair. There seemed to be three distinct sections, the front and two sides, each built several inches from her skull, and the texture was that of spun glass. You could actually see through parts of it, tiny warrens of curl. Her friend's coif had waves, little white caps, varnished into place. Staring through the wrap-around sunglasses, it struck him that perhaps he wasn't getting out enough. The beautician nearest turned his way.

"You like it? We do each other's," she explained, lifting a cream-filled donut to her lips. Her long fuschia nails wore miniature silver stars.

Mr. Raymond had to remind himself of who he was underneath it all. Using his gloved index finger, he punched a hole in his own donut, broke off a section, and sniffed it. The waitress caught him and rolled her eyes.

"Is there anything you need? Something you're missing?" the waitress asked, oozing concern.

The intruder put down the donut and sipped at the coffee. The java was fresh but a lower-end brand, one he'd tried at his store and replaced. Smacking his lips, he searched for an aftertaste. For some reason, though, the coffee tasted better than it should have. Smiling, he replied, "I'm fine." Bouncing a bit, he gauged the comfort of the stool.

"Are you sure?" persisted the waitress. She drifted to the corner where a police officer sat with his partner, and threw a glance Mr. Raymond's way.

"Fill it up, Melissa," the cop said to the waitress and then whispered, "I've got an eye on him."

Mr. Raymond stared up at the menu board and made a mental note of the prices, about a nickel higher than his own. Without his glasses it was difficult to see the cost-per-dozen sign. Boosting himself forward, elbows akimbo, he knocked the beautician's ample bosom.

"Sir," she whined, more annoyed by his sudden lack of attention than the jab to her breast.

Her hair glistened under the fluorescent lights, which faltered for just a second. She tapped a wrist ornament that seemed a cross between a watch and a compass.

"Do you have trouble with electrical objects?" she asked. "I'm picking up a strong force field."

In a conciliatory gesture Mr. Raymond offered to buy her another donut. She ordered two for herself (cream-filled) and two for her friend. Mr. Raymond groaned slightly, dismayed that he was feeding his competitor's profits. From the back of the shop, a baker grinned merrily. Dozens of golden donuts progressed down the conveyer belt and, coaxed by flippers attached to the machine's end, landed on empty trays. Mr. Raymond had inspected the contraption, a German invention, at the annual doughnut convention in Atlantic City. Otherwise the store's layout, he observed, bore a striking resemblance to his own shop.

The beauticians said good-bye and indicated that Mr. Raymond would pick up the tab. The waitress added the bill gleefully and presented it with a flourish, along with a free frisbee. Reluctant to leave, he asked for a tall glass of cold water.

"And another donut," she strongly suggested, "—lemon, raspberry, blueberry, pineapple, apple, peach, spiced apple . . ."

"You're one heck of a salesgirl," Mr. Raymond said, his altered voice sounding odder and odder. "Ever think about working for anyone else? I know of a good night job, with benefits."

The policeman placed a hand on his shoulder. "Could I see you outside for a minute, buddy?"

"I'd like him to pay first," insisted the waitress.

"I'm not going anywhere," replied Mr. Raymond, his tone changing once again. "I'm not finished."

"Just for a minute, bud. There's something I'd like to discuss. Need your opinion on something," coaxed the officer.

Mr. Raymond reached in his wallet for a five-dollar bill and two ones, yanked on the correct leg, and limped out. The cop followed a few yards behind. The high school that sat between the two shops had let out for lunch, and dozens of students poured into Daisy's space.

Bending over as if he'd been taken ill, Mr. Raymond ducked through the teenagers' legs, pushing them, determined to make an escape. For a moment he was sixteen and stealing third. The kids shouted and shoved one another, adding to the confusion. At the same time Mr. Raymond managed to strip off the glasses and hat. The officer, more amused than angered by the man's performance, shouted into the crowd.

"You! Mr. Raymond! Take it easy, will ya?" the cop said, marveling at the older man's speed as he raced to home plate.

Mr. Raymond, winded from his flight, was both terrified and elated by his brush with the law. His legs tingled with excitement and his hands, which had beat the air like oars, were a vivid cherry. Why hadn't the cop followed him? And what had the officer shouted into the crowd? Was he now under some type of surveillance? Dropping what remained of the disguise into the dumpster, he entered his shop's back door and stood by the time clock, catching his breath. For the first time in a decade he phoned his wife in the middle of the day.

"How are things?" he asked in a tone so solicitous she failed to recognize his voice.

"You must have the wrong number," Mrs. Raymond answered, hanging up the receiver.

He wondered if she'd been talking in a kind of code. Sitting at his desk, he sketched Daisy's interior as he recalled it, estimating the square footage in its storefront. Daisy had perhaps a yard and one-half additional counter space. Walking out front, he surveyed his own counter. In the corner sat a classmate from high school, a purse factory worker who always could be counted on for at least a half dozen doughnuts at a clip. Mr. Raymond grabbed the stool next to her. Her bottom was nearly large enough to cover two places. She was one healthy woman, Mr. Raymond observed.

"Tell me, Margaret," he said, motioning for the waitress to bring him a cup of coffee. "Tell me something."

"Drove a needle through my nail this morning," she offered, pointing to a blackened forefinger. "Those leather handles at the factory are murder."

"I meant I had a question," he said sincerely. "How many of our doughnuts have you eaten in your lifetime? Any idea? Dozens? Hundreds of dozens?"

She scratched out "6 × 5 days = 30; 30 × 50 weeks = 1,500;

1,500 × 30 years = 45,000″ and handed him the napkin with her math.

"That doesn't count weekends," she added.

"Have you ever regretted a single one?" he asked earnestly.

"Just this last batch," she said and walked out.

Mr. Raymond stood on his front lawn patting his cannon. He had been outside for several hours, ever since his wife had fallen asleep. At 2:00 A.M. a police car patrolled the street and he thought about hurrying inside, but instead he stood his ground. At three he drove to his shop to make sure it was locked and passed Daisy Donut on the way home. Daisy was empty, though he could see by slowing down a bit that the cash register drawer was wide open. Apparently the Greek's shop had been robbed.

Mr. Raymond's legs began to twitch as he speculated about the waitresses; had they been abducted or hurt? Pulling into the parking lot, he circled the store, driving onto the walkway. When his headlights hit the far side of the shop he caught a glimpse of the figure crouched by a trash basket—a small man holding a gun. The glare from the shop lights and the glass front made everything seem unreal; his own shop and Daisy and the horn on the steering wheel were miles away.

Mr. Raymond wished they had never built this damned store. He wished his wife had chosen the putty-colored linoleum over that faux pink, and that he'd learned to play golf. He wished his daughter Doreen were interested in taking over his business. He wished that he'd kissed the beautician's hair. He even let himself wish he had never become a doughnut man. The bullet, meant to scare him off, shattered the windshield, passing so close to his ear that he heard it whiz by. The headrest halted its journey.

By the time the police arrived Mr. Raymond had untied both the waitress and the baker, who were in the back, sitting in a pile of donuts. The automatic conveyer had continued to push out the donuts which had then flowed onto the floor. Even in this most desperate moment Mr. Raymond could calculate the carnage—about 120 dozen.

After filling out the police report, Every Day's owner drove directly to work. The conquering hero, he thought. Hail Caesar. He had taught them all something about professional courtesy. Two salesmen, Marcus and Josh, stood in the back, loading up their deliveries, and Mr. Raymond stopped to tell them they were both good boys.

"He must be sick," said Josh. "Everyone knows he can't stand me."

Some hours later, after Mr. Raymond had woken his wife, told her what happened, and showered and changed, he returned to the shop and made two phone calls—one to a neon sign company, to get a price on the word *DOUGHNUTS*, and a second to the owner of Daisy Donuts, who wasn't to be reached. When he checked the register receipts at the day's end, he found that sales were off by only 5 percent. A wave of relief swept over him; perseverance was the measure of every man's mettle.

The owner of the rival shop couldn't meet for two weeks; the Greek was traveling and wouldn't be back in Scranton until the end of the month. Mr. Raymond learned this after calling a half dozen numbers, trying to track the man down. Mr. Raymond hated that Mr. Andropolus had an accent.

"You were the one to first call the police, right?" Mr. Andropolus asked his competitor.

"That's correct," said Mr. Raymond, not bothering to mention that he accidentally had tripped the electrical alarm on his way into the shop. And then, acknowledging that he was above all this pettiness, he added, "It's a shame about your losses."

"We're insured," the Greek explained, unfazed.

Daisy was sponsoring a float in the St. Patrick's Day Parade. A giant papier-mâché donut with a coffee cup built from plywood sat in the middle of a trailer, pulled by one of the employees' cars. There were four waitresses on the top, pretending to eat donuts, occasionally tossing a travel mug or plastic sunglasses to the onlookers. They waved, as did the car's driver, and chanted, "Take a Daisy break. Take a Daisy break."

Three floats behind marched the Veterans of Foreign Wars, Mr. Raymond leading the contingent from the Korean War. Because he no longer could fit into his uniform he wore a short-sleeved white shirt with the Every Day logo, a green tie, white baker's pants, and his officer's cap. His black tie shoes had been polished until they'd become two mirrors. His group stepped the liveliest.

"Come on, men," commanded Mr. Raymond. "Let's show them we still have the stuff."

At the end of the route, as the marchers fell out, Mr. Raymond spotted Andropolus's car. Twice now Daisy's owner had canceled their meeting. Andropolus stopped one of the other vets, who pointed out Mr. Raymond.

"I had heard you were in the parade," said the Greek businessman. "I've been extremely busy. We're looking into other fast foods. But I'd like to buy you a cup of coffee." Mr. Raymond nodded.

Together the men crossed the street to a diner on Lackawanna Avenue. Sliding into the booth, the toes of their shoes brushed each other's, causing both to feel uncomfortable. Andropolus ordered a piece of baklava. Mr. Raymond had a doughnut. Neither spoke until they were almost finished eating.

"We service this place. These are our doughnuts," Mr. Raymond finally said, swelling up. "I'll have another," Mr. Raymond added, winking at the waitress and denying his stomach ulcer.

"You make very good doughnuts," said Andropolus.

"One for my . . . friend, too," said Mr. Raymond, but Andropolus shook his head no. "You've tasted them?"

"A whole box," said Andropolus. "I walked in one morning and bought a dozen. That night, when I couldn't sleep, I ate twelve at one sitting. I couldn't stop myself. I think my waitress's name was Doreen."

"You wouldn't be needing another waitress?" Mr. Raymond joked.

Mr. Andropolus checked his watch.

"You were hurting us at first," Mr. Raymond began. "I can't deny that. I watched people who had sat at my counter for years walk the extra blocks because they liked pink. My girls even wanted your uniforms. I found one of your damn travel mugs in

64

my truck. The kid next door threw a Daisy frisbee on our garage roof."

Andropolus interrupted. "That's not making a doughnut. That's marketing. Promotions."

"You're a college boy," Mr. Raymond remarked, brittle, tempted to digress.

"Business major."

"I never had the opportunity myself," Mr. Raymond explained. "But that's not why I wanted to meet you." He took a deep breath and bit down on his teeth, squeezing the words through them. "I'm not the enemy and neither are you. I thought it was time you were welcomed to the neighborhood."

Andropolus smiled to himself. "It's a difficult business, isn't it? I mean there's high turnover. Rising prices of sugar and shortening. Low profits and long hours," sympathized the Greek. "You must be tied to your work. Life must be hard most days."

"Now, see," said Mr. Raymond, "that's the beauty of it. Life is an endeavor."

The Greek slapped his hand on the table. "Are you looking to sell?"

Mr. Raymond stared in disbelief.

"Are you interested in buying my place, then?" asked Andropolus, adding, "Isn't buying and selling the point?"

With the exception of the annual doughnut convention and his two summer weeks at the Jersey shore, Mr. Raymond had spent every day of nearly thirty-five years at Every Day. He dug inside his coat pocket for a calendar to hand his competitor.

"You can think on it," said the Greek. "I have to be off. I'm on my way elsewhere."

"I believe that to be true," said Mr. Raymond, motioning for the check.

Three months later, as Mr. Raymond drove past Daisy early one morning, he noticed a large van in the lot and several carpenters. He parked his car and greeted the men. Inside, the place was empty.

"Good morning," he said. "What's going on here?"

"We're stripping the place," said one worker. "Taking the fixtures to a store in Syracuse. They've sold this building to a Chicken Delight."

Mr. Raymond walked to his car and pulled a box of doughnuts from the backseat. With a smile he handed it to the carpenters, then headed back to Every Day to check the store.

Carl

Carl Quinlan had been a janitor's helper at St. Paul's High School, so when Mike Vokacik retired after twenty-five years of scraping the doughnut shop's floors, Mr. Raymond tried Carl out. At first the boy claimed he wanted the evening job so he could continue with his studies, thinking that was the right thing to say. But really no one cared about his graduating, least of all Carl, and within weeks, instead of coming in at four o'clock, as agreed on, the sixteen-year-old would show up by two and linger an hour or more at the counter before punching in, smoking a half dozen cigarettes, picking at his nails, sipping a Coke. The factory workers all came here on their breaks and he kicked back and listened to their gossip; he smiled and nodded like he was confirming the rumors about Janette, or Nicole, or Betsy from the handbag outlet and Dave from the bookbinder's, a casanova who grabbed for the waitress's hand as she poured second cups of coffee. Carl felt like he fit right in.

Sweeping up a classroom and dumping the trash wasn't, Carl quickly learned, cleaning. Mr. Raymond introduced Carl to that art. The evening before the health inspectors arrived the owner stayed through the night, working alongside his rookie, nearly

67

caressing each curve of the shop. The boss knew how to tease the dirt from the corners, run a broom along the area where ceiling meets wall, how to steam the sugary floors with buckets of hot water. Removing the fixtures, he plunged small mops into their openings, and he twisted the seats from the stools and soaked them in a bath of vinegar. Mr. Raymond rubbed the machinery with a cloth diaper, urging it to shine.

"Why are you doing this?" Carl asked at 5:00 A.M., as they were finishing up. "You could have hired someone to come in here and show me."

Mr. Raymond gave the stools a final wipe. "Ever buy anything, Carl—a car, a bike, a catcher's mitt?"

Carl mumbled a yeah, wanting the man to get to the point. "You may have bought it, but until you worked on it, I bet, until you fixed up that bike, you didn't really *own* it. You clean something this well, you come to own it," he said, and then, glancing at the clock, added with a laugh, "or it owns you."

The truth was, Carl, who lived at home with his older sister Brigid, had never owned much of anything.

The grease from the fryers and smell from the shortening got into everything—the cleaning cloths, the mops, the machinery, the aprons, the paper hats, your hair. All of the employees had "shop shoes" which they wore only there, knowing that if they strolled outside with those sneakers, boots, or nurses shoes they'd smell like a walking bakery. Carl thought if he scrubbed hard enough he could rid the place of its odor, but that goal was tantamount to changing the surface of the moon. Instead he learned how to maintain appearances and keep the heavy cleaning down to once a week.

To make a good impression, Carl lined up his mops, brooms, and scrapers against the sink each night, checking that the tools also looked clean. His adeptness surprised him—at home he never even had made his bed or rinsed the shower after his use. That he left to Brigid, who wouldn't have it any other way. The siblings were not friends, being bound together more by habit than interests; Brigid, thirteen years older, virtually hibernated and Carl spent few waking hours at home. He'd worked at the school for spending money and now contributed half of his paycheck to the household. Along with this, the only thing Brigid asked was that Carl take out the trash and sweep the sidewalks. Neither questioned the arrangement.

Just before starting his shift, Carl sat at the counter working the baseball gloves bought with his first paycheck. He'd had it with him every day for a month and the leather, pummeled and massaged and soaped by turn, was giving in to the shape of his hand. The skin's color had deepened and the webbing relaxed, so that any ball meeting the leather didn't stand a chance of escape.

The guys from the bookbinder's asked if Carl was on a team. When he joined them for a game of catch one Saturday in August he made sure no one else used what was his. Two of the waitresses from the night shift came to watch the men play that afternoon; they were dating the pitcher and the outfielder. Carl, too, waved hello with his gloved hand held high above his head. When he took the glove home he put it in a place where Brigid wouldn't disturb it.

Carl was sitting on his glove—a tip he received from a double-A third baseman who'd eaten at the shop—when he finally decided to flirt with Gail Tuffton. One of the steadies, Gail had all the appeal of a pretty little cottage too long neglected. Her hair, a butterscotch blond, hung unevenly at her shoulders, the victim of one day at beauty school; her skin, a dull white, would have glowed after a good scrubbing. Fifteen years old and toothless as a newborn, Gail came in everyday with two little sisters in tow, gradeschoolers who were racing to see which one of them would look like Gail first. Carl had watched her for about three months, listened to her easy laugh, which possessed the satiny texture of vanilla icing. They had always exchanged nods, but today Carl decided to offer something more.

"How would you like it," he said, on impulse, "if I bought you a set of teeth?" He tilted back on the stool, excited by his own boldness.

Gail sat there smiling, the little flap of skin that should have been between the front two choppers dancing as she laughed.

"Take a hike," she answered.

"I mean it," he said, wishing he could comb her hair with his fingers, "I want to get you some teeth. I'm *going* to get you some teeth."

He walked to the back of the shop and began buffing the jelly pumps, eager for them to shine.

It didn't take long for Gail to be sold on the idea of having teeth. The magazines helped persuade her—Carl circled the prettiest girls, their mouths parted just enough to expose the rows of white, white that set off their lips, their cheeks, their eyes. Next to each model he'd write things like "Tooth Picks," "Love at First Bite," "Something to Chew On." Gail imagined how her life would change once she walked out of the dentist's office: a reporter from the local TV station would stop and ask her opinion on the new mall; her mother, won over by Gail's sweet smile, would quit drinking and begin minding the younger children herself; the teachers at her old school would commend her on her elocution and insist she take the lead in the annual play; boys would like her. Once she got married, had her first baby, and finally agreed to let the TV reporter write a movie of the week about her life, she'd get five thousand dollars, and out of that windfall she'd pay Carl back. Everything would be even-Steven.

Coming straight out and saying yes, please, wasn't her way. Instead Gail went back to the shop at around eleven, after the kids were in bed, grabbed the ammonia and brown paper towels from beneath the counter, and set to cleaning the cases where the doughnuts were kept during the day. This saved Carl a good fifteen minutes. Wetting down the stools, she checked for chewing gum under the seats and along the counter, scraping it off with an icing knife. Gail performed these duties for a week without ever mentioning the teeth, leaving the shop as soon as she was done. At the beginning of her second week of volunteerism, Carl became concerned, having made no real plans for the teeth, and to slow things down he told Gail he was doing his homework, finding the best dentist in town for the job. That night Gail let him walk her home.

Carl had meant to say nothing further, but her happiness—she moved her body loosely, her head and arms almost flighty—pushed him and he found himself talking.

"You'd better practice smiling. Get that mouth in shape for those pearls. Think of those toothpaste commercials and how sexy the girls look."

Carl flashed his own front teeth, big and white as Chicklets, and thought that Gail had already started to look better, thanks to him. When he got to his own house he ate the sandwich Brigid had left on the table and brushed his teeth before climbing into bed.

Just to get an idea, Gail cut out the models' smiles and taped them over her own. Too small; no matter how she contorted her lips, the flesh showed. Then one of her little sisters suggested she tuck the cutout *inside* her mouth, holding it against the inner lips with her tongue. "Now almost close," the child instructed. "Yes."

Walking ouside, Gail shot a baby smile at a stranger and thought "he believed." Then she went to the drugstore and chose three different toothbrushes she'd buy when she had a reason.

Carl didn't show for a whole day, the longest day of Gail's entire life. Mr. Raymond had changed Carl's schedule that week so he could see his first Phillies game. Gail kept silent vigil all Friday evening, figuring Carl was just late, reasoning that her patience would be rewarded if she didn't complain. Leaving the shop at 10:30, Gail was shaking so violently that she could have been her mother. When Gail got home and found one of her little sisters crying in her own mess and their mother passed out on the couch, she cleaned up the sobbing child, coaxed her into bed, and got her settled.

"Gailly," the child said, clinging to her. "Stay."

Gail tried prying the child's fingers from her shirt and when they wouldn't give, she almost hit her. The gesture was enough to scare the child into letting go. The child's mouth, formed into a lopsided *O*, revealed a row of brown stubs that made Gail stop.

71

The next afternoon Gail got up the courage to ask the waitress, Terri, if Carl had quit—left and taken her new life with him. Terri said, "Our Carl?" as if Carls came in dozens, like doughnuts. "Never. He loves this place. He's just off at a ball game."

Choosing six doughnuts (and then two more for herself), Gail asked for Carl's address—she wanted to drop off the sweets. Terri thought that was cute, wrote down Carl's house number, and gave Gail an employee discount.

Carl and his sister Brigid lived in the rowhouses that ran parallel to the river. Their parents, who had died within six months of each other when Carl was eight, had left Brigid the house and its few belongings.

Gail had no inkling of Carl's living arrangement. He seemed so sure of himself that she figured he was on his own, free from the burden of a mother, father, or younger siblings. The whole way over to Carl's house Gail, comforted by Terri's words, fantasized about becoming a waitress, wearing her hair in a bun, bringing Carl cups of coffee—one sugar, no cream. Customers, dazzled by Gail's new smile, would buy dozens and dozens of doughnuts and leave her enormous tips. With the money Gail would put her mother in the detox, hire a private eye to find her father, and pay the entry fee for the Miss Northeastern Pennsylvania contest.

The lights were off, the door locked, and as Gail pulled at its wobbling knob and then tried the bell, a stream of anxiety shot through her body. She felt the adrenaline pumping her legs and she raced to the back, where again the door stopped her. Hurrying to the basement, she placed her foot on the upper sill, and, throwing her eighty-five pounds into the effort, the girl forced open a window. In a life characterized by doing without, Gail wanted her teeth more than she had ever let herself want anything.

Carl's sister, Brigid, had left home just an hour earlier, walking to the church to make her confession. During the night her mind had produced unthinkable dreams, too impure to put into words, filthy visions that, once in the confessional box, she wrapped in the cloak of the Sixth Commandment, which addressed all impurities of thought, word, and deed. Mercifully, the priest did not ask for details.

That spring Brigid's nightmares had dwelled on the same thing—losing her teeth. She'd bite into a doughnut, a long crueller covered with peanuts that Carl had brought home after his shift, and all of a sudden she'd realize that she was crunching her own incisors. Or Brigid would pass by a mirror and see that her smile had gone jagged, looking like the casualty of a wild punch. In her dreams her teeth were loose as a kindergartner's, wiggling about as she tried to explain that she needed a dentist. They flew out when she asked directions from strangers. They crumbled like graham crackers as she prepared dinner. And that was not the worst of it.

But being Brigid, she told no one, instead reading the dreams as a sign to stop eating things like doughnuts and graham crackers. The dreams were a reminder that there's no substitute for good oral hygiene, Brigid rationalized. When the nightmares persisted into the fourth week, Brigid counted up the money for the household expenses and for the first time in five years went to the store to buy herself something other than a necessity. She purchased a Water Pik.

Then last night, the woman dreamed that just as she was about to place the plastic tube in her mouth, she looked down at her hand and found that the pik had turned into her brother's man hose—his urine pipe. She awoke, terrified, to find her own thumb in her mouth, moist and withered as a date.

Returning from the sacrament, Brigid, wearing a blue-print shift with a belt hiked above her natural waistline and a hat shaped like a saucer, noticed that the screen door was ajar and figured that Carl, home early, had forgotten to close it properly. He'd also left on the light in the kitchen. As she was about to call out, she saw a girl, a tiny strange being with a cup of coffee in her hand. Gail did not flinch.

"I'm waiting for Carl," Gail explained, holding her ground, figuring Brigid was his mother. "I'm not leaving."

"He let you in? Where is he?" Brigid asked the intruder. Normally Brigid would have panicked, but she found herself transfixed by Gail's empty mouth.

"Here," said Gail, doing her best waitress imitation. "I made some coffee."

Putting her hand to her lips, Brigid checked to make sure her own teeth were still intact.

"Oh, hold on," Gail continued, disappearing into the kitchen again. "I brought doughnuts."

Brigid, shaking her head, her hand now glued to her mouth, asked Gail how old she was.

"More than fifteen," the girl replied, practicing an open-mouth smile that summoned up Brigid's worst nightmare.

"Dear God," said Brigid. "He didn't do the nasty thing with you, did he? Are you here about that?" Brigid demanded, her eyes seeking out a curve, a swelling on Gail's tentative body.

Gail found herself calmed by this jittery woman and spent a moment peering into her face, a face too young, she determined, to belong to Carl's mother. Her hesitation furthered Brigid's fears.

"Is this your house?" Gail asked politely, marveling at the cleanliness of her surroundings. "Are you two going together?"

"We're family," said Brigid. Then, offering Gail her hand, she added, "I'm a Christian. I'll try to be sympathetic. Just tell me what's going on."

Gail knew that her teeth were just words away. "He made me a promise," she said, and the tormented Brigid began to cry.

On the ride home from the game it occurred to Carl that perhaps he should ask these guys if they knew a dentist. The rigid glove that he'd transformed into a supple hand, soft as a doe's skin, had caught a foul pop over third base and both the glove and the ball lay in his lap. The car had the smell of stale beer; a half dozen cans rattled at his feet when they hit a bump.

"Hey, Dave," he said to the bookbinder seated up front, tuning in the radio, "I need a dentist."

"Open wide," said Dave, pulling Carl by the neck and prying open the kid's mouth with his thumb. "That will be sixty bucks."

The driver asked Carl what the problem was.

74

"Know someone who needs a set of choppers," Carl explained.

"Your pap?" the driver asked. "Cost him plenty. My mother got dentures and even with Medicaid, Medicare, all that old people crap, cost me four hundred dollars. And she never wears them."

Carl sunk into the seat. "They're not for my folks. My folks are dead," he added, toting up how long it would take him to pay off four hundred dollars.

"Hey, that's right—you live with your sister," said Dave. "She seeing anybody? She a looker?"

The thought of Brigid being involved with someone seemed so ludicrous that Carl forgot his troubles momentarily. And then as the sign for the Pennsylvania Turnpike rose before him his worries rushed back into his head, causing Carl to feel dizzy.

"Anybody up for a road stop? Maybe we'll grab a couple of sandwiches," said the driver, and Carl said, "Yeah!"

No one had held Brigid in the last twenty years. Gail, suddenly seeing the woman not as Brigid but as a needy six-year-old, put her arms around Carl's sister and let her sob. In a few minutes Brigid composed herself with the aid of Gail's tissue ("Just blow," Gail had said) and began apologizing for her outburst.

"This isn't like me," she assured Gail.

Brigid and Gail dined together that evening. Gail knew she'd catch hell from her mother when she got home but she was not giving up on her teeth, not when she'd come this far. At six o'clock, out of habit, Brigid wandered toward the stove and extended Gail the invitation.

Thinking back to high school and her home ec classes, Brigid once again assumed her position of authority and poured Gail an eight-ounce glass of whole milk while reciting the four major food groups to herself.

"Did you have cereal today?" she asked the girl. "Maybe we'll start off with some Special K."

Concerned about Gail's ability to chew and still worried about her own teeth (though she had to admit that Gail didn't look too bad sans bicuspids), Brigid pulled together a casserole of chopped beef, canned tomatoes, American cheese, and noodles. She took four slices of white bread from the freezer and set them on a plate.

"We all need good nutrition," she said. "Here you have your condiments." Brigid pointed to the salt, pepper, and a stick of butter.

Gail sat down to a plateful of steaming food and slurped the noodles while Brigid watched.

"Does it hurt?" Brigid asked.

"Sometimes," said Gail, figuring that was the safest answer.

Gail cleared the dishes, without being asked or told, before Brigid had finished her last bite of Jell-O. The two worked in the kitchen in unison then, one washing, the other drying, Gail bending down to wipe the floor when spots of water landed around their feet. The kitchen was as long and narrow as a hall, with a dove gray light. Brigid performed a little ritual, with her mother's ancient teapot, spreading a new cloth on the table and placing the cups just so. The cream and sugar containers were mother-of-pearl, the latter filled with uniform cubes. The girl admired the set.

"I do this every night," Brigid lied. She had emptied from her mind all thoughts of Carl. "Tea helps digestion."

"That's good for a waitress to know," said Gail, her mind only on Carl. She warmed her gums on the cup's rim. "Mmmn," she murmured.

Crossing the room, Brigid pulled open a table drawer jammed with papers and scratched through the odds and ends for a deck of cards. She scooped up a new deck, in yellowed plastic, and a game of Authors' Rummy. For Brigid, who each day worked as a secretary for the city tax office, one of those solitary young-old women, dressed in maroon or blue, who merely waved hello and good-bye, kept a desk without ornament, and gave up nothing of herself, this evening had become an event.

The woman emptied the box and spread before her guest people Gail had never heard of—Nathaniel Hawthorne, James Fenimore Cooper, Louisa May Alcott.

It was Dave, fooling around in the front, who nearly caused the accident. He was chugging a beer and then pretending to throw up on the driver's lap. The rain, which had come upon them suddenly, made the visibility near zero; several cars were sitting it out on the road's shoulder.

The driver jumped when he heard Dave's gagging, Dave's head knocking the wheel. They were inches from the semi when Carl yelled "Watch out!" and the trucker laid on his horn. The sudden swerve threw Carl to side of the car, where he hit his mouth.

"Shit," said Dave, eyeing Carl's bleeding mouth, "We may all need a dentist. You OK, kid?"

Carl's worry was the glove, flung from his lap by the motion, now on the car floor, stained with beer. He picked it up and nursed it, wiping the glove clean, before tending to his own mouth.

Delayed by the meal stop and near accident, Carl had no choice but to go directly to work. He was two hours late, having promised to be back by six. Grabbing his shoes from his locker, Carl tossed in his glove and ball and quickly set to scrubbing the trays in the sink. The night-shift waitress asked how he'd hurt his mouth. Carl's bottom lip had swelled and become a deep purple and the gums of his front teeth were lined with blood. He turned to the aluminum face of the paper towel dispenser and stared.

"It looks worse than it feels," Carl said, pressing a wet towel to his teeth. "We almost hit this rig." He downplayed the incident, nervous that someone might suggest he not travel with such companions again.

"But your mouth's all right?" the waitress asked. "Nothing loose? My neighbor's cousin's a dentist," she said, offering the man's name.

When she left, Carl ripped a blank page from the baker's log and wrote down what she had told him. He wondered if he could buy teeth in sections, like Lego blocks, building on as he got the cash, or if Gail would be satisfied with just a few in the front. Sloshing a mop on the floor, overtired from the trip, he began to resent the promise, and Gail, for believing it.

At about nine o'clock, well into a fourth game of rummy (Gail had won the first three and only now, out of boredom, was willing to throw the fourth), Brigid went to her bedroom on the pretense of changing into slippers and phoned the doughnut shop. Gail had prompted the call, having repeatedly asked about Carl's absence.

"He should have been back by now," Gail had said, and Brigid, honestly having forgotten, answered, "Who?"

It was the first time Brigid had bothered Carl at work, and when the waitress held the phone up, waving it toward him, his face showed his confusion.

"*My* sister?" Carl questioned. "Are you sure that's who it is?" He pushed the broom across the floor, running behind it on his way to the telephone. "Brigid? Is there something—"

"You're at work, then," she said, her voice shallow. "And you'll be there awhile?"

"I got back late, so I couldn't stop home. I won't be in before two or three. Don't make anything to eat," he added, hoping that was her purpose in calling. "I'll have some doughnuts."

She hung up, deliberately not telling her brother about Gail's arrival.

When Brigid entered the living room, Gail noticed that the woman hadn't changed her shoes. Gail's eyes fastened themselves to Brigid's feet.

Her hostess apologized. "The news made me forget," she explained. "The girl at the shop told me that Carl phoned to say he was still in Philadelphia. He'll be home in a few hours," she said. "I should make more tea. Or some hot milk. Would you like hot milk?" Brigid asked.

Gail, unaccustomed to such mothering, nodded yes.

"And some pillows," Brigid suggested, offering the two from her bed, now reversing the women's roles. "Pillows would make us more comfortable."

In her fifteen years, Gail had never met anyone like Brigid; a woman with a home of her own and no children, who could rattle off the names of dead writers and set a table for tea. Brigid seemed the very opposite of Carl, who was teasing and physical, sure of his needs. The woman appeared now to be as nervous as she had been at the beginning of their meeting, spilling the cup of milk, having filled it too high, bringing out the sugar bowl and a spoon unnecessarily.

"He's at the doughnut shop, isn't he?" Gail asked her, her back stretched out against the couch.

Brigid was mortified. "You heard me?" she asked, the corners of her mouth weighed down by shame.

"I guessed," said Gail. She blew on the milk and offered the woman a sip.

"You can go meet him, of course, if that suits you," Brigid said, expecting her to leave.

Sinking into the pillow, Gail replied, "It's OK. I'll wait with you."

She let Brigid's head rest on her shoulder. The older woman smelled like deodorant soap. Exhausted from her sleepless nights, Brigid nearly drifted off, her entire body listing toward Gail's. She was not heavy or cumbersome. Brigid caught herself, straightened up, settling the collar on her blouse.

"Do you ever dream?" she asked Gail.

"About being a waitress. Or sometimes a mother. Or an actress," the girl admitted.

"And Carl," said Brigid. "Does he know about these?"

Gail had to say no.

"But I do. And I promise to help you. Does that make us friends?" Brigid asked.

Two high school kids had gotten sick on the steps of the shop, right before closing time, and Carl was forced to drag out the hose, hook it up to the outside faucet, and run the mess into the street. Some of the vomit stuck between the rungs of the railing and he drew a rag from his back pocket and wiped the poles. Then he went back into the shop to finish, without polishing up the railing as he might have. It was not worth the effort, he thought. The place wasn't his.

After the night-shift waitress cleared the cash register, Carl walked her to her car and sat at the packing table with a container of milk and four doughnuts. Someone had left him a note saying Gail had stopped by, looking for him. There was no avoiding it—she'd be in every day, reminding him. He had no idea why he'd made the suggestion to begin with. When he bit into the last doughnut, he paused, believing that a tooth in the back, one that had seemed unaffected by the accident, had moved. He rinsed out his mouth in the bathroom sink and tried the tooth's strength by tenderly pressing its edge with his finger. It held. The wobbling had just been his imagination.

Carl crept into the house at around three in the morning, having sacked out for an hour on the doughnut shop cot. The living room light burned in the window, a sign that Brigid had fallen asleep, waiting. Only partly awake himself, Carl had to backtrack and stand in front of the couch to make sure that what he saw was real.

Each woman had laid her head in the middle of the sofa, crown to crown, like Siamese twins attached at the skull. Brigid's legs were planted firmly against the sofa's edge, as if she would sit up at any moment, while Gail's legs, at the opposite end, were tucked beneath her. Both were breathing rapidly, the steamy breath of dreams, eyelids quivering, mouths open, ready.

Leaving

Wade

Wade Lowbar had needed a job bad. Sylvia's welfare check stretched only so far and he hated the way the clerk gawked at him when he tried to trade in the food stamps for chips and beer. Besides, Sylvia didn't like him home all day; she wanted to watch her soaps in peace.

He'd been Sylvia's paperboy—that's how they'd met. For the first three months he wasn't even sure who lived in apartment 3C, one flight up from the B & G Lounge. Sometimes the tenant left an envelope for him at the bar. Other times a teenage girl in stretch pants and a big flannel shirt would pay him on her way down the stairs. Then there was the hand that would snake its way between the chain lock and the door frame. No body, no voice. Just a woman's hand, dropping two carefully folded bills into his palm. The fingertips felt like satin. The hand seemed to emerge from a dimness that made Wade forget the time of day.

Twice now he'd seen the edge of a blue velour sleeve, part of a housecoat, the elastic biting at the hand's wrist. One Wednesday morning he cut classes and stayed in the alley behind the lounge, thinking up ways to persuade the hand to reveal its owner. He could ask for a glass of water or to use the toilet, or cry "fire" in the hall. Wade tried none of these.

Instead Wade put a face and torso together in his head, one he hoped for. That's how he recognized Sylvia, coming down the steps, her right hand holding her coat closed.

"Excuse me, ma'am," he said, rummaging through his brain for a piece of conversation.

She stared at him blankly, then at the toe of her red shoe, which she tipped forward.

"I'm the paper carrier. How come you've never tipped me?"

She offered, instead, to buy him a drink. After that they went back upstairs and made love—his first time. A week later, on his seventeenth birthday, Wade quit school and moved in. With Sylvia and her fifteen-year-old daughter Jennifer.

Wade tried ManPower first, assuming that he could pick up some day work in one of the factories' warehouses. The line was a long one—about twenty guys, all bigger. Wade tugged at the collar of his fatigue jacket and slouched against a pipe. He moved up three places in a half hour; five minutes later, he left. A sign posted at the parking authority advertised for a night guard, but he'd miss Sylvia too much. The paper listed a few possibilities, including a janitor's job at the Industrial Park—no go, since he'd have to take two busses just to get out there.

Before returning to their apartment Wade downed a milkshake at Shookey's Shake Shoppe and walked over to the Court House Square to see a demonstration by the pro-lifers. EVERYTHING THAT GOD MAKES HAS DIGNITY, said the banner.

Sylvia was soaking in the bathtub, a magazine propped on her knees. She glanced up when Wade entered the room, then watched him shrug and stick his hands deep into his jacket pockets.

"We gotta get out of here," she told him. They were two months behind in the rent. "You're the man of the family," she added, sizing him up the way that only she could. "So do something."

He pulled out of his coat, knelt on the dirty tile floor, and, rolling up his sleeves, started scrubbing Sylvia's back with a washcloth.

"I'm serious," she continued, hardly placated by the gesture. The

slope of her spine cut through the pooled water. "Do something."

He handed her a towel, one that had come in a giant box of detergent. It still smelled like the soap. The newspaper was jammed in his coat pocket and he reached for it, turning to the want ads. Moments like these he thought she would stop loving him and he would die, instantly.

"Couple of things in here look good," he said, watching her prance toward the bedroom, dropping the towel behind her and then, without turning back, shutting the door.

The bus to the mall was nearly empty—just Wade, an old lady with a plastic bubble over one eye, and a girl with an infant wrapped in a yellow blanket and a quilted sack thrown over her shoulder. The baby bottle had Mickey Mouse on it and the girl wore a Minnie Mouse pin on her jacket. Wade sat in the last seat, his feet up on the seat in front of him, trying to imagine Sylvia as a young mother, carting her kid downtown or to the doctor. He couldn't picture it any more than he could see himself at any age other than seventeen. Sylvia looked, and always would look, exactly as she did now, her body tall and lean as a python. She had a hard face, with angles sharp as an axe. Sometimes that scared him. It scared him to think that he had touched something so beautiful.

The video arcade had just opened, so he got his hands on the Pac Man immediately. The kids from Valley View were dribbling in, oversize eighth graders, mostly, with football jackets (orange and blue, the school's colors) and Nike sneakers. From the corner of his eye Wade watched them assess him. He had five dollars stashed away for an emergency and he spent all of it, even though that meant he'd have to walk home. The next job he heard about he'd take, no matter what.

Marie Eden, who he'd met on his paper route, told Wade about the opening for a baker's helper. The job entailed picking doughs as they rolled off the cutting table, washing screens, setting up for the next shift. The pay wasn't bad—$5.50 an hour—and he could walk to work. Wade started the same day he had the interview; the owner's daughter, Doreen, threw him an apron and pointed to a rack full of crusted screens.

"Could I use the phone first?" he asked, hoping to give Sylvia the good news.

The phone rang about a dozen times before Wade gave up, figuring that Sylvia must be in the tub taking her morning soak, listening to the radio. Wade really wanted to keep trying; he dialed again but hung up after the fifth ring, concerned that he was making a bad impression.

Hosing down the screens was easy, like running your own car wash, except that the idea was to keep everything else as dry as possible, which Wade wasn't too good at. He spent an hour of his shift mopping up the sugary puddles so the employees wouldn't slip. The bakers wore rubber-soled army boots that sucked at the floor like leeches.

"There's a spare pair of boots in the back," said the baker, eyeing Wade's sopping sneakers, the laces caked with glaze. "Put them on and praise the Lord. Go ahead."

Wade smiled and headed for the storage area, where one of the newer waitresses, Adele, sat on a jelly can, smoking a Kool. She gave him a grin and tapped her ashes into her cupped hand.

"Getting the hang of it?" she asked, crushing the cigarette butt with the heel of her nurse's shoe.

He liked her. In fact, he sort of liked the whole place. The smell of it made him feel secure, the heat a little drowsy, and no one demanded too much of him. He could eat all the doughnuts he wanted (but had to pay for his drinks). Because things were slow, the preaching baker even showed Wade how to roll a dough out, dusting it with flour and stretching the yellow blob into a thin sheet. As Wade punched out, Adele gave him a half dozen doughnuts, leftovers from the day before. He intended to take them to Sylvia but ended up eating all six on his way home.

The lights were off in the living room—even the TV and radio were off. Sylvia stood in the bedroom, tossing her things into cardboard boxes. The only clothes left were Wade's few shirts, his jeans, and the two belt buckles he kept on the dresser.

"Where were you?" she asked, her eyes too lazy to meet his.

"I got it. I worked today," he said, dropping to the bare mattress. "What's going on?"

She threw him the landlord's notice, threatening eviction in thirty days. "I'm moving. I don't need this. Jen's gone to stay with a girlfriend. You can do what you want."

Wade's hands clutched his stomach, as if he'd just been socked. The tears that sprung to his eyes were large and oily, running uncontrollably down his nose and cheeks. He tried blotting his cheeks with his hands, uttering not a sound.

"You're so—intense," she said, heading toward the living room.

Her movement loosened his throat. "I'll talk to the landlord. Tell him about the job. I'll get a loan from the owner." He wanted the words to trail her, even if he didn't dare.

That first night alone he rode the bus to the mall and back, walked into the apartment, threw himself on the mattress, and cried until he felt ill. Wade said Sylvia's name five hundred times, trying to make her reappear. For a few moments, around midnight, he thought she was standing outside the door, but when he went to check, no one was there. The next day Wade called the shop, saying he was sick. "Real bad," he lied, "throwing up." The waitress who answered believed him. Then Wade went to the high school to find Sylvia's daughter.

"I can't stand it," Jennifer said. "You finally get a job and then blow it by chasing Sylvia." She and two friends were hanging by a back door, sneaking cigarettes. The smoke circles drifted over Wade's head. "Listen. I'm going to live with my Dad's mom. She's cool. I can ask about you, too, if you want."

Wade shook his head, his hair wild from the tears and his sleepless night. Jennifer offered him a puff of her cigarette, which he passed up, and spoke to him kindly.

"She'll turn up—she always does," she said reassuringly. "Our stuff is still there."

Her voice drugged him temporarily, but as he closed the school's door, panic spread and he hurried through the streets looking for Sylvia's friends. At around four o'clock, after searching the neighborhood for hours, he tried the shelter. Sylvia was sitting at a card table drinking coffee from a paper cup, playing gin rummy with a bag lady. Circling Sylvia's neck was a red chiffon scarf with black raised dots. It cascaded to her knees. On her feet were the red heels she'd worn the first time Wade met her.

Wade ran to her, exhausted. "I was so worried," he said, reaching for the angular face.

She smiled, distantly, and wagged her head. "Kiddo. You're adorable," she said softly, kissing him.

The bag lady blew her nose on the queen of hearts.

Wade promised to find them another apartment, one where Sylvia wouldn't have to worry about the hot water running out or guys from the bar following her home. He had three more weeks before the landlord would post the eviction notice. By that time he'd have a paycheck and better connections. Maybe someone at the shop would help him.

Once they were settled in a new place, Wade would make Sylvia marry him, so there'd be none of this running away. That night, sleeping alone and soundly at the old apartment, Wade dreamed that the bartender from the B & G performed the wedding ceremony, inside the doughnut shop. Everybody wore their whites. And they ate a doughnut cake.

At the shop the next day the workers actually seemed concerned about Wade's health, advising him not to push it if he still felt sick. They scratched off some of his duties for the shift and let him make up a batch of chocolate icing, his favorite task. Twice the baker saw Wade in the back, sitting on the jelly cans, sipping a Coke. Branley just waved, like the whole thing was fine with him. Adele, the waitress who'd given him the doughnuts that first day, made Wade some instant tomato soup. Wade confessed that he had to move from his apartment—that his landlord was a real creep.

"I'll write you up a note for the bulletin board," Adele said. "Somebody's bound to know of a place you can rent."

The apartment was on the other side of town, a bus ride away from the shop, but Wade decided to look at it anyhow. He wouldn't mention it to Sylvia beforehand—she'd be disappointed if things didn't pan out. It was a walkup, four rooms above a discount clothing store on Archer Street. The last tenants had left some Uncle Ben's rice in the cupboard and a closetful of shoes. Several were in good shape and Wade was tempted to fish out a pair when the landlady turned to close the door. Sylvia would have died for the thigh-high blue suede boots lodged on the shelf. They were almost enough to persuade Wade to take the apartment.

For $120 a month, plus utilities and heat, the place was his.

"No pets, no kids, no parties," the landlady said, patting her underarms with a pink tissue. She wore a green stretch sweatsuit and a pair of men's loafers. Wade weighed her in at around 250. Sylvia would have called her gross. He poked his head into the bathroom to check the tub—big and deep, the kind with feet and two spigots for water instead of one. It had been three weeks now since he'd watched Sylvia bathe and the memory made him ache. Even so, he remembered to ask how high the heating bill ran and whether the owner would put on new locks. Wade felt, well, like an adult, a grown man making sure his family would be safe. When she asked again if he wanted the rooms, he nodded.

They (he) moved in the middle of the night. Wade tried to borrow the doughnut truck, offering the salesman a date with Sylvia's best friend, but he couldn't persuade Marcus Tucker to hand over the keys, which infuriated Wade, since he was the better driver. The baker had bible class and by the time Adele learned of Wade's dilemma, he'd become so embarrassed that he lied and said Sylvia's brother was lending him a pickup.

Wade borrowed three shopping carts from the guy at Food Fair, tied them together, loaded them with the boxes of Sylvia's clothes, dishes, and knickknacks, and dragged the caravan across town at one in the morning. The two round-trips he made cost him four hours. Coming down the hill on Ash Street he looked like a musher being dragged behind an aluminum sleigh. He'd allow the fleet to carry him forward a bit and just as things started to rattle, he'd stick out his foot, using it as a brake. By the end of the trial the treads on his sneakers were worn to a smooth plain. Halfway through the second trip the wheels on one of the carts jammed. Pulling the carts into an alley, he worked on the problem in the pitch dark. At one point he thought he might need to empty the cart out, push it on its side, fix it, and reload again. That was the only time he wanted to quit. Instead he kept kicking the wheels with his foot. They finally gave.

Sylvia said she loved it. Coming over on the bus, Wade told himself that if the driver got six green lights in a row, Sylvia would like the apartment. They sailed through the city streets and Wade felt even better than he had the day he landed his job at the doughnut shop.

"Cute place," Sylvia said, and Wade beamed.

She threw her purse on the low-slung coffee table, the only furniture in the living room, and walked through the hall to the big bedroom. On the mattress lay a box, wrapped in foil and decorated with a spray of silk flowers. Inside were the blue suede boots. Wade held his breath. Sylvia removed her espadrilles and laced up the boots. Without breaking the motion, she lifted her hands to the nape of her neck, unzipped her dress, and let it fall, along with her panties, to the floor. For a moment Wade thought he'd been struck blind. And if he had, it was worth it.

Nobody would ever love another as much as he loved Sylvia, Nobody, no how, he said, floating above her, then finally coming to rest at her side.

The first two months were great. Sylvia spent her days decorating, arranging, and rearranging her knickknacks, including the porcelain dog family. The couple bought a second-hand couch at the Goodwill and put money down on two chairs they fell in love with at Kaplan's Furniture. Wade worked overtime and bought Sylvia a bouquet of flowers every week. Sometimes they made love three or four times a day. Afterward he'd watch Sylvia lying there, her face cutting into the pillow, her brown hair swirling across the case. That's when he began to pray—a simple "Please, God, take care of her" prayer. "Please, God, don't let this be the last time."

Sylvia got friendly with the store owners downstairs and began working a few hours a week in the clothing shop. She gave freely of her fashion advice, unabashedly pushing her taste on anyone willing to listen. Within a month, half of the women in the neighborhood were dressing like Sylvia. Even those who didn't have the legs for it. She did so well that the Kosnicks asked her to consider a part-time job. As a bonus she'd get 25 percent off anything she bought. But Sylvia didn't jump at the offer—the commitment would mean missing her soaps a couple of days each week and the work entailed doing chores like watching that the teenage girls didn't stick any jewelry in their pockets.

Wade overheard Sylvia's phone call with Mrs. Kosnick. Her leg was up in the air, dangling a high heel, like something out of a fifties movie. Sylvia was saying, "Well, maybe if I could come in after 'The Bold and the Beautiful,' we could work it out."

Placing the flowers on the kitchen table, Wade waited for Sylvia to finish. He opened the refrigerator, gulped a mouthful of milk, and, gagging, spit it all over the curtains. Then he rinsed his mouth in the sink, grabbed a bottle of ginger ale, and gargled with it to kill the sour taste. He spit that out, too, out of anger. Sylvia put down the receiver.

"I don't want you working," he said before she could even get through the doorway. "No wife of mine is working."

Lifting the flowers to her face, she answered, "I'm not your wife. So stop getting crazy, Wade. This isn't 'Father Knows Best.' "

He couldn't let go of the argument; it had a hold on him he didn't quite understand.

"You're supposed to be here for me," he said. "That's the deal. You've got a color TV. You can sit here and watch whatever you want. You can play cards. You can invite your friends in. You can take a bus to town, or the mall, or even hang out at Kosnick's. But no job, understand?" He was trying hard not to let his voice crack. "I'll do the working."

For a minute she just stared, her face harder than he'd ever seen it. Not just hard, he thought. Mean. Plain mean.

"Is that what your father did?" she asked.

He hit her. He realized he'd done it after he heard her scream and watched her fold like the fender on a small car. He had no recollection of making contact, but the blood from her nose was all over her hands and face—even splattered on her halter top. Suddenly she was huddled against the legs of the table, holding onto the seat of the chair, screeching. When he extended his hand to help her up, to begin apologizing, she bit him. So hard that she, too, drew blood.

That was the first time he walked out.

In the back of the doughnut shop was a small army cot that a baker occasionally would sack out on. It was really nothing more than a piece of canvas stretched over six wooden legs. Wade rolled up his jacket as a pillow and threw himself onto the cot. For three hours he tried sleeping. He listened to the sound of the screens hitting the grease-filled fryer, the noise of the baker's rubber-soled shoes sucking at the floor as he moved from the cutting table to the fryer and then, finally, to the glazer. Only those sounds kept him from crying.

One of the salesmen, Marcus, bent over the little bed and asked if he could buy Wade some coffee. Wade turned slowly, so the cot wouldn't tip, and stared hard into Marcus's acned skin. Just looking at the man made Wade feel better about himself.

"I'd like a hot chocolate," said Wade.

They sat together in silence, sipping the drinks. Marcus was twice as disheveled as Wade, even though Marcus insisted that he'd gotten a good night's sleep, and the crumbs from two dough-nuts outlined his chapped lips. His partner stood by the door waiting for him.

"Take it easy, buddy," Marcus said to Wade.

At six in the morning Wade walked to the bus stop and waited until the first bus to the mall came by. When he got there about an hour later, there were three elderly men who had set out lawn chairs in the parking lot, to take the early morning sun. As he passed them Wade noticed that they were all reading newspa-pers—all from different days. Digging a quarter from his pocket, he lifted the rack on the paper machine, pulled out a *Tribune*, walked back to the three, and started reading, too.

"A fight with the missus?" one asked him.

Neither Sylvia nor Wade brought up the incident. Sylvia stayed in the apartment until her eyes returned to their normal color and Wade slept on the couch for six nights straight. Marcus offered his place as an option, but Wade declined. He was, after all, paying the rent. On the seventh night, after Wade heard Sylvia breathing deeply in her sleep, he slipped in beside her. In the middle of the night, they both awoke. Wade climbed on top and they made love until dawn, without speaking a word. At nine Wade got up, yanked up his baker's whites and rubber-soled boots, and kissed Sylvia's collarbone. Three hours later she got up, took her bath, and headed for Kosnick's. The store was filled with boxes of new stock and Sylvia dove into them, occasionally plucking a scarf and wrapping it around her waist or neck or tying it around her head. That afternoon she sold twenty scarves, a record. Mrs. Kosnick was so pleased that she served Sylvia coffee. When Wade came home they were sitting in the store window, sipping from tulip-shaped cups. He waved, went upstairs, called Adele the waitress, and asked if she'd meet him in front of the fountain at the mall.

Wade wasn't one for discussing his problems. In the third grade, when the teacher asked him why he hadn't changed his clothes in a week, he shrugged, said they were his favorite clothes, and never told that he, his three sisters, and his mother had moved at dawn the previous Thursday to get away from his father. They'd left nearly everything behind—it wasn't until his mother spoke with the Salvation Army lady that the kids had "new" clothes. Wade's father hadn't exactly done anything wrong. It was more like he just hadn't done anything, period. In years. Except to disappear every once in awhile. The last time Wade had seen his dad the man was lying on the couch at a friend's house, watching a kung fu movie. Mr. Lowbar barely looked up from the set, and when he did he asked Wade to buy him a beer.

Adele was wearing her uniform. Actually, Wade could smell her before he saw her, that sweet odor that scented everyone who worked at the shop. That smell alone made him smile—it reminded him of the time, on a dare, that he'd stuck his whole head into a pitcher of Kool-Aid.

"Hi," she said, drawing a cigarette from her pocket. "Why don't you tell me about it."

Wade shrugged his shoulders, ran his hand through the stagnant water in the fountain, fishing for a nickel. His hand seemed to swell in the bad light.

"Sylvia—" he began, his stomach growing queasy at the thought of badmouthing her.

"How old is she, anyway?" Adele asked, flicking the ashes into the fountain. "I mean really, Wade. I think you could do better."

Adele reached for his hand and laced her fingers between his. She was only the second woman to have ever done so—even Wade's mother hadn't hugged the boy since his childhood. "You're true blue, aren't you? Listen to me," she continued, squeezing his hand emphatically, "that pain won't last forever."

Just north of the fountain, in the center of the mall, was an organ display. Adele took Wade's arm and led him to the tester, where she poked out "Twinkle, Twinkle Little Star." Then she turned the sheet music to "Roll Out the Barrel" and guided Wade's index finger through the first verse, while he smiled. A Polish couple started clapping.

"Don't worry," Adele said. "Your heart will sing again."

Every morning in the shower, Wade cried. Sylvia was spending more and more time at Kosnick's, and Friday night she'd arrived home at 2:00 A.M. Her restlessness was growing. If Sylvia heard his cries, and she probably didn't, she chose to ignore his sadness. One day before dawn he awoke and, while watching her sleep, tried to draw her face in his mind. First the brow, then the eyes, her nose, and the lines to her mouth. When he left he thought he had seen her more clearly than ever before. He knew that at any time in the future he could summon up that picture in his mind, more truthful than a photograph. On his way to work Wade stopped at the bank and closed out his savings account, all three hundred dollars of it. The teller was maybe twenty, small-framed, with no makeup and a long red ponytail. She smiled at Wade when she went to get the bank officer to help with the paperwork. Wade smiled back, remembering Adele's words.

On the bulletin board at the shop was the notice about the car—a 1972 Valiant that ran but needed body repairs. Neither of the doors opened easily and the front one on the passenger's side was tied to the chassis with clothesline. The car had belonged to the deaf baker's son, who'd enlisted in the army. Wade believed that the car had good vibes. For $200, the baker said, the car was Wade's. Wade looked at the $300 in his hand, the most money he'd ever had, and asked if the baker would go down to $150. The baker took $100 and handed Wade the keys. Wade breathed in the shop's smell, sniffing his jacket to be sure he carried the aroma with him.

Sylvia had left a note saying she'd gone to the mall to buy stockings. In an envelope on the kitchen table he placed his remaining two hundred dollars. Walking into the bedroom, he stuffed his belt buckles into a paper bag, along with a pair of his jeans, his fatigue jacket, and a book on rock stars that his secret Santa (probably Terri Kudja) had given him for Christmas. Wade peered into the closet, started to take the blue suede boots, and then reached for the long red scarf Sylvia was wearing the day he was sure he'd lost her. He also took the two rolls of quarters they'd saved for the laundry.

He'd parked right in front of the building. Wade held the steering wheel so tightly that he thought his fingers would begin to bleed. The knuckles bulged, whitened by his grip. The radio still worked and he played it soft, real soft. And as he drove down the street, headed for the highway, he found himself singing along.

·

Marcus

The story that got to everybody, the story everyone wanted to hear, was about the time Marcus lived under a bridge. It wasn't the first thing out of his mouth but it wasn't the last, either. Marcus Tucker, age nineteen, aspiring doughnut salesman, delivering his goods throughout the greater Northeast, somehow knew when to pull that story into the conversation and show it off like a two-headed calf. Once he started parading it around the yard, no one cared why his training partner, Josh Steele, a Phi Beta Kappa, would-be financial analyst, left a kick-ass job in New York City to deliver doughnuts at five in the morning. As far as Josh was concerned, Marcus upstaged him every time.

As Josh often pointed out, it wasn't as if the guy had been under that bridge forever. By his own admission, he'd stayed there only nine months, maybe a little less. For nine months a person can stand just about anything—living alone in a cave, collecting tolls at a highway booth, sitting at home with another creature inhabiting his or her corpus. So why does hanging out under a bridge make folks who otherwise don't give a damn roll over and offer their paw?

That's how Marcus got with the company. He told Mr. Raymond about his dream to be a trucker, unfurling the certificate from the correspondence school saying he'd completed the courses. Marcus mentioned how he'd run away from home at fourteen to escape his father, who liked to diddle him, how he'd panhandled for a year and flopped at night at some youth shelter in the Bowery. Tucker hauled ass out of there when his friendly night supervisor started pulling the same Uncle Ernie number. He got placed in a group home for six months and finally ended up under a bridge in New Jersey. Set up house like something out of *The Hobbit*; used the water under the pilings to wash in a wuss of a river that not even once threatened to flood the guy out.

Josh Steele was a junior at the University of Chicago around the same time Marcus had saved enough money doing yard work—handyman jobs—to rent a post office box and enroll in the International Correspondence School for truck drivers. At that time, one man never guessed that the other existed. While Josh pushed toward Wall Street, Marcus dreamed of easing his Levis into a big rig, an eighteen-wheeler with a squawk box, surveying the country's low roads from a high seat—high enough, he'd say, to be safe from those who might try to pull him down again. The only problem: Marcus had yet to take the road test. You'd think he was young Abe Lincoln the way he told it, studying first by candlelight, then by a bare bulb after he shimmied some electric pole and ran a straw down to suck the juice. The Every Day waitresses rubbed up against that story aching for more, more—finally one morning Josh put an end to it by asking Marcus if his madre was Nancy Hanks. Never heard of her, said Marcus Farkus.

On the surface, at first glance, Marcus didn't have a lot going for him—skin so bad it could take a lesson from ground chuck, and his hair, a stringy mop with a head for a handle. He'd never read the employee manual, which stresses a neat and tidy appearance. Josh, atoning for the sin of once having left the area in search of something better, followed the rules, got a buzz cut, shaved in the dark before going on a run. ("Expected that from a boy raised on a farm by good parents, my own kin," said Mr. Raymond. "A boy who was *once* a member of the Wall Street community.") Nobody expected anything from Marcus—except Marcus.

What Marcus had going for him was rock bottom, and a truckload of stories. And Josh got to hear most of them during the three weeks they trained together. Halfway through the morning Josh would tell Marcus to put a plug in it, but he had to admit that the Life and Times of Tucker the Trucker made him forget he was stuck on the backroads of hell, delivering fat-infested cruellers to the heftiest people on the planet. ("Never touch 'em," the clerks at the grocery stores and waitresses at the diners would tell you. "Those little gems are for our customers. Got any doughnut holes with you?")

The two men, four years apart in age, were teamed to compensate for Marcus's lack of driving experience. Josh, the owner reasoned, could coach this worthy young Marcus, this unfortunate, while learning the run. Marcus tried to be glad for the chance. But once in the truck, he confessed to Josh his disappointment.

"Landing this job," he said, "is sort of like waking up on Christmas morning to find a tricycle with training wheels under the tree instead of a ten-speed."

"Right," said Josh.

The first three days the sales manager took the boys out to lead the way; they drew lots and Josh sat in the seat next to the boss man, while Marcus rode in the back with the doughnuts. Day four and beyond, Marcus did all of the driving—couldn't shift gears worth shit and Josh was sure he'd drop the transmission, but, hey, it wasn't *his* truck.

The twosome would start out in the near dark, the time of early morning when the sky looks like it's been bled of all its color. Josh arrived at 4:30 and Marcus would be there an hour already, counting up his orders and loading them into the truck. He wasn't looking for the extra cash—never once punched in before five o'clock, the official time of departure. Until they made it out of the city, though, Marcus would scrunch up his face, lips eating themselves as the tires bit into the pavement. All Josh needed to say was "Quarter of a mile to the blue route" and those lips would stop, having sucked themselves dry so they could chap on the trip back home.

They started calling the stories Sufferin' Tucker's Scab Collection. Seems that on Christmas, Toddler Tuck could count on Santa for about four items: a new shirt (or jeans), some kind of tool that was really his daddy's, a board game, and a car—Matchbox, model kit, whatever. He'd walk through the trailer into the living room and start to unwrap the gifts, and when he was through, his mother gathered them up and put them on a closet shelf. "It wouldn't be nice if your cousins were to see them," she'd explain. "They didn't get nothing this year." By the time Marcus was seven he'd told his folks to give them to the cousins instead.

Josh, always looking for life's report card, started rating the stories on a scale, one to ten. Marcus gawked at Josh like he was some grade-school teacher handing out gold stars for good behavior and barreled ahead. Age nine and at the state fair, Tucker crawled out of his seat on a ferris wheel, having planned on sliding down the spokes to escape his daddy. Figured Father Fiddle couldn't follow (he was right); the guys at the controls had to shut the thing off and call the fire department to help get the child down. Marcus had his first audience and the hell beat out of him when Papa hit the ground. (Why, oh, why didn't he just throw up on the ride like every other kid?) Josh awarded a 7.6 for content, 6.5 for delivery, 8 for entertainment value.

How Marcus hooked up with that blind guy and Dim-dim Jim was a story in itself. One day Marcus was riding a bus to Pennsylvania, next he's training at the doughnut shop, third he's moving in with two lost souls he met while swallowing his lunch on a bench by City Hall. The triumvirate parked their sorry carcasses in an apartment two stories up from a pizza place. The smell must have driven the blind guy nuts. We-are-fam-il-y.

At the end of the day, home from the run, Marcus would ask for some of the stales—day-old doughnuts normally sold to the pig lady. He said the blind guy toasted them in the oven and they tasted nearly as good as fresh. (The owner did *not* appreciate hearing that. His livelihood depended on folks wanting just-baked goods and nothing less.) The three roomies would trade off fixing dinner, Dim-dim making his contribution on Saturday night because it took him most of the day to figure out the formula for macaroni and cheese. The housekeeping fell to the blind guy, since he worked only three days a week, weaving brooms in some sheltered workshop. Place was so neat, Marcus said you could eat off the floor. For all Josh knew, they did.

Of all the places the two delivered to—diners, grocery stores, hospital luncheonettes—Marcus preferred the supermarkets, which the Every Day salesmen serviced before the stores opened up to the public. There'd be a few vendors, unloading the goods, a manager, and maybe one checkout lady, so the opportunity to steal was great. But the floor was so spanking clean, the shelves so orderly (no cereals left in the dairy case or canned fruits in with the breads) that a working man just didn't want to tamper with stuff. Like some grocery god had organized this universe, had ordained that the tea was in aisle four and the carts belonged up front.

The store managers ran this world, as everybody knew. Marcus and Josh hung back at first while the bread guys made the most of the quiet—talking sports (local), cars (theirs), and wives (somebody else's). Halfway through the conversation they'd suggest that the manager stock some additional items—pies, hamburger rolls, whatever. To managers, Marcus served up his sheepish grin, quietly unloading the goods, silently stacking them at the markets, getting across somehow that the clients were too special to spend their time rapping with him. Sort of stutter out a "sir" for affect. Tucker had more extra orders than the bread guys. Josh couldn't bring himself to congratulate his partner.

"Everybody can afford to back a loser," Mr. Phi Beta Kappa observed. "It's the winners people have trouble with."

As if to prove Josh's theory, pretty soon the checkout girls, particularly those at the Pump 'n' Pantry, started wooing Marcus. Making little sandwich packages ("Oh, these are for Marcus," they'd say. "Deli counter's over there on the right if you'd like something"). It may have had something to do with his clothes. You can buy a guy like that a thousand-dollar suit but you can't wear it for him. Tucker had a talent for making a brand-new shirt look like it had spent a decade in a Goodwill box. The Pump 'n' Pantry girls wanted to run out and buy him another, each thinking that her touch would turn him into a prince.

Josh consoled himself by saying that the hick chicks used ol' Marcus just to get to the real royalty. They saw how Josh protected his partner, always watching over him on the road. After all, Josh was the one toting up the receipts each shift, trying to introduce Marcus to the wonderful world of two times two. But when Tucker began dangling those stories in front of the short blond, mentioning that he might ask her out, Josh said he had no choice. He had to tell Marcus the truth about who she really wanted. They probably made it anyway.

Of course Marcus's luck couldn't hold. Any fool could see that. But the owner was pleased with Marcus's improvement—called him into the office to tell him so. The blind guy's daughter had stopped by to say how happy her father was with his new living arrangements and gave Marcus a five-dollar gift certificate to the monogram shop ("You Name It") where she worked. And Thumbelina at the Pump 'n' Pantry was showing more and more cleavage.

One morning, their last week out, Marcus and Josh walked to the lot, reached the truck doors, and found the windows wearing doughnut holes: perfect circles of condensation, weird as those cornfields in England. No way they happened on their own—some moonstruck artist had used a stencil or a compass. Front, sides, and back, dead center, rings that wouldn't disappear until you got in the truck and started hauling.

"Spooks the hell out of me," said Josh, who wanted to erase them.

But Tuck the Buck kept trying to prolong the rings, slowing down when he saw their edges beginning to fade. "I like them," he said. "They're odd."

Two days later it happened again. "I'm not getting in that truck," Josh said. "Somebody's sending us a message. Could be wired to a bomb."

Josh stomped his feet on the pavement, figuring he'd get Marcus to confess to the crime, or at least postpone their run. But Marcus was as unshakable as concrete, doing his duty to God and his country, making sure those plumpsters got their doughnuts on time.

"Neither snow nor rain nor heat nor dark of night . . . aye, Marcus?" Josh began.

"Huh?" said Marcus.

They finally climbed up into the truck and took off, neither one speaking. Twenty minutes out of town a fox bolted out of the woods and into the two-lane roadway. Its eyes glowed a bottle green and Marcus braked to avoid him, sending the packages of doughnuts flying all over. One box clipped Marcus in the ear, another flew in his lap, and two hit the windshield. Josh ducked. The fox hopped a minute, his tail sweeping the air, and skidded back into the bushes. Marcus's clean shirt and his company jacket were dusted with powdered sugar and coconut stuck in his hair. Straightening up, Josh rolled down the window and cursed out the critter. Marcus put the truck in park right in the middle of the road, got out, and shook himself like a wet dog.

"Should have hit it," Josh yelled, and Marcus started with his lip thing.

That whole day, then, Marcus seemed strange (funny to say that about Marcus, as if he could ever be otherwise)—hypervigilant, poising himself for surprise. Even his nostrils were anxious, pulling at the air each time he left the truck. Came out of Walls Store in Falls, a trailer turned convenient mart, and said, "I think I know who drew the circles."

"It's the kid janitor on the late shift," Josh guessed, riled. "I'm reporting that little . . ."

Marcus, now still as wood, shook his ugly head. His hair followed after.

"Granny Urghardt."

Of all of Marcus's stories, this was the one that garnered the gold: a wild-ass tale of his motorcycle grandma, who'd crossed the country with the Hell's Angels more times than she could count. (Then again, no one in Marcus's clan was well acquainted with the higher functions.) A sixty-three-year-old leathered biker who tracked Marcus down every five years or so to give him some birthday money, and let him know when his dad was on his tail, so to speak.

"They in town for something?" he asked, referring to the group she hung with. "Some kind of convocation?"

Josh ignored the question and carried a tray of doughnuts into the diner. The place was empty except for the world's largest waitress standing in a corner, peeling the leaves off a head of iceberg lettuce and eating each one, tip to stalk.

"Where's Marcus?" she asked.

Shoving the doughnuts under her nose, Josh said his partner was back in the truck. Yanking off another piece of lettuce, she pointed to the window and sighed, "Ain't no truck out there. You do something to him?"

By the time Josh whipped around, Mark the Lark had disappeared. Vanished. Josh asked Miss Iceberg for a fresh cup of coffee. "They're all fresh," she sassed between bites.

Half an hour, another lettuce head, and two customers later, Josh got antsy. Called the next stop, a mom-and-pop restaurant, to see if Tucker had been by. No go. Took out his book and phoned up the rest of their customers, saying they were behind schedule. Then he called the shop's owner.

First thing out of Mr. Raymond's mouth? "What'd you do to him? This running off must have to do with you—not us." He was angry now, his voice one long yell. "We've done everything we can for the boy. And he appreciates it. He knows the value of a good job."

Something had spooked Marcus, and he was hating all of those people who'd been sitting in the cheering section. Only one person had a chance of finding him, someone who didn't really care whether he came back or not, someone who had more to gain by his leaving, someone who had run from something, too. And that was Josh.

Josh's story was short and to the point. He'd left New York after only six months on the job. He'd gone in with great enthusiasm, committed to eighteen-hour days, and through his diligence had uncovered the "improprieties." Sitting on the information for a month, he checked and rechecked what he knew to be true. When he told his boss, the man thanked him, asked him to remain silent, and within twenty-four hours had Josh escorted from his office. Josh stayed in New York until his money ran out. He went home because they had to take him in and, to bury his pain, he went to work at the doughnut shop. There, he told himself, he'd be a favorite son, an inspiration to all, someone who'd risen above a tragedy. But it didn't work out that way. Somehow his trouble didn't make much of a story—not when it knocked up against Marcus's life.

Both the blind guy and Dim-dim hung out at the shop until midnight, hoping Marcus would turn up. Sometime between three and five in the morning the truck appeared, magically, with a full tank of gas and the key tucked into a hole under the passenger's seat cushion. The phantom driver left it in back of the shop so that no one would notice until it was time for the deliveries. Josh went on the route himself, making the run in half the time, though it seemed twice as long as usual. Every place the questions were the same—"What you doing here alone? Where's Marcus?"

At Pump 'n' Pantry, Thumbelina had her neck halfway out the window, straining for the sight of her ever-loving Tucker. Josh nearly passed the stop, wanting to avoid the abuse. The other Pump 'n' Pantry princesses were gathered round her outside now, the hems of their little checked aprons jittering in the wind, a scene from *Lassie Come Home*. Josh stopped the truck on a dime, jumped to the back, threw open the side panels, and began tossing their order into their laps.

"He's on spring break," Josh yelled. They caught every last crueller.

When Marcus was seventeen, or so the story went, he met a woman working as a telephone linesman, a big Bertha type lodged in a plastic bucket high above her truck, an official New Jersey Bell vehicle parked just yards from his bridge. Once she and the giant wash pail made it back to terra firma, he asked her to lunch. She didn't refuse him—he must have bathed that day—she just packed up her stuff, half listening to the story about the time that Marcus, at seven and a half, watched as a telephone guy took the phone from his parents' trailer, saying, "Company property." Marcus ran after the man, offering instead his dart gun, a broken wrench, and some Boy Scout pencil he'd taken off a rich schoolmate. "We didn't want the damn thing anyway," his mama shouted.

That touched something soft in Bertha (there was a whole lot of it there), and the next thing she knew, she was dining al fresco, in the land down under. Twenty-six years old, living with her mother, she'd never had a boyfriend. "A woman that big," said Marcus, "can squeeze all the hurt out of you."

She called him Kid Dangerous, on account of the dart gun. Started by bringing pillows, a raintarp, and, of course, an unconnected phone. One afternoon they sat under the bridge, the rain pounding the tarp, each of them with a phone in hand (she'd brought along a spare), pretending to have a long-distance conversation. Marcus called her from a truck stop in Cheyenne, Wyoming. He rang her hotel room in Paris, France.

"Bon jour," she answered. "How'd you know I'd be here?"

"If you really want to find someone," Marcus commented, "you can always find them."

A perfect ten, Tuck. A perfect ten.

Josh returned from his run at around noon. Granny had parked her Harley six inches, maybe seven, from the front window. On the corner stools sat Mrs. Urghardt and her boy Roy, Tucker's daddy. Grimier than a machine shop, holding the coffee mug in both hands, he was asking the waitress when Marc was due in. Roy turned around to watch Josh unload the truck—hard to believe it, but Marcus got all the looks in the family. Sleeves rolled to the elbow, Mr. Tucker displayed a tattooed wrist—you couldn't make out the picture—and a forearm so lily white that at first it seemed to belong to Granny. Granny had her own badge of courage—a skull and cross bones stamped on her left shoulder. Her skin had grown so loose that it looked like the skull was frowning. Marcus had beat them by a full day.

For the first time since Josh had started, a waitress was pleading with *him* for a favor. "Come talk to them," she said. "They're Marcus's people."

Washing up, Josh did his tallying for the day, chomped on a doughnut, and, when he was good and ready, sauntered out to the front of the store where the customers sat.

"Hello, son," said Mr. Tucker, and Josh stuffed his hands into his jeans to avoid a handshake, nodding in response to the greeting. "I understand you've been training my boy."

"We trained together," Josh replied.

Mr. Tucker took the correction well. Granny's lips were whittling themselves. Josh saw the behavior as genetic.

"Too bad you missed him," Josh said. "He left on the five A.M. bus to Baltimore. Dropped him at the station on my way out. There's some trucking school down there he's applied to. But of course you know all that."

The waitress gasped, glaring at Josh, "How could you!" and threw down her cleaning rag. "Your boy," she said, shoulders back, chest out, "was one of the finest workers we ever had. And if we'd teamed him with the right person, Marcus would still . . ."

Of the four in the party, only Granny smiled.

Driving the route the next morning, Josh did the stops in reverse order, last one first. A third of the way through the trip he parked the truck behind one of the supermarkets and told the manager he needed some air.

"I'll be back in half an hour," he explained.

"Marcus never got car sick," the manager replied.

Walking down route 611, along the shoulder, Josh kept peering into the woods, looking for the spot where the fox had bolted. Downhill, past the guardrail and a clump of brush, snaked a small stream with some kind of storage hut nearby. There was a figure, a human, sleeping alongside, and Josh knew it was either Daniel Boone or Marcus. Crouched in the bushes, he waited for the sun to wake his partner.

Josh had just about given up, decided to stretch his legs, when Marcus came running toward him.

"Anyone with you?" Marcus asked.

Josh shook his head no and headed toward the highway. Glancing backward Josh saw his partner, arms flailing, then hands cupped around his mouth.

"Any more messages?"

"Yeah. The boss says you're fired," Josh lied.

Two months went by and Mr. Raymond was still mourning Marcus. Thumbelina had quit her job and the manager at Walls in Falls canceled his order. "Don't like the way you stack things," he said to Josh. The waitress, who'd written to Marcus in care of the trucking school in Baltimore, had her letter returned, marked addressee unknown. Josh worked the route alone, and six years later, after a short jail term for a crime to be described later, Mr. Raymond made his own kin, heretofore unappreciated, *top* sales manager.

Evelyn

Evelyn was attending her second church service. She sat in the front row with Branley on her right and Wade Lowbar's pregnant, unmarried sister, Elizabeth Rose, who also had just found religion, on her left. Last Sunday Branley had coaxed three customers, among them a trucker with a glass eye, to join in, too. Evelyn had found that first service slightly more appealing. At least she could watch the trucker without being watched. Wade's sister's eyes were everywhere.

Things picked up when Branley stood to give his talk. He publicly acknowledged Evelyn and Elizabeth Rose, whom the rest of the congregation pursed their lips at in disapproval. He talked about sinners, which Evelyn liked, and people becoming as innocent as little children, which she tolerated, and then heavenly reward, which she dismissed. This religion bit was wearing thin. Furthermore, it was cutting into her overtime at the shop.

"We must become good, because goodness is rewarded. The Lord Jesus gives to the good," said Branley, and Evelyn thought, Baloney.

Two followers rose to give their testimonials.

"I had wealth—three motor vehicles and two houses with a

girlfriend in each, all gotten through unethical means. So I was poor in the spirit. Today I live in a trailer with my dog Ronnie and the Lord Jesus Christ, earning my keep selling door-to-door. I've been blessed with a clean slate."

"Better hang on to it," Evelyn whispered. She found the second story equally uninspiring: a former female bartender, "as thirsty for Satan as the people I poured for," caught in a brawl one night and rendered unconscious, woke three years later in a nursing home. During those lost years a kindly church member, a total stranger, played a cassette of hymns to the patient every morning. Although she walked with two canes and had pain "twenty-three hours a day," she, too, was moving to her own trailer.

"Do they give out trailers here?" asked Elizabeth Rose.

Evelyn did not stay for the social and its attendant rewards.

The next day Evelyn decided she'd had her fill of religion.

"I think I need a break," she said when Branley asked about the Wednesday night prayer meeting. "I need some time to let what I've heard sink in. But I'm sure Elizabeth Rose would love to go."

Elizabeth Rose had shared with Evelyn her wish to give birth inside a church. Unbeknownst to Branley, the girl was attending services at three different sects.

"It would be just like the Nativity," the fourteen-year-old had said, confusing her stories.

Branley, not yet abandoning hope of formally converting Evelyn, let her remarks pass and consoled himself with his newborn doughnuts. Evelyn swung by the shop's office, close enough to hear Doreen Raymond being bawled out for not wearing a hat. The paper crowns were the bane of every waitress. Evelyn herself was bareheaded but somehow had escaped notice. One of the other waitresses had considerately left her a note, attached to a creased crown, saying, "Mr. R. on the warpath—use mine." Instead Evelyn took her chances.

At home Evelyn cleared her desk of the Bible studies pamphlet, deposited the clutter in a wastepaper basket, and opened her mail. There was *Time* magazine, with a cover story on "Chaos," a new scientific theory, three bills, a form letter from her congressman, and a registered letter that her downstairs neighbor had signed for. When she read the document telling her of the inheritance, she immediately thought of Branley's system of checks and balances and wondered how he would square this one. Evelyn couldn't dismiss that this happened just after she had turned her back on religion, and she wondered if hers could be a new kind of testimonial.

"I said faith be gone, I am no believer, and the money floated downward like that manna stuff."

After the inheritance tax Evelyn would have enough to erase her debts and maintain her life style for the next decade without having to do so much as lift a doughnut. This she did not find rewarding. A waitress for twenty-six years, the last fourteen at Every Day, Evelyn knew that serving coffee was in her blood.

She craved waitress stories, scavenged for them the way other women did for costume jewelry. Her one complaint with the famous Marcus Tucker, former doughnut shop demigod, was that he never told a single tale of a waitress. But she had other sources.

At the grocers she picked up a TV dinner, which she did every Tuesday, the day the *Enquirer, Globe,* and *Star* came out. Out of habit she had pulled a Swanson turkey dinner (Thanksgiving sealed in an aluminum tray) from the freezer case but then, in her elation, tossed it back and retrieved a Le Menu with baby carrots. With the package proudly tucked under her arm, she grabbed for her papers and, while still in line, flipped through the pages for the true-life happenings of her servile sisters.

There was a story that took place in Florida, in a doughnut shop that had been closed down by local authorities after making scads of money. The waitresses had been serving customers topless. No pictures. In Kansas a waitress at the Tornado Diner had saved two children, caught in a twister, by telling them to hang on to her hair. From the photograph Evelyn could see that the waitress's cap was only a little larger than the one Evelyn was forced to wear.

In a third story, a coffee shop waitress "in the United Kingdom" read people's fortunes by the stains in the bottom of their coffee cups. She had correctly predicted two surgeries (gallstones), one marriage, and a visit by a long lost cousin. The quality of the picture was so poor that all Evelyn could make out was the uniform's V-neckline and the pocket hanky.

She finished the three papers before reaching the register, and stuffed them all into the same slot. But she did buy the *TV Guide*, to see if the talk shows were featuring waitresses.

Her favorite TV segment of all time was "Waitresses From Hell," women who had knowingly poisoned the men who'd scorned them, including a few nontippers. Evelyn had it on tape. Just for the show, the prison had let the women wear their waitress uniforms. One lady from Texas even had a ruffled apron.

The following morning, after a discussion with the lawyers, Evelyn started to tell the girls at the shop about her fortune. Then she decided that the effect would be greater if she showed them instead. She received a copy of the will and taped it to the living room wall until she could get a proper frame and invited people over, one at a time, to see for themselves in black and white. The overdue Elizabeth Rose was left out of it, Evelyn not willing to play midwife.

"The Lord heard your prayers," said Branley, carefully reading the copy, and Evelyn pointed out that the will had been drawn up two years ago, long before her brief interest in churchgoing.

Doreen Raymond and Marie Eden arrived one after the other, reeking from the Ring King. Doreen's hem, which she'd stapled mid-shift, had tumbled down for the umpteenth time and Marie's hair had a crease from the paper crown. Evelyn was struck by their shabbiness, perhaps because she'd just viewed the waitresses tape. All of those women had been wearing brand-new uniforms.

Fingering the corner of the photocopy, Doreen said, "It's like something you'd read about." She sucked on her diet soda. "Maybe they'll write you up."

She then went on to tell Evelyn about the latest battle with her father.

"He won't give up on those stupid hats. He said, 'Doreen, can't you set an example? Can't I even count on my own?' When I told him I couldn't find a hat—that we were out—he found this in the packing room. He stuck the crown on my head. Right in front of the Buick boys," Doreen added, thoroughly humiliated.

The crown's points had been flattened and someone had colored the letters in the words *Every Day*. A magic-marker sun set in the hat's corner.

"I'm taking this home and burying it," Doreen vowed. "Lucky you. You can quit tomorrow and never have to look like this again."

But Evelyn told her supervisor, Marie, that she had no intention of foresaking her career. In private, Marie postulated that Evelyn would hang around just to be contrary.

"So," Marie asked, "what have you decided on, then—a new apartment? How about a cruise vacation? Lester could make some calls for you. There's a trip where you drive to the ship. Maybe Les and I could go and take our honeymoon," Marie mused.

"I'm content right here," Evelyn replied.

Evelyn clipped an item from the *Enquirer* on the top-ten jobs for women. It compared the occupations of women in 1990 with women in 1940.

1940	1990
1. Servant	1. Secretary
2. Secretary	2. Cashier
3. Teacher	3. Bookkeeper
4. Clerical Worker	4. Registered Nurse
5. Sales Worker	5. Nursing Aide
6. Factory Worker	6. Teacher
7. Bookkeeper	7. Waitress ***
8. Waitress ***	8. Sales Worker
9. Housekeeper	9. Child-care Worker
10. Nurse	10. Cook

She tacked the list to the employee bulletin board with the message "Here YESTERDAY, TODAY, and TOMORROW."

"You can leave that all behind," said Terri Kudja. "Break out on your own and have a business. I'd help."

"Or at least buy a van," said the deaf baker. "Something from the Buick showroom. We could all go for a spin."

This game of what-I'd-do-if-I-had-your-money annoyed Evelyn; she found the activity asinine, since not one of the speculators was likely to ever have an extra nickel. She had no intention of squandering the cash on their desires.

Instead she did what any truly dedicated waitress would do: she bought a new uniform.

Boarding the bus to Lackawanna Avenue one Saturday, she sat in the back, where she could rest her purse beside her. Of all of the riders, Evelyn conjectured, she was the only one who didn't have to take the bus. The thought was delight enough. She watched a cosmetician, dressed for work, get off, an ankle bracelet fastened over her stockings.

Evelyn walked into the Scranton Uniform Supply Store, right past the windows filled with mannequin student nurses, restaurant waitresses, beauty shop operators (you knew their trade by the prop in their hands, their head ornaments, and the style of their nylon hair), past the sale rack and irregulars, to the register, where a woman in navy blue slacks and a pink pilled sweater stood on a small platform. The clerk had mannequin arms and wrists which were poised above the cash register's keys.

"Waitress?" she guessed as Evelyn fingered a contoured poly-blend with razor-thin pockets and a collar with needle-sharp points. "You're in the wrong section. That's career apparel. Head-nurse wear." She wagged a milk-white hand toward the 'seconds' area. "Try service dress."

Instead Evelyn upgraded to a starched cotton uniform with latex insets at the waist. Disregarding the price tags, she pulled four of the store's best dresses from the wall and slung them over her arm.

"They're not wash 'n' wear—they'll retain food stains," warned the clerk as Evelyn started for the dressing room. More bored than annoyed by the waitress's gesture, she decided to let the customer indulge herself. It would give her the chance to finish her nails. "All right, all right, go for it. And take your time, honey," she added.

Evelyn accepted the clerk as she would have accepted truckers

114

at the doughnut shop; this behavior came with the job. Ascending a tiny stage, she concentrated on the uniforms, the three mirrors her audience. Grabbing the material at her waist, she pulled the fabric taut around her middle and behind and posed. She almost looked dishy. Then, to get the full effect, she took the paper crown all the waitresses wore from her purse.

"Enjoying yourself?" the saleswoman called.

"I could use a little assistance," Evelyn replied, her nascent kindness strained.

The clerk strolled toward the dressing room.

"Hold this here," Evelyn instructed, pinching the cloth.

"Excuse me?" the woman said.

"Oh, I see," said the waitress, observing that the saleswoman was quite tall. "Just scootch down. Or kneel if it's more comfortable."

Evelyn placed the crown on her head, attaching it with bobby pins. "I'd like this uniform, but custom made. And a crown cut from the same cloth, with detachable tortoiseshell combs."

"Queen for a day," the woman smirked.

Evelyn lightly tapped the clerk's head, as if to knight her. And on her way out, she casually placed the high-priced "career apparel" in with the sale dresses.

Evelyn had never received more mail and phone calls; she was besieged by insurance salesmen and brokers. A couple of regular customers had even proposed—including one of the bookbinders and a seventy-seven-year-old woman who still worked every day in the purse factory. "Two women," the lady customer said. "It's legal in some states. Maybe California. I saw it on Donahue. We could go there. Raise something."

As an act of revenge, Evelyn tried to match up the two suitors, telling each one that the other had sent over a doughnut and a cup of coffee. The customers sat at opposite ends of the counter, nodding cordially for a week.

Elizabeth Rose offered to name her offspring after Evelyn.

"Girl or boy," she promised. "If it's a boy I'll shorten it to Ev."

Evelyn tried to be gentle, which was against her nature. "Stick to your original plan," she said, referring to the girl's intent to name the baby after the church she found herself in when labor began—Pres for Presbyterian, Luther for Lutheran, Union for Unitarian, or Babs for Baptist. "I'm not any fairy godmother," Evelyn added.

During the weeks following her news of the inheritance, all of the help at Every Day seemed amazed that Evelyn could keep her head while her bank account swelled.

"I don't know," admitted Marie. "I think I'd be tempted. She didn't so much as glance at the brochure for the Poconos condominium. It went right in the basket."

"She could be saving it for the Lord's work," said Branley. "Those who protest the loudest are often the most devoted."

Overhearing them, Evelyn wondered if the fog around Branley's head would ever clear.

Standing on the corner, Evelyn watched an elderly woman dig deep into her black plastic bag for a bus pass. A middle-aged couple, husband holding his wife's purse, which had orange-and-purple balloons and oversized handles, argued. "You bring this," the husband said, shaking the pocketbook, "and then you're always sorry."

There was also a grocery checker and a young woman, dressed in a pleated skirt with a red sweater vest and matching beret, who worked in a clothing store downtown. She'd pinned some kind of gold bug to the front of the hat. Evelyn noticed a small hole in her hose that had been covered with nail polish.

Except for the husband's charge, there was silence. The checker looked at his watch and said aloud, "Shit. He's running late again."

Evelyn waited until several of the riders became impatient and then broke the snake-shaped line they had formed. She called a cab to take her to the uniform store.

To make sure everything was just right with her new outfit, Evelyn had requested two fittings. For the first one, a tiny Italian woman, who may in fact have been a midget, wrapped a tape measure around Evelyn's bust, waist, and hips, her upper arms, the length between her shoulders, the span from shoulder to wrist, calling out the numbers as she worked. Her lips moved carefully, to prevent the straight pins from falling out.

"Your right arm longer," said Mrs. Maroni, and Evelyn insisted that she measure again. "No, everybody. Everybody," the seamstress explained. "Georgia Patterson, three inches longer on the left. She tall. She's can carry it off."

"Change it," Evelyn said to the seamstress, "so that both arms are the same."

"It short-sleeve," said the seamstress. "It no matter." Then she smoothed a piece of cloth over Evelyn's stomach. "It will be beautiful. You see," she said, as if consoling her. She climbed down from her stool and drew herself up to her full three feet ten inches. "Let me tell you," Mrs. Maroni observed. "These things are not everything. Being the same is not everything."

Evelyn's second fitting lasted only a few minutes, with Mrs. Maroni making some minor adjustments to the hemline. The waitress inspected the crown while she waited. Even the saleswoman had to admire the craftsmanship. Evelyn guessed that the saleswoman's sudden civility stemmed from the realization that Evelyn had money.

"The color of that turquoise stripe is perfect," the waitress said. "It matches the doughnut shop counter."

"Now that we have your size down, let's put in an order for three or four more," suggested the clerk. "And you've got to visit our foundation department," she added, as if the section were blocks away instead of within arm's length.

A headless, armless bust sat atop the bra display, strapped into a heavily wired undergarment. Next to it a torsoless leg covered with support hose thrust its jaunty foot into the air.

"I wear them myself," said the saleswoman, running her hands over the pink sweater and along her rib cage. She had the same build as the student nurse dummy.

"Your bra strap's showing," Evelyn said, and she paid her bill.

Once she got home, Evelyn tried on the uniform and a new pair of pantyhose, her nurse's shoes, and the crown. Modeling the dress, she picked up her dictionary and pretended to read it in front of the mirror. She then took a paper cup, filled it halfway with lemonade, and said, "Here's the sample, doctor." Standing on the seat of a chair, her hand on the wall for balance, she twisted her waist to better contemplate her backside. Then she raised one foot, slowly, to get a view of her shoes. The shoes would have to go. Pushing back the crown ever so slightly, she removed a pair of dangling jet earrings from her pocket and placed them in her ears. Then she waltzed over to the wall that held the will, apprising her of her new wealth.

"You're small potatoes," she said to the still-unframed document. "I look like a million bucks."

On the way to work Evelyn was asked out by a meter reader (from the Pennsylvania Gas and Water Company), a teenage athlete wearing a gold-and-white football helmet, and a passerby in a blue pickup. A deer, legs bound and hanging from a frame, swayed in the back of the truck. She had worn a pair of black suede shoes with three inch heels, which set off her ankles and the white stockings. The crown rode in her pocket, wrapped in a plastic baggie. The meter man was the most sincere.

"I've never done this before—stopped someone on the street," he explained. "But I knew if I didn't at least say hello to you, I'd never forgive myself."

When he lifted his hands to his glasses she noticed that he was missing the top of his thumb.

"I've got to get to work," she said, heading in the direction of Every Day Doughnuts and concluding that if he were smart enough he'd figure out where she waitressed.

Evelyn punched her card into the timeclock and ignored the stack of aprons returned from the laundry. In the ladies room she fixed the crown to her beehived hair. The small rhinestones she had glued to each of the crown's points glittered under the washroom's bare bulb. Out front, two Buick boys leaned on the counter.

"Hubba hubba," said the mechanic. "Where've you been hiding it?"

Evelyn tried to act as though the dress made no difference. At the coffee machine she could feel the men's eyes appreciating her rear. She poured two glasses of ice water and took mincing steps, so as not to fall off her heels. Her thighs, thrown together by the incline of her shoes, scraped one another and the starched fabric of the uniform gave off a "sckt-sckt-sckt" sound from beneath her skirt.

"Stick it in here," she said, handing them the glasses, her trademark meanness masking her pleasure.

The other waitresses were visibly disturbed by Evelyn's transformation. Doreen wrapped her own apron more tightly around her waist, trying to bind her middle, while Marie and Terri straightened their crowns.

"Well," asked Evelyn, "what do you think? Isn't this something?" she coaxed, modeling before the group. She walked around the jelly and icing machines, over to the Ring King, and back to the swinging door.

Marie, who was filling doughnuts, paused to lift a stray hair with the heel of her hand. Evelyn lovingly adjusted it behind Marie's crown, bending at such an angle to place her own tiara in Marie's face.

"My, my," said Marie, stepping back for a better view. "You've got the real McCoy."

"You look so different from the rest of us," Doreen said. "Is that really a uniform? How did you find one that fit like that?"

"I think this sets a new standard," Evelyn said, her heels clicking on the linoleum as she pranced out front.

Marie followed her, flicking an apron. She waited while Evelyn finished up with a customer, then handed the long white cover-up to the employee.

"Not on your life," said Evelyn, smiling widely, and Marie responded, "Fine. It's your cleaning bill."

The meter man was in the corner, waving at Evelyn, his half thumb poking at the air. "Sensational," he said under his breath. "Sennnsational."

Branley glanced at Evelyn through the glass partition. The uniform hugged her body into a perfect figure eight. All he could think of was Mary Magdalene. He hurried back to the cutting table and furiously began punching out the circles of dough.

Doreen and Marie had steered clear of Evelyn throughout most of the morning, marveling as she avoided percolating coffee, spilled colas, exploding jelly doughnuts, and puddles of grease. Doreen and Marie's aprons looked like first-graders' finger paintings. Evelyn had managed to keep her uniform spotless throughout the entire shift. Even the shoes were holding up, though Evelyn could feel large blisters blossoming on her heels.

"It's miraculous, isn't it?" asked Doreen. "I mean, she's doing as much as ever. The crown hasn't budged, her shoes are still on, and the uniform is snow white."

Marie, who usually kept any cynicism in check, let loose. "The Immaculate Deception," she said. Then she stared at the toe of her brown orthopedic shoe. "I wonder," Marie added, "if I could have a pair made in white."

The genuine compliments came from the customers. A Buick boy, watching Evelyn's shape beneath the tight white fabric, had called her a sex goddess. Three strangers asked her to dinner. And when she counted up her tips for the shift, Evelyn was up by five dollars over the day before. At the end of her eight hours she rested for a moment by the front window and waved to the three teenage boys ogling her.

The other waitresses punched out without saying good-bye and Branley did not dare let his eyes leave the fryer.

When Evelyn got home, she carefully checked the dress for any marks and hung it in the bathroom to air out. One shoe's toe had been gouged and, working the suede with her finger, she soothed the wound. The crown rested on her dressing table.

Sticking a Q-tip in a bottle of ammonia, Evelyn shined the small rhinestones. It occurred to her that the crown's effect might be enhanced by larger gems placed on either side. Raking through her jewelry box, she found two loose stones, both rose colored, and carefully glued the gems to her hat.

In the bottom of the silk-lined box lay a turquoise necklace, sent to her by her younger sister, who'd once stayed on a reservation in New Mexico. The color was slightly deeper than the stripe on the crown. Retrieving a needle and thread from a sewing kit, Evelyn draped the necklace over the embroidered stripe and stitched it into place. Then she turned on the radio and went into the bathroom to soak her blistered feet.

The newscaster told of a waitress at the Hole Truth Doughnut Shop in Tennessee, mother of four adopted children, living in two rented rooms, who'd just learned that her daddy was a famous country and western singer. Some equally famous lawyer had taken up her cause, forcing blood tests all around.

"I just want us to be a family again," said the waitress, whose voice had a musical lilt. "I want him to know his grandchildren." The waitress had spent years wondering where her talent—she sang at weddings—had come from. At the end of the newscast the waitress sang one of her father's songs. Evelyn wished she could see what the waitress was wearing. She had a good idea that the woman was in uniform.

Sorting through her closet, Evelyn yanked out two old uniforms, one from when she was fifteen pounds heavier that would probably fit Doreen. She also grabbed three calf-length wool skirts that did nothing for her. Maybe the girls at the shop would appreciate those, too.

The meter reader was parked in front of the shop, his radio blaring.

"Listen to this," he called as Evelyn walked by. "I phoned the station and dedicated this to you."

The first chords of Roy Orbison's "Pretty Woman" were the backdrop to the deejay's prattle. "This for a lovely lady at Every Day from a guy who wants to run your meter."

" 'No one could look as good as you,' " the gas man sang along. " 'Mercy. . . . What do I see? Is she walking back to me? Yeah. She's walking back to me.' "

"Big deal," said Evelyn, feigning indifference. "There's no drive-in service here. You'll have to come inside."

Evelyn had walked to work in her sneakers, changing her shoes when she got to the shop. Leaning on an old sofa Mr. Raymond had brought from his home, she slipped the pumps over her bandaged heels. Doreen had tucked a lace hanky into her uniform pocket. Terri Kudja wore her crown slightly to the side with a spray of hair sticking out of it. Terri had several wet spots on her dress where she had washed off blobs of jelly and chocolate, having attempted to work without any apron. Doreen's skirt, too, was covered with water stains. Only Marie wore a cover-up.

"The gas man waiteth," Marie, barely civil, said to Evelyn, shaking her head at the crown's additions.

"I love turquoise—it's so mystical," Terri sighed. "I wish she'd given that to me."

Evelyn tiptoed around a stream of glaze and squeezed by the doughnut racks. Elizabeth Rose, eight days overdue, squatted on the first stool, listening to Branley.

"Tonight at seven P.M.," he instructed her. "You're sure you're up to this?" he asked. "There will be prayers and a Bible lesson, so it may run a little late."

"Oh, yes," said the exhausted Elizabeth Rose. "I'll come."

When Branley left, Elizabeth winked at Evelyn and Evelyn winked back. Carefully wiping up the counter, catching the crumbs with her hand and then shaking them into the sink, the waitress asked the meter reader for his order.

"I'd like a cup of coffee and a date," he said, and the other customers hooted.

"We'll see," replied Evelyn and she walked over to the doughnut case.

The man waited a half hour for the shop to empty out, helping the burdened Elizabeth Rose to her feet when she decided to leave. Evelyn gave her admirer a quick test.

"What happened to me recently?" she said, trying to discern if it was her money or her body that he was after.

"You graduated from high school. Won the lottery. Ran for mayor," he rattled off.

Obviously, no one had told him about the will.

"I have cellulite," she said. "Picture it. More dimples on my thighs than craters on the moon."

"I have two bridges," he replied, pointing to his upper and lower teeth.

"You're on," she said. "What should I wear?"

"Anything," said her suitor. "Just be sure to bring the crown."

For a full week she'd managed to keep the uniform clean. With each passing day her coworkers grew more and more remote. Doreen hurt most of all by the offering of a hand-me-down. When Marie finally pulled rank and said that Evelyn must wear flat shoes, the heels posing a safety hazard, Evelyn took a cab downtown and bought two pairs of sneakers, one white leather, trimmed in gold, and a cloth pair with sequins.

After two dinners with the gas man she'd given up the relationship. When he'd invited her in for coffee after their second evening, she noticed that the walls of the living room, bathroom, and bedroom (yes, she peeked) were covered with photographs of women wearing crowns. There were twenty-three shots of Princess Di alone, no two taken from the same angle. On his closet shelf he kept a red velvet crown, shaped like a muffin, with a gold cross on top.

"What's a queen without her king?" he had asked, rearranging his hair to accommodate the ornament.

She didn't dare mention this to the other waitresses. The anecdote would have made them feel justified, made them feel that Evelyn had gotten what she deserved. She had begun to nibble away at her inheritance—the uniform, the sneakers, a dozen pairs of seamed hose (one on her, one in her purse, in case she got a run), and this seemed to aggravate the others far more than if she had blown it on the purchase of a Cadillac or a vacation to Disneyland.

Keeping the dress in near-mint condition required an extraordinary effort. Evelyn now performed any risky task—carrying a tray of glazed doughnuts, icing the chocolate cruellers, pouring a hot tea, with her arms extended as far from her body as humanly possible. At times she had to tip herself forward like a teapot, her butt pushed out, her back a table. No one out front objected. This feat did not satisfy her, however, and Evelyn found herself longing for something to happen, for a circumstance to arise where she could exhibit those characteristics possessed by the waitresses she'd read about. God knows she was dressed for it.

One morning at around eleven there was nearly such an opportunity. A customer, a schoolmate of Mr. Raymond's, had switched her longstanding order that day from a half dozen sugar doughnuts to a dozen dough-netts, the fried holes. Tossing them into her mouth like kernels of popped corn, she'd accidentally lodged one in her windpipe. Evelyn envisioned her own name and picture in the paper, having saved the woman's life with the Heimlich maneuver, which was detailed on a white laminated card taped to the phone. Instead Doreen Raymond thumped the lady once on the back and the soggy bullet went flying, straight into the coffee cup of one of the bookbinders. All Evelyn had managed to do was avoid being splashed.

"How did it happen?" Doreen asked, pouring the victim a glass of water.

"I just wasn't concentrating," the woman admitted. "I was admiring Evelyn's uniform, wishing that I could look that good. It's really terrific, isn't it?" she asked, and Doreen smiled sarcastically.

"We could all look that good if we had her money," Doreen said to the coffee machine.

That same week, on Thursday, both Doreen and Terri reported off. Marie had driven two hours south to visit Lester's great aunt, recently widowed and living in a nursing home. All three of Terri's children had the flu and Doreen claimed she had a case of food poisoning. Evelyn, serving the customers with the help of Russell, the packer, an eighty-plus senior citizen who moved at an unhurried pace, concluded that the absence of her coworkers was deliberate.

"I'll show them," she said, whirling around to avoid the stream of jelly shooting from the doughnut caught in a toddler's fist.

Russell had returned to his orders, a part-time girl was due in within the hour, and Evelyn's single brush with disaster had been some powdered sugar, which she quickly dusted off when Elizabeth Rose waddled through the front door. The girl looked as though she'd been up all night. As she placed herself on the edge of the stool, she sucked at the air.

"I think there's something wrong," she said, her hair and brow damp and tears rising in her lower eyelids. "I thought for sure at last night's service I was ready, but nothing came."

Evelyn realized that except for Branley and Russell, the two women were alone in the shop.

"I'm calling a cab. You should be in the hospital," Evelyn said, terrified, and Elizabeth Rose let out a scream as though she'd been stabbed. She shook her head furiously.

"OK. Here, I'll get you some tea," the waitress offered. "You're probably just tense."

The girl turned her head and vomited. "It's too late," she gasped, her cries becoming like the yapping of a small dog. "The baby's coming. It's moving down. I can feel it moving," she said again, "down."

She grabbed Evelyn's hand and stretched her back against the counter.

"Branley," Evelyn yelled. "Branley. Call nine-one-one. *Quick.*"

The preacher, propelled by the sound of Evelyn's pleas, raced to the front. Elizabeth had her right hand between her legs.

"Tell, t—ell him," she said, puffing.

Evelyn, not comprehending the demand but still holding the girl's left hand, said, "What? Tell him what?"

"Where, where I want the baby . . ."

"A church. She wants to go to a church," Evelyn spit out for her.

Elizabeth Rose was crying now, long strings of tears, and Branley got behind her to support her. Russell, shaken from his tomb in the back, dialed the paramedics. The girl pressed her hand again between her legs and whimpered. "No, no."

"Evelyn. You're going to have to look. To see how far along," Branley insisted. "Now. Right now."

The waitress lifted the girl's dress and pulled her stained underwear to the side.

"Oh, dear God," said Evelyn. "She's been pushing in the head. The head is showing."

Branley told Elizabeth Rose to repeat after him. "It will be just like church, I promise," he said. " 'I love the Lord, for He hath heard my voice.' "

" 'I love the Lord,' " repeated the young mother.

Evelyn grabbed a stack of aprons and a scissors, which she plunged into boiling tea water. In the time it took for her to walk to the other side of the counter, she had unbuttoned her uniform and stripped to her slip. The sequined slippers were kicked to the side.

" 'I will offer to thee the sacrifice of thanksgiving,' " Branley was saying, and Elizabeth Rose, her fingers wrapped around the underside of the stool, did her best to keep up.

The baby's head was clearing the opening, and Evelyn held it, firmly, guiding out one shoulder and then the other. It appeared as though someone had smeared the infant with jelly; in fact, most of the gunk reminded Evelyn of doughnut filling. She knew she had to clean the newborn's mouth and wait for the cry. The cord looked like a greasy rope of unbaked dough.

"Alleluia," shouted Branley, hearing the kittenlike "waa," and Elizabeth Rose weakly mimicked, "Alleluia."

The slip Evelyn wore was soaked right through with blotches of red and gray. Elizabeth Rose's jumper was wringing wet, too. The waitress lay the infant in the girl's arms.

"Are you cold, baby?" Elizabeth Rose asked sweetly, and Evelyn pulled her clean uniform around her namesake's tiny form.

The newspaper article had a picture of little Evelyn Rose, eyes closed, fists tight. Evelyn and Branley both received a mention, with praises and thanks from the new mother. Even the paramedics were laudatory. "That waitress [Miss Evelyn Caine] should be working with us. She's a natural. We couldn't have done a better job ourselves."

Evelyn asked Mrs. Maroni to sew a tiny uniform with a cap as a baby gift, a replica of the outfit she had worn. Then she took ten thousand dollars and put it in a savings account for the little girl and her mother. Until she could have another uniform sewn, Evelyn borrowed back one of her old ones from Doreen (who had decided that they were decent, after all). No one said a word about the cloth tiara, which now also sported a genuine blue sapphire, just the color of little Evelyn's eyes. When Evelyn Caine left two months later to work the night shift at the Bluebird Diner ("things are getting just too routine here," she explained, tapping the toe of her gold-trimmed sneaker), she had the waitresses draw lots for her crown. And of course the meter man asked out the winner.

Coming and Going

Beatrice and Audrey

Every morning at 8:00 A.M., Mrs. Bea White stopped by the doughnut shop on her way to the Cathedral. She ordered a plain doughnut and tea with nothing in it. Regular enough to set a clock by, she waited six inches from the register, never moving further into the shop or entertaining the notion of taking up a stool. While Marie got her breakfast Mrs. White counted out the exact cost of her purchase, sixty-two cents. Not once in five years had she broken a dollar bill.

Reaching into the brown bag for her drink, she stood at the shelf that rode along the window, cut a small hole in the cap of the cup, retrieved the doughnut and paper napkin, and folded the brown sack into quarters. This went inside her purse. The doughnut sat atop the tea while she pushed on the door with her right hand; if someone offered to hold the door for her, Mrs. White looked right through the Samaritan, paused until he passed, and continued her routine.

She ate and drank during the remainder of her walk, sipping twice for every bite. Her meal lasted for three blocks. Stuffing the napkin, now marked with the faintest trace of lipstick, and the plastic lid into the cup, she dropped her waste into a blue-and-white trash can. On either side of the bin were advertisements for the Guild Studios, which sold religious articles.

Claiming the last aisle on the Blessed Virgin's side, the middle-aged woman set down her navy blue handbag, the most expensive purse that the local factory manufactured. She sat far enough away from the altar to insure that the priest's words couldn't reach her. After Mass she waited for ten minutes, in which time the priest would turn down the church lights on his way back to the rectory. Then, dusting off the pew and the kneeler with a tissue, Mrs. White would leave. The janitor would say "Good day." Though physically capable, she had barely spoken to anyone in five years, including her husband and son, with whom she lived.

People generally spoke well of Mrs. White, describing her as a model wife and citizen.

Audrey Voxe had been a telephone operator for fifteen years. When she ordered her morning beverage and doughnut from Marie or Adele, the sales manager always popped out, just to enjoy Audrey's voice. Since birth he'd been missing an outer ear (his inner ear functioned perfectly) and he believed that this "defect" accounted for his perfect pitch. Audrey's words were round and warm, sounding as if they had passed through a reed. Every syllable was clear without being exaggerated; her speech was so lovely that she'd done three radio commercials for the phone company and had been on a local version of "What's My Line?"

For a month now she'd been frequenting the shop; she began the ritual when she changed to night operator, a job that set her free at 7:30 each morning. The caffeine and sugar jolt kept her going. She preferred to stand (having sat all night) as Marie fixed her order, but several times Audrey rested on a stool, particularly if the waitresses were busy, and talked with the sales manager. Inevitably, upon hearing the waves of her words lap at his ear, a trucker would ask Audrey to say his name.

"It's fine," she'd reply, laughing a bit with embarrassment. "It happens all the time."

She would talk about her job and the calls that had come in the dead of the night. Twice in one week people had phoned back to tell her how calming her voice had been during an emergency.

"I guess it's reassuring," she said.

She told the sales manager, and anyone else who would listen, that she loved her job. Occasionally the help would sneak an extra doughnut into her bag, tempting Audrey with a new flavor, but her request was always identical: tea, plain, and a plain doughnut.

Audrey walked home, having taken a cab to work the night before ("It's really safer," she'd explained). Her path was the same as Mrs. White's, though they traveled in different directions; once when Audrey crossed to the opposite side of the street to avoid some construction, she passed a stern-looking woman dressed in a tan raincoat and a black hat and said hello. She received no response.

No one appeared to miss Mrs. White's conversation. Even before she gave it up altogether, she'd been tight-lipped; throughout her childhood and adolescence and early years of marriage, the tiny stream of her utterances diminished, finally, willfully, drying up. Once, just after the birth of their son, Mr. White heard his wife crooning and he laughed with delight. She mistook this for criticism and never sang again. Friends whose wives had venomous tongues, incessant gossips that poisoned the town's grapevine, told Mr. White how lucky he was.

If a new waitress was on, Mrs. White would vocalize her request, forever using the same words, "Tea with nothing in it and one plain doughnut." The "to go" was understood, since she made no effort to sit. On those rare occasions when her voice took to the air it sounded as ordinary as the tea she drank, though she herself knew it had journeyed miles to get there.

Mrs. White first became vaguely aware of Audrey Voxe the day the deaf baker, urged on by the route sales manager and Marie Eden, asked if Audrey would give him speech lessons.

"I hear you have a beautiful voice," the baker said, his own filled with echoes and murmurings, the hum of a whale. "I would pay, of course, and I would practice."

His desire so moved Audrey that she sunk to a stool and

lingered for a half hour over her tea while eating three doughnuts.

"But I'm not trained. I have no teaching skills," she explained as he sat with her on his coffee break.

He placed two fingers on his throat and asked if she'd allow him to touch her neck as she spoke.

"Sure," she said, and the flour-dusted fingers settled just below her larynx.

"Say something that sounds nice," he requested.

She thought it over for a minute. "The rain in Spain falls main-ly on the plain."

"I understand," said the baker. Getting up from his seat, he added, "Please think about it. You don't have to say yes right now."

In desperation Audrey turned to the woman who flanked the far side of the register. Her posture erect, her hat perfectly flat on her head, she seemed the very soul of composure.

"I don't think I can teach someone to speak," Audrey said, her voice filled with concern. "How do I get out of this?"

Mrs. White's expression remained unchanged and Audrey, too upset to realize she'd received no guidance, dug for her wallet. But Mrs. White had heard the question and when she claimed her breakfast, she shoved the change into Marie's hand with a bit more force than usual.

Mrs. White tried to leave the woman's question behind, but it dogged her all the way to church, partly because of the voice that had posed it, a voice so clear and distinctive that it had etched the phrases in her mind. She didn't enjoy her doughnut, having eaten it much too quickly, thrown off her regular pace. Hurrying the tea to her mouth, Mrs. White burned her tongue, which lay in her mouth swollen and pained. She sucked in air to cool the injured tip.

Each time the tongue touched her palate or the back of her teeth, she shuddered. To prevent this from happening she took the white hanky from her handbag, one she'd washed and pressed into a neat square, and stuffed it into her mouth.

*   *   *

134

Audrey dialed the operator and asked for the continuing-ed number at the local college. Of course the woman recognized Audrey's voice.

"You know that I'll have to charge you a quarter," she said. "I'm sorry."

"Not a problem," said Audrey. "That's the least of my worries."

Audrey was hoping to find a public-speaking course for the baker. The man in the registrar's office said he'd send her a catalog.

"I'd better stop by and pick one up," Audrey explained. "I need to know right away. Can I get it from you? What's your name?"

"I'm Ernest," he said, so timid that he could have used the course himself. "Ernest Lee."

The skies had begun to cloud over but because it was warm, Audrey decided to walk. Moving at a brisk pace, she made it within fifteen minutes. The woman at the front desk asked what she needed. Ernest Lee, who sat behind her, jumped up.

"It's here," he said sweetly. "I have it for you."

"Are you matriculated, miss?" the secretary asked, determined that nothing would happen without her say so. "What will you be using the catalog for?"

"Why, a friend," said Audrey, her voice patient and comforting.

"Oh, yes. OK, Ernest. No need to dawdle," responded the secretary as Ernest handed the catalog to Audrey.

"Thanks very much, Mr. Lee," Audrey said.

Ernest, thrilled by her tone, was inspired to sing as he reloaded the office's Xerox machine.

As Audrey started home a drizzle of rain began, just enough to hurry her along. She placed the catalog closer to her body, folding her arms over it and lowering her head. Audrey felt the thud, the smacking of her right shoulder against a rigid object, and heard a muffled "ohhh," all in the seconds before she actually saw the woman, the same woman she had spoken to at the doughnut shop earlier that morning.

Mrs. White, her mouth still filled with the cloth, glared at the telephone operator. Apologizing profusely, Audrey slid her hand over the woman's shoulder.

"Oh, gosh—please forgive me," she said as they stood face to face in the rain. "I hope I haven't hurt you." Then, trying to lighten things, she added, "Twice in one day I've bumped into you."

Mrs. White's stone eyes left Audrey's friendly face and traveled to the catalog, which advertised the public-speaking courses, along with computer literacy classes, on the front. Fat raindrops bounced off the rim of her hat as she pushed Audrey out of her path. The hanky, her tongue's wet bandage, had started to taste the way the fabric softener smelled.

Bea White could not, for the life of her, understand why this was happening.

When Audrey visited the shop the next day, her intention was to simply drop off the catalog with a note saying "See page 23." But then she saw the baker waiting, back pressed against the wall, his paper hat tipped forward on his head. Greeting Marie and placing her regular order, Audrey added, "I'll have it here." The baker waved hello, as if their meeting had been pure coincidence. Audrey motioned to two stools.

"What's your name, anyway? I don't think we were ever properly introduced," said the woman.

"Walter," he said, though it came out sounding like "Water."

"Well, Walter," she continued, pushing her voice to sound even more helpful than usual, "I've found a course—I've even talked with the instructor. It's a little pricey but if you're really interested—and I'm not saying you have to be—this is probably the best way to go."

He dropped his big head so far forward that the hat began tumbling downward. He caught it and held it in his lap.

"Now I can help some—I'd be willing to go over things with you, say, twice a week, so there'd be someone to practice with," Audrey said, knowing that this was the consolation prize.

Because his head had been lowered, his eyes averted, he didn't catch the last part.

"Were you speaking?" he asked.

"That's a good example of how inept I'd be," Audrey added, embarrassed by her own waffling. "I didn't even realize you weren't watching me just then. I'd been saying that I'd be a—a tutor, I guess, if you need one."

The baker thumbed to the course description. A black-and-white photo showed a handsome man in a suit, arm lifted, filled with poise, talking before a group comprised mostly of women.

"I'll take it," he said. "If I need help, I'll tell you."

Visibly relieved, Audrey nodded and finished up her tea. She missed Mrs. White by five minutes.

Mrs. White couldn't remember the exact moment she had stopped speaking. It seemed that that decision had been made little by little, over the course of her entire life. At first being "closemouthed" was fine because she was a girl, and shy, and this was acceptable, if not laudable. Then, as a teenager the teachers mistook her reticence for intelligence. She was not as smart as they thought and did not make even salutatorian—a good thing, since she never would have been able to give an address.

Small events robbed her of her speech—a complaint by a stranger who told her to hush as she rode the bus home from class one day; a loud-mouthed cousin who said Mrs. White's voice suffered from "emotional lockjaw"; the laugh from her husband; her son at four, saying, when she had tried to correct him, "I hate you. Just shut up. Shut up, you bad mommy." Once a police officer, writing out a parking ticket, joked as she began to stutter a protest, "What's the matter, lady? Cat got your tongue?" If she glanced back even further she could see herself in the play yard, at four or five, rhyming words—*boat, doat, coat, loat, foat, moat, rote, toat*—slowly and carefully, and a clique of tiny girls, maybe one year older, mocking her, their voices high and chimelike.

Over time the resolution came to say as few words as possible, to measure them out like drops of blood. The silence, the vow to keep still, became the template of her life, the very form that allowed her life to continue.

Mrs. White saw Audrey leave the shop. Audrey had made such an impression that Mrs. White could now identify her even as she walked away—the long, slight frame, reddish-brown hair worn in a page boy. It was touched up, Mrs. White believed, though she'd never inspected Audrey's roots. And Audrey's raincoat had several oil marks near the hem.

Wordlessly, Mrs. White went through her routine, the waitress bringing her order directly. No one would disrupt her, not even that horrible speech lady, who seemed to be everywhere she went. No one would make her speak. During the remainder of her trip to church Mrs. White looked around three times for any sign of her nemesis and, satisfied that she was alone, ate her doughnut and drank her tea in peace.

When she entered the church, however, for the first time in years she heard—vaguely—the voice of the priest. Without realizing it she stood throughout the entire Mass, stiff as a cross, while the other parishioners knelt and sat and stood.

At two o'clock in the morning Audrey got the first of four distress calls. Initially her party mumbled between gasps; not the regulated, lascivious moans of a breather but the panicked, choked talk of someone taken ill; the call lasted less than twenty seconds. She prayed that her caller would either dial the police or phone again. Nearly five minutes later a call came in where the party refused to say anything—Audrey had begun with her usual "Good morning, this is the operator," her spiel ending abruptly when the caller slammed down the phone. The third call followed a three-minute delay; Audrey, acting on instinct, immediately asked the silent dialer to please stay on the line, so she could send help. In the background Audrey heard a muffled cry; the caller hung up. But two minutes later the last call came, and although the person (Audrey *thought* it was a woman) said no more than "He's . . ." Audrey kept the party on long enough to trace the number, find the address in the company's reverse directory, and notify both the police and the ambulance company.

"Hang on," Audrey said, her voice firm but calm. "Just hang on. That's all you have to do. The rest is taken care of," she had said, over and over.

Earlier that same night, Mrs. White had knelt on her bathroom floor, scrubbing the tub. She did this each time her husband or son used the shower, up to four times each day. The son was spending the night with a friend and, after setting the breakfast table, Mrs. White, who always went to bed before her husband, pulled down the coverlet on her twin bed, placed her rosary beneath her pillow, and fell asleep.

She woke to the sound of her husband struggling with the phone as he held his arm and chest. He was motioning toward her, sweat soaking his cheeks, and she dashed out of bed and into her son's room, forgetting that he had left. She hurried to the coat closet, pulled on some boots and a jacket, and ran to the neighbors', who failed to hear her knocking. By the time Mrs. White got back upstairs Mr. White was begging her to dial the operator, and his arm shook and his breathing grew more labored. At first she thought he was saying, "Please, please," but he was actually calling out her name, "Bea, Bea."

She finally picked the phone up—Mr. White had knocked it under his bed and she had to dust off the receiver—and dialed O. The voice, *that woman's* voice! How could it be that out of all of the voices in the world that might have answered, it had to belong to the woman who was forcing her to speak? Had she somehow planned this? Mrs. White put down the receiver, tried moving her husband, getting him to his feet, and in desperation he hit the phone with his hand and placed his finger in the O slot.

When Mr. White began to lose consciousness she made herself call back, hoping that another voice would answer. Hearing Audrey again, all Mrs. White could say was, "He's, he's," believing, with all her heart, that Audrey was responsible for the world falling apart.

When Audrey got to the doughnut shop that morning, she forgot to ask the baker about his class, though she'd intended to do so. Instead she told Marie that she had a really intense night and ordered a Sanka so she could go home and sleep. Marie coaxed much of the story from her; Audrey's voice sounded terribly weary, almost pained. One of the truck drivers had to look twice to make sure it *was* Audrey.

"The person's alive," said Audrey. "The police phoned me back to let me know they'd taken him to the hospital. A minor heart attack. This Mr. White had a minor heart attack."

The waitress and the sales manager looked at each other.

"It's a common name," said Marie, shrugging it off.

The manager offered Audrey two jelly-filled doughnuts and she took them without arguing.

Mrs. White's absence that day went unnoticed; three days later, when the woman resumed her normal schedule, Marie realized that she'd missed seeing the customer earlier that week. Because Marie knew she would not get a reply, however, she didn't ask Mrs. White where she'd been.

Audrey had been plagued all week by a sense of uncertainty, as vague and as annoying as the beginnings of a cold. Had she left the burners on? Was the door locked? Faucet turned to the far right? Matters that had never entered her consciousness now shadowed her.

At first she attributed the feeling to the baker's lessons, but they were going fine—Audrey had held two tutoring sessions, which she'd really enjoyed. Teacher and student sat in the far corner of the doughnut shop, facing one another, during the baker's fifteen-minute break.

"Give me a raspberry," she'd say, while trying to demonstrate the *th* sound in the word "thick," her teaching instincts absolutely correct.

"Bite down on your back teeth. You want the *d* in 'doughnut' to be clear as a bell," she'd add, and the baker would comply.

Coming away from their meetings, she began appreciating her own voice, acknowledging that perhaps it was, indeed, a gift. She had always entertained the thought of doing voice-overs for national commercials and was inspired to begin looking into this possibility. The sales manager, whose brother-in-law sold space for a radio station, suggested that Audrey update her recordings of various endorsements, "The Diamond Czar on the boulevard in Dickson City," or "Kaplan's, the store above the mall. Them all." The manager would then get the tape listened to, because he had connections.

Maybe it was the idea of radio work that was making her feel a bit off. She tried blocking the whisperlike feeling in a safe and methodical fashion; before going to work one night she unplugged all of her electrical appliances (except for the fridge), hoping that this would bring her silence.

Mrs. White had no strong feelings about her husband's survival. In the first few minutes of panic, when he was thrashing about in his bed, reaching for the phone, she thought she should want him to live. Later, in the ambulance, still angered by the voice of the operator, she wished him dead. Their son was twenty-one and could survive without a father. The house was paid for and there would be insurance monies to live on. Her silent nature would be interpreted as grief.

The most annoying aspect of Mr. White's illness: his hospital stay had disrupted Mrs. White's daily routine. For two days straight she was obligated to appear at his bedside at 7:30 A.M., when the doctor made rounds, and listen to the physician assess the man's condition. The doctors found Mrs. White delightful; she listened carefully, so carefully that she never had to ask a single question. But the doctor's visit meant that Mrs. White had to forfeit her morning doughnut break and head to church on an empty stomach. She tolerated this for as short a period as was socially acceptable.

On the third day she resumed her regimen, though after Mass she made the trek to her husband's bedside and stayed there, devotedly, until 4:00 P.M. By day six, partly due to Mrs. White's "attentiveness," said the doctor, Mr. White was ready to go home.

The speech lesson had been delayed by ten minutes, due to a problem with the dough. Audrey stood by the window, eating her plain doughnut, watching the rain dance on the cars' rooftops. The baker shouted from the back, "Two more minutes, Audrey." She looked at her Timex. Having promised to meet a friend at 8:15, she knew she'd have to speed through the lesson if she was to be on time.

Taking a seat and leaning on the counter, elbows akimbo, she tapped the top lightly with her ring.

"What a beautiful ring," said Adele. "Oh, I just love it."

Audrey glanced downward. "Would you like it?" she asked.

The waitress shook her head, embarrassed by her own desire. "No, no," she answered, her eye on the stone.

"My grandmother used to say if someone really loves something you own, you should give it to them," Audrey reasoned, slipping the ring from her finger. "I never wear it. Enjoy it."

Adele tried returning the gift, but Audrey refused to listen. "Honestly," she said, "keep it."

The baker, a fine dusting of flour over his forearms and face, sidled into his corner. They were going to work on the *w* sound. Audrey described it to Walter; pretend you are sucking a plum, breathe in, and then blow out, releasing the fruit.

"Whisper," she said, and in hushed tones he repeated "whipper."

Audrey laughed. "I'm sorry. Repeat the word aloud. Whisper."

They tried why, while, wheel, when, whistle. Audrey glanced at her watch. It was eight o'clock. "White," she said distinctly, and then, before realizing it, added, "Mr. White."

On the far side of the register, at strict attention, was Mrs. White. The voice pierced her shroud of silence.

"White?" asked the baker.

"Yes, white. White," repeated Audrey.

Mrs. White held tight to every fiber of her being. She stood as the waitress fixed her order.

"I have to run," said Audrey. "We can pick this up tomorrow."

Audrey nodded to the customers on her way out, saying to Adele, who was still thanking her for the ring, "It's yours. I'm happy you like it."

The rain had grown steadier and she turned up her collar and paused before crossing the street. The sense of uneasiness seemed to overwhelm her and she turned to her right.

"Oh," Audrey said to the woman beside her, the same woman she'd seen in the shop several times now. "I didn't realize you were there. Good morning."

Mrs. White returned the greeting with a look of absolute hatred.

"My gosh," said Audrey, "Are you all right?"

Two words came, words pronounced distinctly, in the voice of a teacher giving a lesson.

"Mrs. White," said Mrs. White.

"Are you—is your husband—why are you staring at me like that?" asked Audrey, the rain now pouring down her face while Mrs. White opened an umbrella and shaded only herself. "I'd like to speak with you sometime—I've got to run—I hope everything is OK. We must speak, because I'm concerned. We have to speak," Audrey continued, stepping out into the street.

Mrs. White looked past Audrey at the oncoming car, its wipers swishing wildly. She searched for the words to warn the younger woman, but she had just spent all she had.

The driver dashed from the car, frantically, and placed his fingers on Audrey's neck, hoping for a pulse. Mrs. White, managing the doughnut, tea, and umbrella quite adeptly, continued on her trip to church. By the time the others hurried from the shop she was well on her way.

Once in the cathedral she moved to a center aisle. The Mass passed without incident, until the Kiss of Peace, when Mrs. White joined with the congregation, turned to her neighbor, and said in a voice as lovely as Audrey's, as she grasped the woman's hand, "Peace be with you."

Frances

Once a week Frances Cabrine drove to town to pick up her pig food. When she got to the back of the doughnut shop, where they kept the stales in sacks the size of a small woman, someone would shout, "Here's the pig lady, jiggity-jig." She'd grown accustomed to the name, no offense intended or taken, just the quickest way of identifying her connection with the purchase. She knew Russell the packer, the bakers, even Mr. Raymond, and talked to each one as she stapled the bags shut and then dragged them to her station wagon, a car without a backseat. Loading the sacks took some effort but Frances was sturdy and hard-working and never expected a hand. Besides, the doughnuts were worth the outing; cheap and filling, they fattened the stock and, more to the point, made her pigs taste sweet, or so the other farmers claimed. She'd mix the baked goods with grain, milk, stale bread, and spoiled produce from the supermarket dumpster.

For her trip to town Frances always wore a dress, starched and ironed, and when the weather was cold she covered it with her good coat. Her blue-black hair was strict, clean, and parted in the middle, pulled behind her ears. She looped a brown handbag over her arm, just above the wrist. Considering the purse part of her outfit she didn't set it down; the pocketbook batted against the doughnut sacks as she pulled them to the car. Frances had school-teacher shoes, black-laced oxfords—in fact, her whole demeanor, refined and friendly without being intimate, put the workers in mind of a teacher. They looked forward to seeing Frances Friday mornings; she noticed things, such as haircuts or new shoes, and occasionally she brought fresh brown eggs or vegetables from her garden. One fall she had a bumper crop of cucumbers, foot-long and crisp as an autumn dawn. She carried them into the shop in a cardboard box, bringing enough for everybody, even those workers she hadn't met.

Scrupulously honest, Frances twice reminded Mr. Raymond as he said good-bye that she had not paid him. She opened the clasp on the top of her purse and withdrew a clutch attached to the larger bag by a leather cord. The dollar bills were faded and limp but not dirty. Russell emphasized that the pig lady was very much a *lady*, though she never considered herself above any type of labor. If boxes were blocking the pig food and people were too busy to move them, she moved them herself. The time a sack split open, its belly leaking doughnuts, she found a broom and swept up. She would have washed the spot clean if Mr. Raymond hadn't stopped her.

Unlike some livestock owners, she hadn't ever raised a pig as a pet or entered one in a competition. She wouldn't give her stock people names. (A high school friend of Frances, Mary Agnes, had named her prize pig Mr. Bobby G., Jr., after the love of her life. Frances couldn't see it.) Even with this detachment, Frances hated to have the animals slaughtered. As a matter of course she ate very little meat.

Frances asked after Mr. Raymond's business, and Russell's health, without fail. If Terri Kudja strolled to the back while Frances was there, the pig lady wanted to hear all about Terri's kids, Mandy, Daniel, and Kenny, the baby. Terri had given Frances a wallet-size photo of the three children taken just after Kenny's birth. The woman displayed the picture on her refrigerator.

"How are those pretty children?" Frances would say. "Tell me what they've been up to." She remembered their ages and the school they attended.

The pig lady listened attentively, even as she filled her wagon with doughnuts. But she never loitered. Once, after Branley Orbis had made his preaching public and his orations could be understood throughout the shop, Frances heard him at the fryer, firing up his faithful. His voice had a rhythmic quality, clear and lulling as any minister who spoke on the radio.

"You have the gift of speech," she said to Branley. "You sound just wonderful. That piece about the willow is stirring," she added.

Branley, who'd had his share of disappointments, thanked her.

"It's true," Frances said kindly, without exaggeration. "I wouldn't say it if it weren't true."

It was amazing how good the pig lady could make you feel.

Frances couldn't forget a face and often surprised people she'd met in passing with her excellent memory. She'd done volunteer work for the Red Cross, helping out with the county Bloodmobile, and recalled each of the donors, including those from twenty-five years back. She wasn't squeamish about needles or blood, understanding both to be necessary. When Mr. Raymond introduced Frances to his wife one morning, as the three stood in the shop, Frances recollected that the women had met previously.

"Aren't you Rh-negative?" Frances asked, recounting Mrs. Raymond's Bloodmobile visit twenty years earlier. Frances had given Mrs. Raymond a cup of orange juice. "There used to be a great need for that blood type. We'd ask for it over the radio—emergency cases, you know." Frances then let the incident drop, seeing Mrs. Raymond's embarrassment at failing to place the pig lady. "You have a good day now. See you all Friday next," Frances added, handing Mr. Raymond the cash. Her fingers were remarkably strong.

Before she left the pig lady would take a folded blanket from the front seat and cover the bags completely, tucking the blanket's woolen edges underneath. She was driving through downtown Scranton on her way home and wanted things to look presentable.

She loved seeing the passing pedestrians and the few store windows, the traffic lights.

Generally Frances made it back home by midafternoon, but even if she was running late she emptied the car. The one time she'd left the doughnuts in the wagon overnight, a bear forced his way through the tailgate window (it was ajar), breaking the glass with his weight, feasting on the sweets, pulling the blanket halfway into the woods. The bear returned two nights later and Frances, not willing to hurt him, shooed him away with a rake and a holler. She saw him again, rambling through the pines, but she kept the doughnuts away and he kept his distance.

The pig lady's contact with the other food stores—the bread factory and the supermarket—was limited. The bread place stored their stales in a shed, which she'd been given a key to, and she emptied it out every two weeks, leaving the small payment in an envelope slipped under the office door. She waved to people, even if they failed to wave back. The supermarket managers just tossed the spoiled produce into an open dumpster, which Frances picked through before the Food Fair opened. There was no charge—the manager merely tolerated her behavior.

But the doughnut shop was different; for Frances the business call was close to an education. Every Day seemed a hive of activity, what with doughnuts being fried and iced and served or packed, orders being phoned in, deliveries made. A whole slew of people. The word that came to her was industry, industry in the old sense, diligence in an employment and pursuit. Industry and husbandry; that's how she thought of her relationship to the shop. But more than that, because of the friends she'd made—and she felt they were her friends, always glad for the visit—hers was a social call, a morning out. Everytime she saw these people she was glad.

Because she paid in cash, no one knew Frances's last name. They knew the car and her first name, her Friday morning routine, that she raised pigs and vegetables and had worked for the Red Cross, her nature at the doughnut shop—and that was it. That was the sum total of their knowledge of Frances. On account of the simplicity of their knowledge, she seemed as constant as the sun, as reliable as the hills.

Mr. Raymond and the others hadn't a clue as to how solitary her existence was. She'd been married for more than twenty years, a quiet, comforting match to a man as taciturn as a field after snowfall. Her husband had run a small dairy, by himself, Frances helping out when he needed. The dairy went to auction the month after Frances found him slumped under a cow (had he been checking a hoof? Her bag? There was liniment nearby but none on his hands), Patrick dead of a heart attack, the doctors told her, at the age of forty-four. The dairy sale paid their debts; she was able to keep the pigs and her garden, the house, and two acres of land. For ten years she also saved the big crimped tube of liniment, placed on a bureau shelf, dusted once a week, then finally put to rest in the root cellar.

He died on a Monday, lay in the ground on that Wednesday, and on Friday Frances was at the shop (having driven a little more slowly than usual), asking after the others, gracious and gentle. She had only just started buying the doughnuts and didn't feel right saying anything; besides, the hum of the place soothed her aching heart.

Most days, even the hardest ones, during the sale, Frances was grateful—that she had been married, that Patrick had been kind, and they'd known happiness. Her expectations of life were basic, as fundamental as those that inspire a seed of grass to grow. During her dozen years of solitude (forty-eight seasons was how she saw it, her marriage having thrived for ninety quarters), anger shook her only once.

When the river flooded and the rats traveled to higher ground, they lodged in her feed bin. Opening the lid, she saw them scurry and she screamed, though she had no fear. In no position to lose her feed, she had little choice but to grab each one by the tail, stunning it on the side of the bin and tossing the carcass, fat from its last meal, onto a pile to be burned. As she did so she cursed Patrick. And she may have wished, though she couldn't rightly remember, that someone had been there to hear her.

*   *   *

149

Frances was lucky enough (that's how she saw it) to be on hand the morning the shop's new glazer arrived. Everyone seemed to be turned up a notch, moving more quickly, Mr. Raymond acting especially animated. The bakers and Carl, called in to help, were to complete the glazer's assembly between baking shifts, but first the men had to drain the old machine of its icing, store the sugar mixture in buckets, clean the machine's square tub, and then break it down into parts, dragging those pieces to the back of the shop.

Mr. Raymond nodded hello to the pig lady, his face flushed with pride over his new possession.

"I'll be through in ten minutes," Frances promised, taking a new path to accommodate the workers. "That's some machine. You certainly have a wonderful operation," she said.

Beaming, Mr. Raymond leaned over and whispered. "It's a matter of doing what you know. And I know doughnuts."

Frances, too discreet, would not say that her pigs agreed. After she'd finished loading up, she returned with a small box and placed it on a packing table.

"Tomatoes," she explained. "Good luck with the new equipment. All the best."

Getting into her car, she tried turning over the engine, to no avail. She sat a moment, composed herself, and tried again. Pulling on the hood release, she walked over to the front of the wagon. She saw the problem immediately—a loose battery connection, easily fixed. It would take her no more than five minutes. Hearing the voices of the help inside the shop, she paused to enjoy the sounds of camaraderie. She thought of how much silence filled her own life. Maybe she would take up her Red Cross work once again.

"You're still here?" said Carl, tossing some refuse into the dumpster, as Frances, having made the repair, was now fussing over her cargo's blanket. "Well, come see. Mr. Raymond said if Frances is still here, have her come see."

The stainless steel contraption, set just beyond the fryer, radiated newness. The final bolts were being tightened. The owner, polishing cloth in hand, was erasing some of the fingerprints, small rainbow-colored blotches on the hardware. He looked up to see Frances's sweet smile, cheering them on.

"If you wait," said the baker, "we'll give you a doughnut from the very first batch."

Making herself useful, Frances helped with the cleanup while waiting.

A walk in the field south of her garden usually gave Frances that sense of belonging most people find in others; her community had been, for years, her land. The cross-hatching marks of pheasant feet on the snow kept her company, as did a clouded sky or the wind's moan as it bent the pine branches.

On a Tuesday morning, early, after tending to the pigs, she broke from her regular schedule and walked the two miles to an old friend's house. The grass had the clarity of spring water; morning light, Frances knew, was the most revealing. She raised a hand to her face to chase an itch and from the corner of her eye she saw the tiny hairs on her fingers, now unmistakably white.

Her friend Agnes also had animals—one milk cow she'd called Veronica and a family of swine named the Crosbys, each with its own first name and birthday celebration. Frances couldn't bother to keep them straight; besides, new Crosbys, of course, were always being born and older ones sold.

Frances had brought her girlhood friend a loaf of cinnamon bread, which had risen overnight and been baked at five this morning. Agnes would allow herself only a sniff and then share the loaf with her family, but Frances took it along anyway. When Frances was just about one hundred feet from the porch Agnes heard her, listening with that deep suspicion often possessed by those who've lived alone too long.

"You walked?" said Agnes, as if continuing an ongoing conversation.

"Good morning, Mary Agnes," Frances replied, her social grace forever intact.

"I'll be in the kitchen. I'm fixing little Lawrence his bottle," Agnes said, releasing the screen door.

Three ceramic bullfrogs occupied the corner of the steps, one higher than the next, ready for a game of leapfrog. Agnes had a kiln in her cellar. Frances lifted the frog, yet unweathered, from the top step. It sat in her hand like a clean stone.

"Take him," said Agnes, a piglet now under her arm. "He's not from the same batch as the others. I won't feel bad separating Freddy the Frog." She snatched at the bread, put it to her nose, and, tearing a piece from the whole, dipped it in her cup of milk. "OK, little one," she said, the bread lifted to the piglet's snout.

"You're well, Mary Agnes? Your feed holding? Any supplies I can help with?" Frances asked, settling herself on a cane-bottomed chair.

"We've had no sickness," her friend observed. "The vet's been out twice but just for vaccinations. They say every year now. Poor Veronica, who hates a needle."

The piglet sucked noisily on the rubber nipple. Its skin had the sheen of newness, nearly translucent. The women headed out toward the barn. Agnes, as always, seemed to be in her own space, and none the worse for it.

"Mary Agnes," Frances began, "I've been thinking of buying a TV." The admission hurt her.

"For the girls?" Agnes asked cheerily. She referred to Frances's stock as the girls, even though Frances raised both sows and boars.

"More for the company. I have the radio, of course—it's just a thought," Frances explained. Then, venturing further, she added, "And I've thought of maybe taking a job, some part-time work. Not the Red Cross," she said, preempting her friend.

Agnes was gaga over a fine shoat, singing him "Pig o' My Heart" under her breath. Frances needed to start back home, to begin the rest of the day's chores.

"I'll stop by toward the middle of the month," Frances told Agnes. "Make a list for me if you need anything." Agnes's hair, still a chestnut brown, gleamed in the sun. "You look wonderful," Frances said.

Agnes let go of the pig. "Thank you, Frances," she said, smiling. "I appreciate your goodness."

* * *

More often than not Frances left her weeding for the late afternoon, but today she wanted the sun's relentless heat on her back and head, her forearms. She started out wearing her hat and a pair of coarse cotton gloves, the ones with fat and rounded fingers. When she got to the squash section she stripped off the accessories, loosened her dress at the neck, and lay down at the garden's edge. First Frances took in the scent of the grass, sweet and dry, and the fertile smell of the soil. A breeze stirred the air and she watched the sky, as farm folk will, for the next day's weather. There was a change due and Frances understood enough to know that change was healthy and, too often, rare.

She took herself into town the next afternoon, Wednesday. Both the pigs and the air were skittish so she was ready for the thunderstorm, the lightning cracking the sky, but not the hailstones, now popping against the car's roof, frantic on the hood and windshield. The hail, big as cherry tomatoes, was a surprise. It labored her driving, making the two-lane road toward the highway seem much longer than usual. Frances laughed aloud at one point, wondering if mother nature were handing her a reprimand for breaking her routine.

The trip was more impulse than plan. In downtown Scranton the skies were untroubled and the teenage girls bare shouldered. Everyone moved in clusters. Frances tried backing into a parking place, but the traffic was too thick. She drove into a lot, handing her keys to the attendant. Once in the Globe, the city's sole department store, she rode the escalator to the top floor, personnel, and asked for an application. There were no openings for sales positions, but Frances took the application anyway and placed it inside her purse, proudly. She wanted to see how it felt to carry the form around.

Walking through the store, she watched the sales clerks posed behind the counters, waiting for customers. An elderly lady stood at the candy counter and an old man was trying on a pair of shoes. At three in the afternoon there was no bustle, no real movement. If Frances had wished to enjoy a still life she could have stayed home. She paused at the escalator for a moment, noting that the mechanism didn't function unless someone climbed aboard.

Frances decided to drive by the doughnut shop. She wouldn't be disruptive, checking in the back for stales; nor would she sit out front with the public. The entire front was glass, as was the partition separating the work area from the store, so she could see the baker baking, the glazer dipping, right from her car. She'd simply drive by, inconspicuously, to enjoy the scenery.

Passing slow enough to aggravate the driver behind her, Frances turned the corner to the shop's back door, planning on a second pass. Mr. Raymond stood along the curb, checking the tires on one of his trucks. She stared straight ahead but he'd spotted the station wagon and waved her to an open space.

"Frances," he called, happily. "Why, it's not Friday, is it?"

Embarrassment plastered her hands to the steering wheel. She finally opened her window and smiled.

"In a hurry?" Mr. Raymond asked. "Why, then, just come in for a minute. I'll be right there."

She found it hard to refuse the invitation. Now Terri Kudja, finished with her shift, was at the back door, waving to Frances as well.

"What a treat," Terri called and then, coaxing someone inside the door, said, "Look, I've got Kenny with me. My sister just dropped him off."

In a second Terri had the child riding her hip. Since no one pressed Frances to explain her visit, she made no excuses.

"My," Frances said, beaming at the child, "you are one big boy. And handsome, too." She placed her hand on his sneaker and wiggled his small round foot. "Are you taking care of your pretty mom?"

The boy snuggled his face against Terri's uniform.

"Honey," Terri said. "Do you know who this is? This is the pig lady, Frances. She's our friend."

The child lifted his head and stared at the woman incredulously.

"I have a whole bunch of pigs," Frances explained.

"Any with you?" Kenny asked.

* * *

154

Carl was hauling some garbage bags and Frances held the door. One of the salesmen, Josh, had just come in from the road.

"Hey, Frances," he said, his hands filled with receipts. "Did you hit that hail coming in from the country? Did you see that stuff? Wicked."

"Yes, it was." Frances laughed. "It was positively wicked."

To keep out of the way Frances followed Josh into the office. A pad of employee applications sat on a shelf. She read the first few questions as she asked about his sales. There were spaces on the form for schooling—grade school, high school, trade school, and other. Then, waiting until Josh's back was turned, until he was at the adding machine, totaling his sales, Frances peeled the paper from the tablet and placed it inside her coat. Never before had she taken something without asking.

Branley Orbis was on his platform, passionately frying his doughnuts, and Adele the waitress was in the next room, pumping them full of jelly. A baker's helper, Wade's replacement, was whipping up a batch of vanilla icing, his arm a mixer. Branley called for another box of shortening and Frances, seeing that all were occupied, took the initiative, pulling down the thirty-pound block from the top of a small pyramid and pushing it over to Branley.

"Jesus loves you, Frances," said the preacher.

Certainly she could be of use here.

She heard a bear that night, rummaging about hours after she'd fallen asleep. Identifying the noise right off, she stayed in bed, figuring he'd soon be on his way. When he continued thrashing about, she slid the curtain across the rod. A black cub, no bigger than a female Labrador, had dragged a trash bin from around the back and was banging it like a bongo player.

"You'll wake the neighbors," she hollered, sorry there was no one near to arouse. Frances looked at the creature, now on two legs, and he appeared to look back.

Her largest boar had rutted up the pen and there was a hole in the barn roof to patch, so Frances completed her run to the city as quickly as possible on Friday. She hadn't had a chance to read through the application, though she'd stashed the paper in a top cupboard for safe keeping.

When Frances returned home she spotted Agnes's pickup in the driveway; Agnes stood on the porch, struggling with a mammoth brown television. The tube jutted out, a mound of metal, and some kind of silver brackets hung from the side.

"Go back," Agnes was saying. "This is supposed to be a surprise. Go back."

The woman placed her knee under the chassis as support and extended her little finger to catch the screen door. Frances hurried from her car. She took one end, Agnes the other, and they set the beast in the living room.

"It can't stay there. We got to hang it," Agnes said, lifting the television's silver arms. "These here are to hang it up."

"Where ever did you get such a . . . large one?" Frances inquired carefully.

"The county hospital. They're replacing the old ones; I found the advertisement in the *Pennysaver.* You can lie down and watch," she said proudly, and then, more apologetically. "It's second-hand. They said 'like new,' but it's second-hand."

Frances dusted the cabinet with a hanky. "Why, Mary Agnes. It's spectacular. It's one of a kind, now, isn't it?" She walked around the knee-high eyesore, acting pleased, genuinely touched. "Let's have some coffee—to toast it. Christen it, maybe? And I have a spare loaf of cheese bread," Frances said, knowing that Agnes would end up sticking the loaf in her pocket.

Agnes plugged the television's cord into the wall and fooled with the circular antenna screwed to the set's back. She switched the channels and the screen filled with snow. Finally the picture cleared.

"Look," she yelled. "It's channel twelve in Binghamton. You get channel twelve. That's your channel."

Frances had placed the coffee cups and bread on a tray and carried it into the living room. The women drank the hot liquid and listened to the farm report.

"See how useful a TV will be?" Frances said to her friend encouragingly.

"You know all that," Agnes said quietly, tucking the cheese bread in her pocket. "You don't need a farm report."

After they finished their repast, Agnes picked out a corner of the room where the brackets would hold to the wall and Frances carted her tools from the shed. She fetched a piece of pine to bolster the set. The effort took the women half an hour, both being handy with screws and drills. The task completed, the television's vast blank face staring downward, Frances walked Agnes to her pickup, holding her hand, thanking her.

"I took the bread," Agnes confessed, and Frances said gently, "I'd hoped so. I made it for you, Mary Agnes."

"You're so good, Frances," Agnes said, as if explaining her own gift. "They say goodness fills us up, but I think goodness can make you lonely. I didn't want you to be so lonely," Agnes added, climbing into her truck.

The Friday before the butcher was to come by her farm, Frances bought three dozen fresh doughnuts, along with her usual stales. Terri tried to give them to her, Mr. Raymond seconding the motion, but Frances insisted on paying.

"Well, at least let us give you an employee discount," Mr. Raymond said, and Frances, happy at the thought, acquiesced.

For the past month she'd made subtle inquiries about the staff and the work load. She remarked on leadership and the problems of turnover. Mr. Raymond had not caught on, taking the questions as part and parcel of the pig lady's kindness. On a whim she'd also applied for a sales job at the mall—a place she'd frequented only twice—and mercifully was turned down due to her "lack of experience."

"I hope those are for you," Mr. Raymond said, pointing to the box of just-fried doughnuts.

Frances had planned on bringing one dozen to Agnes's stock. "They'll be polished off in no time," she assured the owner.

That afternoon Frances looked over her pigs a final time. Five she'd keep—two sows and a boar for breeding and a pair for Agnes, to replenish her stock. As Frances had suspected, Agnes had traded two of the Crosbys for the television set. Frances had potatoes and squash to store in her root cellar, two pumpkins to make into pies for the grade-school fair, and the hen house to tend to, but she stood along the pig pen, October blowing in her hair, and hand-fed fresh doughnuts to the seven pigs she was selling. Never in all her years on the farm had she done such a thing. The pigs' breath, as they gobbled the sweets, warmed her hand.

"I'm sorry," she said to a plump sow.

Before retiring for the night she poured part of the bag of stales in among the pines, for the bears. They didn't come.

She'd always hated this part of farm life, even when Patrick was alive. The butcher was wiry and quick, his arms cutting the air like knives, as he herded the animals up the ramp to his truck. Before he was in the drive the pigs began to squeal. Agnes always said that they smelled the blood. Earlier Frances had penned off the ones that would stay behind and so now she and the butcher were placing peach baskets over the doomed pigs' heads and shoving the animals onto the ramp. The only way to get a pig to cooperate was to blind it.

Frances tried to make conversation, first about the weather and then about the man who read the "Farm Report," but the butcher was grunting as much as the animals. Out of the need to hear another voice, she asked about prices.

"Neither one of us will ever get rich doing this. You know that, Frances," he said matter of factly, closing the pickup's tailgate against the last swine.

Going to the porch, Frances handed the man three bottles of her best preserves for his wife. Then she asked about his arthritis. He held up knobby fingers, which he flexed easily in the air. There was no use talking over the pig squeals.

"I can't do it," she said, but he was already in the truck's cab.

After he'd left, she let the remaining pigs run into the pen. She would visit Agnes tomorrow, dropping off her new pair. Unbuttoning her sweater and leaving it in the barn, Frances strode across the field to feel the frost of fall, to find her sense of belonging. She stood at the edge of the pines, taking in their moans, their smell.

It wasn't enough.

158

For a moment she thought of taking the pigs to town, of borrow-
ing Agnes's pickup and driving through the city, showing the
animals how the other half lived, as it were. She'd stop by Every
Day; it would take no effort to get the swine inside. Picturing the
scene, with Mr. Raymond and Terri and maybe her children (hadn't
Kenny asked that Frances do this?), the pigs running amok, Frances
began to wonder about her sanity.

Returning to her house, the walk home having comforted her,
Frances made the pies, as promised, the television on in the next
room. She delivered the baked goods to the school's fair, bought
a seven-year-old's watercolor of a city skyline, praised the third
graders' puppet show, and drove home at dusk, glancing along the
roadside for deer.

The night was cold but she rested on the porch anyway, knees
under her chin like a schoolgirl wishing for a suitor, actually
hoping for her bear. Resigned, Frances looked up and watched as
channel twelve in Binghamton signed off. Before going to bed she
sat at the kitchen table and filled out the application for work at
the doughnut shop.

After Frances loaded the station wagon with stales, she went to the
office to pay her bill. Mr. Raymond was alone, behind his desk,
talking on the phone. He smiled at the pig lady, neat as a pin, and
motioned for her to wait just a minute.

"Some arrangement's got to be made," he warned the caller.
"You better get a plan for yourself, some organization."

When he hung up, she was the first to speak.

"Starting next month, Martha Amble will be stopping by—that
is, if you're interested in selling her your stales. She has a farm, a
large one, about twenty miles west of mine, and I've told her all
about mixing the baked goods with feed. I didn't talk price, seeing
as that's your prerogative. Martha's reliable, and good-humored,"
Frances said without emotion. She offered her cash before the
owner had a chance to respond.

She had not anticipated his anger, which even now she thought was part jest. His eyes narrowed and his brow grew pink. He looked a little like a pig.

"Do you think I'd want a stranger coming in here, wandering around, privy to my operations? Do you really think I'd allow such a thing, Frances?"

The application, which she'd been about to hand him, was slid into her pocket. Mr. Raymond had caught the action, recognizing the form.

"May I?" he said, easing up a bit, aware of her shame.

Frances lifted her head with dignity and gave the man her application. There was not a mistake or an erasure on the paper. He sighed and stared up at the office door, where he'd tacked a nature calendar. Frances was patience incarnate.

"Forgive me," he said, liking the woman too much to torture her. "I was thinking of Terri Kudja. That was her on the phone."

Frances immediately forgot her own predictament. "She is all right? The children?"

"She's out at least once a week. They moved back to the projects six months ago and the kids have been nothing but trouble. Fights. A small fire. The other kids won't accept them back. Or so she says. It's neither here nor there."

Mr. Raymond made a few notes on Frances's form. "Cabrine," he said. "All these years, I never even knew your last name. Widow," he read aloud. "You ready to move to the city? Give up the pigs and that country air? It would be hard to commute if you were working full time," he advised.

Hesitating a little, Frances replied, "If the situation were right, I'd consider relocating."

"I'll see what I can do," said Mr. Raymond. "I know the owner."

On the trip back home Frances drove through the city with an eye toward living there. She was amazed that she could count the trees, a feat she could never consider on her own land. Taking a detour, she passed through the city's projects, brick cubes whose only distinctive features were the painted doors. Although she felt she might be overstepping her bounds, she asked a child on a bicycle where the Kudjas lived.

"That one with the red door," said the boy. "Number nine."

Terri opened the door, more frazzled and worn than Frances had seen her. Kenny was at her knee and her daughter was propped up on the couch. A packet of ice sat atop a small goose egg rising from the girl's forehead.

"Look," squealed Kenny. "It's the pig lady."

Frances found the quarters incredibly cramped. There was only one window, with a view of the parking lot. Terri kicked a toy out of the pig lady's way.

"You can see," Terri said, forcing good humor, "that I wasn't prepared for company." Then, with pride and conviction, she added, "You know we won't be here forever. We left once."

"Oh, God, Mom," interrupted the girl. "Will you get real?"

"No, I think your mother's right—it's Mandy, isn't it? I love that name. It suits you, you know? It's strong, but it's pretty, too." Then, turning her attention to Kenny, Frances asked, "Have you ever ridden a pig? Do you think you're big enough to stay on?"

Kenny raised his fist, attempting to make a muscle.

"Could we two talk, outside?" Frances asked Terri.

Mr. Raymond agreed to the arrangement, willing to try it for six months. This alone was testimony to Frances's popularity. Of course, Marie Eden ironed out the details, so that Terri could drive in from the farm Monday, Tuesday, and Wednesday, and weekends when needed, working a straight shift, with Frances filling in at the shop on Thursdays and Fridays. That way Frances still picked up the stales for the pigs on schedule. The kids gave their pigs dogs' names—Rover and Spot and Shadow—which pleased the pig lady no end.

161

Ernest

Adele started calling him Professor, which may have been the beginning of the end. He never asked for the title, simply had it handed to him early one morning along with his black coffee and jelly doughnuts, a commoner knighted by a waitress looking for a fifty-cent tip and perhaps a chance at a third husband. Protesting—"No, no, I only work in the college's admissions office"—didn't help, nor did his efforts at shrugging it off. Adele insisted, pronouncing the word very distinctly, and in the presence of other customers. After about a month's time he stopped trying to correct her and settled into the role she had arbitrarily chosen.

One Tuesday in January, as the man was leaving with his order and an extra dozen glazed for the staff (Adele's suggestion), Le Mans, Terri's ex, poked the Professor with an oil-laced finger. "What's this about the ozone? Who's really responsible—you college boys or us? Huh?"

The Professor appeared startled, pushing back a bit on his heels and adjusting his glasses by wiggling his nose.

Le Mans continued. "Now, I've read where there's good and bad ozone. Couldn't you come up with another name for the smog stuff? My mother had fourteen children and none of us has the same name. Got an answer? Huh? Didn't think so."

"Excuse me," said the Professor with as much dignity as he

could muster and backed into the door, using his hind quarters as a lever to open it.

"Hey, woman," Le Mans cried to the waitress, "don't pour that stuff into the Styrofoam. Here's my thermos."

When the Professor arrived at work he turned on the lights and set the doughnuts out in the coffee room. Straightening the paper cups, he wiped down the plastic tablecloth and pulled the filters and coffee packets from the cabinet beneath. The coffee packet read "For institutional use only." Still upset by the Le Mans episode, he nearly forgot the sugar and Creamora. He took the Sweet 'n' Low out of its hiding place behind the medical forms in the supply case. If he didn't hide it, the secretary, Mrs. Domko, would take the extras home with her. He counted ten envelopes, which he arranged in a row next to the stirrers.

The copying machine clearly had been touched after he left last night. A stray paperclip sat atop it and the paper drawers had been closed improperly. With the precision of a surgeon, he opened the machine's face and peered at its innards. Pressing on the plastic handles, as directed, he released yet another set of drawers and traced the path of the last sheet of paper. Three pieces were folded around the metal bar that rested against the feeder. Two additional pieces were jammed behind the sign that read CAUTION: MACHINERY MAY BE HOT. He was dislodging those, with care, when his boss walked into the office.

"Ernest," he called. "What are you up to?"

"I'm at the copier, Mr. Munsch," he answered, trying to sound upbeat.

"For chrissake, call the repair guy. It won't be right otherwise."

Mrs. Domko, entering the front door, asked her boss where everybody was.

"Ernest's in the Xerox room," he replied, rolling his eyes, and she tsk-tsked in sympathy.

"Good as broken now," she muttered, removing a bagged lunch from her fat black purse and then stuffing her pocketbook into an open drawer.

The machine had hold of Ernest's hand and he longed for the

copier to swallow the rest of him, for its metal mouth to devour his arm and shoulder, the head and torso then following along willessly. When he looked up from his reverie he saw Mrs. Domko standing over him, a glazed doughnut pinched between her pink fingertips, the Sweet 'n' Low packets poking out of her sweater pocket.

At home, Ernest changed the water in the canary's cage, opened the mail, and listened for a half hour to his language tape, conversational Italian. His comprehension was good, his reading vocabulary growing quickly, but never once in three weeks of studying had he spoken the words aloud. They remained locked in his head, one sentence flowing into the next with a perfect accent.

To organize himself for the morning he lined up the borrowed library books—a travel guide to Rome, a volume of Pliny, a paperback entitled *Getting Along With Any One!*—and set out a white shirt, pale blue boxer shorts, brown socks, brown tweed jacket. He would wear the same pants he had on today. During dinner he turned on the radio, always tuned to the same classical station, thought how wearing the music selection was, ate a baked potato, a single slice of ham, and a pineapple ring. While washing his dish he remembered an old girlfriend and the way she looked in a very compromised position, particularly the luster of her back. In the course of the day and night he had uttered, at most, two dozen words. No one called at the door or by telephone. Just before bed he overheard a conversation between two people in the next apartment and paused to put his ear to the wall, half smiling at their conversation, but within a few minutes he realized that he was listening to a television program.

Even when the shop was packed with customers Adele could spot the Professor's car half a block away. Because it was a two door and foreign (Japanese) she dubbed it Sporty; she alone thought so. His driving, more than his car, signaled the Professor's approach, since he crawled through the intersection, traffic or not. Adele had his order ready ("Don't want to keep those students waiting") when he walked cautiously through the door.

165

"What are the noodles called?" Adele asked Marie, who was restacking the coffee cups.

"Italian," Marie answered.

"They have another name—" she said, handing the Professor his breakfast.

"Fettucine?" he offered, and Adele beamed with delight.

"How do you say it?" she asked again, adding that she was making the dish for a church supper.

"Fet-tu-cheeeni," he said with a flourish, and for the first time sat down at the counter. "Ribbons. Ribbons cut from dough."

"I couldn't fit a word that long in my mouth," teased Adele. She rushed to get him coffee—"Tastes so much better in a real cup," she whispered—and handed him a newly filled sugar bowl.

He felt more solid than he had in years, as if his feet had just grown roots and his limbs had taken on the toughness of a trunk. When he went to pay, Adele insisted that she buy, and when he left he said good morning to two people he'd never seen before. Out in the parking lot a homeless man pushed a cart to which he'd tied a totem pole built from stuffed animals, bunnies without eyes, limp-backed dogs, a bear that had lost his snout, a green-velvet cat, a monkey suffering from the mange, and a bird with a head twice the size of its body. The basket itself carried a bundle of clothes, shoes, and newspapers.

Resting his cargo against the curb, the owner paused to bow to his menagerie. Ernest glanced upward but met the man's eyes anyway, two almond-shaped sores blistered with the crust of sleep. Yesterday, and probably tomorrow, the Professor would have uttered, silently, "But for the grace of God there go I," and would have branded his mind with the man's image so that he could refer to it throughout the morning. But today he said, "How unfortunate," and drove his car around the back of the building so as not to further disturb the traveler.

Mrs. Domko rapped the top of the desk clock when Ernest arrived, prompting their boss to say, "Must make an effort to be here on time, people."

"It's fast," challenged Ernest.

Mr. Munsch, mystified, said, "What?"

"It's fast. She set it ahead to make herself look good," Ernest replied, waiting for his superior to pull out his pocketwatch. Then, as if the strain of talking had weakened him, he went to the back room to make the coffee.

As Mrs. Domko listened to the water run through the machine and begin filling the pot, she asked her boss, ingratiatingly, "May I get you a cup?"

He nodded yes. Ernest's ceremony with the stirrers and sugar packets was nearly over. Butting him with her bottom—deliberately, Ernest thought—she twisted the words "Excuse me" in her mouth, which he chose to ignore.

"I said, 'excuse me,' " she repeated.

A phrase from his childhood—no excuse for you—rang in his head, but he stopped it there. His seeming indifference plagued her with the meanness of an itch she could not scratch. To gain some relief she scrutinized his actions until, predictably, he spilled the box of coffee filters.

"Sad," she sighed and placed her heel just fractions of an inch from the fallen papers. Busying himself with the counter, he waited for Mrs. Domko to move.

"I'll be right in, Mr. Munsch," she said with exaggerated desperation. "There's just a bit of a mess in here." And then, lowering her voice, she added, "Two messes. Ciao."

Unwittingly, she sashayed out of the path of possible destruction; now on his knees, Ernest began to lick the carpet, as he had countless times before. As a child, taunted by his schoolmates and unable to retaliate, he'd run home, race upstairs, and run his tongue over the floor, swallowing the dirt, hoping that the offering would be adequate to suffocate their cries. Had she stayed, Ernest would have pulled Mrs. Domko to the ground, too, and held her mouth against the black surface.

After work on Tuesday, as was his custom, Ernest visited his mother and grandmother. They lived in a high-rise (twelve stories) for the elderly two towns away from the college. The drive took about twenty-five minutes and his relatives always prepared a cold dinner, which sat waiting on the kitchen table, the women having eaten at five o'clock.

Mother and daughter talked at each other incessantly, their voices as chirpy as a parakeet's. Ernest's mother, Clementine, had just served as a juror in an armed robbery trial.

"They had it on videotape. The fellow turned around and stared right at the camera while he made that poor clerk crawl on her belly to the Slurpy maker. Bold as brass. Always thought those cameras ruined the appearance of a convenient mart but now I understand their usefulness," Clementine added.

"You can't believe a machine," said the grandmother. "They might have mixed up the film, or the camera could have taken a bad picture. You never look like your pictures."

Ernest's mom continued, her diatribe unbroken by her son's entrance. He tapped both women on their shoulders to say hello and headed for the kitchen, where their words were still audible.

"His attorney made a big deal about it being a first offense. 'Robert Halbin's character should not be judged solely on this unfortunate event. Bob Halbin's character is the character of the American people—caring, concerned, a model citizen, government worker, scout leader, and a man who, like all of you, was just a little tired. Tired of higher prices. Tired of trying to make ends meet. Tired of pouring his hard-earned cash into big business's bulging pockets.' "

Slicing into the cup of canned peaches with his spoon, Ernest read over the list the women had written for him:

1. change lightbulb in hall
2. get Mother's spring hat from top shelf in closet
3. check ant traps under kitchen sink
4. move refrigerator to find Mother's pearl button
5. rehang knickknack shelf
6. lift TV so we can dust stand (needs it badly)

Who wanted the hat and who'd lost a button was unclear, since each lady referred to herself as "Mother." Putting the peaches aside, he placed his dishes in the sink and then checked underneath for ants. In the living room Clementine and Anna discussed the criminal's clothing, his wife's humiliation (her father had once run a convenient mart), and the defense attorney's brown teeth.

"Looked like he chewed on a bushelful of lies," said Clementine, and Anna, who'd sat in the audience throughout the trial, agreed.

List in hand, Ernest finished his chores, then nodded to his relatives and dutifully lifted the television set. His mother closed her mouth, sponged off the stand, wiped it dry, and thought to ask him how his job was.

"Fine," he told her.

"And how's that nice Mrs. Domko who sometimes answers the phone? Her voice is so sparkly."

He pictured Bob Halbin, the robber, and wondered who, of the two of them, was more tired.

All of the morning regulars had picked up Adele's habit of calling Ernest the Professor. He helped a seamstress from the shirt factory with a crossword puzzle called "La Dolce Vita" and explained the duties of the Roman senate to Terri Kudja's nine-year-old, after which he felt so good that he deliberately swaggered into work five minutes late. Adele shared these achievements with her customers, some of whom also had begun quizzing the Professor. But they did so randomly, as he was getting into his car or was just about to place an extra order, and Adele thought that a system should be established. Taking a half-dozen doughnut box, covering it with brown paper, cutting a small round hole in the middle, she labeled it ASK THE PROFESSOR. She intended to attach the question box to the wall on the register's far side, so people would pay their bill first.

The day before the box went up, Adele followed the Professor to the parking lot, figuring she'd need his permission. She pointed out that by receiving the questions ahead of time (she'd drop them off at his apartment, after her shift) he could better prepare his answers.

"Not that you don't have them on the tip of your tongue already," said Adele.

He resisted less than she'd anticipated. To keep things orderly he suggested that the questions form a theme, say, Italian cities, which also would fit with the Italian festival taking place downtown for the next two weeks. Adele loved the idea, said she'd print up a card reading TODAY'S TOPIC: ROME and tape it to the box.

After work he stopped by the college library and took out six books on Italy, including a history of the Roman Empire. (Someone had ripped out all of the pictures and maps in the travel books, so Ernest relied on his imagination.) Preparing a dinner of spaghetti, he turned on the language tapes and, unconsciously, started repeating the phrases aloud. When he realized what he'd done, he looked around to see if the sounds had somehow changed the room. Then he lowered his voice but went on.

The promise of the question box made Mrs. Domko seem tolerable and the day's work less dreary. Adele had placed a sealed envelope in his mailbox, which he opened even before opening the door. Four handwritten messages greeted him, four people who expected him to know. In all his life he had never experienced such support. He touched the papers again and again, rubbing them between his fingertips until they became slightly damp and flaccid, and when Ernest discovered that he could satisfy each request without consulting his references, he lifted the last scrap of looseleaf to his lips and kissed it.

Milan, Venice, Florence, Naples, and Sorrento met with equal success. Arriving twenty minutes earlier at the shop each morning, he held court at the counter, reading aloud question and answer, then tacking the written query and reply to the bulletin board. A jubilant Adele scurried about, pouring coffee refills, gasping theatrically when she thought the question too difficult, applauding the Professor's response.

"Venice," he warned, after fielding the questions on gondolas, "is sinking. Sad to say, but it's so." He lifted his hand to his forehead as if the burden of this truth were weighing on him.

Two older men nodded their heads. "The world," said one, "is going to hell in a handbasket."

"But," interjected the Professor, seeing Adele's cue to pick things up, "Venice still enjoys ten million visitors a year. Think of it," and he looked around him to make sure his audience did.

Then the Assisi incident occurred. An eighty-six-year-old woman walked from the south side of town just to drop her question in the box. She didn't even bother to buy a doughnut, or a coffee, asking only for a glass of water. Since this was the single entry for the day, Adele decided to read the question before leaving it with the Professor. In chicken scrawl the note said, "Is my cousin Gina Masiello, born in Assisi, still alive?"

She couldn't simply leave the question in the mailbox, so instead Adele waited for the Professor to arrive home. From six until seven she stayed in her car; then she stood in front of the building until eight. Back in the car for another half hour, she decided she would hold the question until tomorrow if the Professor didn't show soon.

He returned from the mothers' apartment, where he had told them he was hiring a handyman to help them out once a month. Adele, dressed in a lemon-colored pantsuit, leaned against her car, a cigarette between her fingers. Usually her hair defied gravity, piled high on her head, impervious to wind, rain, or sleet, but tonight it fell around her shoulders, vulnerable as silk. Ernest didn't recognize her at first.

"I think we may have a problem," she said, her voice husky from the cigarette and the night air.

Sotto voce, thought Ernest. "Please," he said, mindful of the chill and the lateness of the evening. "If you'd like, you can step inside."

Adele settled herself on the couch, grabbed the pillow that decorated the arm, and placed it on her lap. She put her hand to the side, a gesture to the Professor, but he chose a straight-back chair and waited for her to speak.

"I knew you were very neat," she said, taking in the orderly bookshelves, polished desk, a small dining table and chairs. "I just knew it."

He relaxed a little, more comfortable with her than he had expected. Waving the notepaper in her hand, she added, "I feel responsible." She hesitated before surrendering the question. Reading it carefully, he then glanced at his watch.

"Three o'clock there. We shouldn't try before seven," he said, reaching for the telephone book to look up Italy's country code.

171

"What?" she exclaimed. "She probably married and took her husband's name, moved to—moved anywhere, for that matter, Rome, or France, or America," she complained, tired of waiting.

To soothe Adele, he took her hand, patted it, and placed it tenderly on the pillow. It had the sweet smell of the doughnut shop; he squelched the urge to lick her fingers. "I'll get a list of Masiellos from the operator. If that fails, I'll try the department of records at city hall. It's a city of saints. Someone will help," he explained, listening as a stranger would to the confidence in his voice. "You of all people should believe in me," he added, scolding playfully. "You were the first."

Even as she leaned into his kiss she thought perhaps she had done a dangerous thing.

Ernest set the alarm for 2:00 A.M. The trill woke him instantly and as he breathed in the night air he felt wonderfully alive; he gazed down at his bare chest and could not help himself—he thought of the statue of David, displayed in Firenze. Dialing the overseas operator, he said to the world, with the tongue of a native son, "Buon giorno!"

Rosa Rinaldi and Gina Bruno (nee Masiello) spoke by phone, their first conversation in sixty-five years. Doughnut sales rose for two weeks straight, and Mr. Raymond was so pleased with Adele's innovation that he agreed to an ad campaign called "Ask the Professor." WHO HAS THE BEST DOUGHNUTS IN TOWN? the legend read. ASK THE PROFESSOR. Remarkably, Ernest said he'd pose for a photograph and wear a mortarboard. Adele helped select the photo they printed: the image was grainy enough to render him unrecognizable, which she thought was for the best. Having conquered Italy, Ernest moved on to the topic of famous fruits, Mr. Raymond suggesting that the subject tie in to a special on apple doughnuts. Adele dissented, saying the Professor should choose the category himself, but Ernest saw no problem. A tiny part of the world had become friendly—strangers and acquaintances alike said hello when he was in the doughnut shop; Le Mans, the

172

mechanic who initially challenged him, now popped him playfully in the gut.

Mrs. Domko noticed a change in Ernest, a starchiness that was not unattractive. On more than one occasion he had spoken at length and done so with authority. When Mr. Munsch was planning his European vacation Ernest had a conversation, a dialogue, about Italy and gave specific advice on tours to Assisi.

"Make sure you see the Piazza del Comune," said Ernest. "It's where the Temple of Minerva once sat."

Then, one morning last week, Ernest and she walked out together, and he paused to give his opinion on professors' salaries and ask what she thought. He had left the box of Sweet 'n' Low out on the counter all the day before, and she found herself offering to take coffee duty next week.

"Good morning, Mrs. Domko, Mr. Munsch," he said, his voice as deep and clear as a spring-fed lake.

Both Munsch and Domko, still a little surprised by this newly hatched Ernest, said hello in unison. Each day he took an unexpected step forward.

"I thought I'd tackle those old files today—see if I can't get them ready for the warehouse," he offered, taking on a job that they all detested.

"You'll probably need help—you should take Mrs. Domko with you," said Munsch, and the woman found herself nodding willingly, almost cheerfully. She could have sworn that Ernest winked at her when he added, "Teamed up we'll be through in no time."

At home, he dropped to the couch exhausted but in good spirits. He had stayed up most of the night researching his new topic, mythical creatures, and this concerned him, but as Adele said, heck, one can't know everything. The customers, consciously or not, seemed to be raising the ante, some days changing the game from Ask the Professor to Stump the Professor.

Lifting the envelope from the desk (he'd given Adele his spare key), he shook it to guess at the number of entries. Not overwhelming—maybe six, he estimated, opening it. The initial contact still thrilled him. He felt like a well-loved performer welcomed back by his audience. "What's the flying horse's name, used to be on gas station signs?" "Where does the Loch Ness monster live?" "How big are Bigfoot's feet?" There were three others, just as he had guessed, and he knew all of the answers instantly, as well as he knew his own name. Professor.

Since the Assisi question Adele had been reading through the slips before giving them to the Professor. Twice there'd been crank questions, which she discarded, one on Liberace during famous fruit, one on a customer's mother-in-law when the topic was mythical creatures. This question, which she now held in her hand, was sick, the product of a twisted mind, and she considered burning it to rid herself and the world of the sentiment. The printing was much neater than usual, and the author had chosen all capital letters, blocked out in two perfectly straight rows:

WHY DON'T YOU
KILL YOURSELF???

Doreen saw Adele turn the note over, looking for a signature, and asked to see it. "No peeking ahead," Adele said, and as soon as Doreen left, she placed the paper in an ashtray and put a match to it. Later, wiping out the ashtray, Adele convinced herself that the question had never existed and by the end of the week, when the Professor took her to the movies, she'd forgotten all about the incident.

But a week later, on a Monday, the same day the note had appeared before, the question was raised again. The writing, hurried this time, spilled off the edge of the paper, the letters nearly tumbling one over the other:

WHY Don't
you kill yourself?

Crushing the paper in her fist, she began throwing all of the slips into the garbage. Then, when a customer spotted her, she made a joke of her actions by saying with a laugh, "If I had a brain, it would be lonesome, don't you think?" The customer laughed along with her and helped her snatch the questions from the trash, except for the offending paper, which she'd stuffed in her uniform pocket. Throughout her shift Adele wrestled with whether or not to tell the Professor or to get the owner's advice; the most satisfying action of all, she decided, would be ripping the box from the wall.

"Ask the Professor" was no longer fun. The Professor took the whole thing too seriously, considered it more than just a game, which it was at best—and now this. While punching out at the time clock she suggested to Mr. Raymond that the idea was getting stale, that customers weren't into it, but he dismissed her, saying she was responsible for a great success and he intended to keep the game going as long as the public was willing.

"Besides," the owner told her, "that guy who plays the professor—what's his name?—lives for it."

So she tried watching the box more closely, between serving customers, to uncover the culprit. She distracted the customers so they'd forget about the game and twice covered the hole, supposedly by accident. Finally, after thirty-six hours of intense guilt, she took the most drastic of measures: she stopped screening the Professor's questions.

For two months now Mr. Raymond had made a point of speaking to the Professor each morning. Sometimes the exchange was little more than "Great job, they love it," but Ernest warmed to the owner's attention, however slight, and this approval from management also helped the customers see the Professor as a credible source. Ernest was beaming over his most recent mental triumph—answering all of the questions in the U.S. capitals series—when Mr. Raymond pulled him aside.

"You feeling alright, Prof? Everything A-OK?"

Ernest nodded enthusiastically.

"Adele thinks maybe you and the customers are getting a bit burned-out, but I say we may as well go for broke, right?" the owner remarked.

175

The Professor gave Adele a look that cut right through her, that cried traitor, torturer, and heathen all at once. He cleared his throat, another form of reprimand, and winked at the owner while adding, "You know how silly women can be. Studies have shown." The two men, having bonded sufficiently, parted ways, Mr. Raymond returning to the back of the shop, the Professor taking his rightful place at the end of the counter. When Adele, who had a good idea of their conversation, tried talking to the Professor, he ignored her and asked Doreen to pour him another cup of coffee, this one to go.

On the drive to work he kept telling himself that Adele's support was inconsequential to his success. She was probably just tired of dropping off the questions—he'd go back to the shop and pick them up at each day's end. Certainly the customers showed no symptoms of "burnout"; just yesterday there were twelve slips in the box, a dozen voices waiting for reply, hungry brains to be fed. Even if Adele doubted, and yes, it hurt to think so, the others surely, by their actions, believed.

Ernest was so distracted by his own consolations that he failed to notice the homeless man with the shopping cart, who had migrated to the university, the totem pole of stuffed animals exchanged for one of empty cans and bottles.

"Professor—you, Professor," the man cried, trudging up the hill a few yards behind Ernest.

Ernest thought he heard a student calling for one of the college professors. Outside the confines of the doughnut shop no one— save Adele—would address him that way.

"I has a question, a question about my animals," the wanderer said. "I'm not walking back to any doughnut shop. You answer me now."

Finally turning around, Ernest, cowed by the man's insistence and concerned that he'd cause a scene, replied, "Fine, fine," and then, in a near whisper, "what is it you need?"

"Where are the animals? Who chased them away?"

With deepest conviction Ernest replied, "They're right there," and pointed to the pole filled with empty containers.

The man shook his head in disgust. "Man, what you think I am, anyway?"

Ernest hurried along so as not to be late for work. At lunch he called the doughnut shop to let the waitresses know he'd drop by for the questions. Adele nearly got on the phone, then thought better of it, figuring he needed some time to forgive her.

"How'd he sound?" she asked the waitress.

"Odd, as usual. The guy's plain weird," the woman answered. Then, unable to resist, she added, "But I'm sure he has his assets."

Adele had studied every customer that April morning; no one the least bit suspicious had approached the question box. She decided to put in her own question, a first, hoping it might ward off any evil doing. When Ernest arrived that evening Adele had long gone, her shift over at three.

He quickly glanced at the slips while still in the shop. "Piece of cake," he told the waitress.

For fourteen days—almost three weeks' worth of questions, since he only answered them Monday through Friday—no untoward incident had occurred, and, in fact, Adele and the Professor had reconciled. On a Friday night they had dinner at the shopping center's Chinese restaurant, the Professor making a great show of his adeptness with chopsticks and Adele, to please him, making a great show of her inability to use them. The restaurant's waitress, who was Hawaiian, complimented him, saying he was the only patron all evening who hadn't used a fork.

"Ah, so," the Professor said, and the three of them laughed.

He seemed so solid, so sure of his place in the universe, that Adele decided to unburden herself regarding his hate mail and explain why she had spoken to the owner.

He took the news calmly, dismissing the slips as some teenager's "rebellion against authority." Pleading a headache from the MSG, Ernest dropped Adele off early and headed straight for bed, where he stayed round the clock for the next two days. At three on Sunday afternoon, disgusted by his lethargy, he dug his fingers into his face and scratched the skin so severely he bled.

As if on cue, the recurring question appeared Monday. Adele

never saw it. Ernest read it after supper, the last of five questions, more difficult than most, on American comedians. It was Jack Benny Day. Ernest had asked himself the question—WHY DON'T YOU KILL YOURSELF?—so many times that he could have written the message himself. It didn't escape him that the hand was nearly the same as his own. For about a minute and a half he wanted to suspect Adele, but the idea was too unkind to stay with him.

The time was after midnight when he finished neatly printing out the replies to the four answerable questions and placed them in an envelope marked "Adele." Entering the dark bedroom, he faced the shadows from the buildings across the way, stretching from the wall to the ceiling. During his three months of playing the Professor he had secured the answers to every question save two—the one posed to him by the homeless man and now this last one. The Professor, he thought, had a pretty good run, a near-perfect life. Far better than Ernest.

On his way to the doughnut shop that night he drove recklessly, speeding through the intersection, cutting off a car filled with teenagers riding around after the prom. He took the graduation cap he'd worn in the picture, a copy of the advertisement, and the envelope for Adele and left them by the front door. He parked the car in the lot, figuring that the mothers could at least sell it, and headed on foot for the bridge that lay between the shop and the college. The students had renamed it Jump Street. Mrs. Domko would claim that she had known all along Ernest would end up this way. The spring air slapped his face as he fell forward, reawakening in him the protracted pain called life, which was as frightening and much more cruel than the moment of his death.

The Regulars

The automobile club was organizing trips to Hawaii. The employees were selling hard, saying that the chance for a free tropical vacation came with a new membership (or a renewal). Milo insisted it was some kind of scam.

"Who'd want to win?" he asked, his index finger crooked around his sixth cigarette. "The place is a concrete jungle."

He picked up the granulated sugar doughnut and chased the tobacco taste from his mouth. Three other customers sat down at the counter, greeting Milo and the waitresses. They were regulars. The regulars owned the shop between seven and eight o'clock each evening.

"Joe Bruno is retiring," said the fifty-year-old redhead, opening a baby-blue cigarette case and offering her brand to her two companions, a man and another woman. "His daughter bought him a cottage up the lake. It has a basement."

"She married good," said Milo.

"That's kaput," said the skinny brunette, her face a perfect heart, the pointed chin balanced in her palm. "Maybe the house was part of the settlement."

A fifth customer, wearing a green-plaid hunter's cap, joined the party. His hands were large and dry, the skin broken into flakes. "How ya doing, everybody? How ya doing?" He patted Milo and the other man on their backs and grinned at the ladies, who had pushed up the sleeves of their sweaters and held their wrists against the counter's ledge.

Doreen Raymond, recently moved to the night shift, looked quizzically at the second waitress. Doreen was hoping the night job would make her feel more independent, free from the eyes of her father. "He takes it black, right?" Doreen asked. "With a vanilla cream–filled doughnut?"

"Hold on, hold on," said the customer. "I think I'll try a hot chocolate."

"He's been saying that for a month," said the redhead.

Doreen placed her finger against the button on the cocoa machine and pushed.

"On second thought," he said, "I'll have a coffee. Coffee always tastes right."

"The Karpovich boy won a scholarship to someplace in England. It's in tomorrow's paper," said the brunette.

"All the kids leave," said Milo.

"My own Charlene," commented the man in the cap, the one who'd changed his order. "All the way down to Allentown. She says, 'Dad, there's nothing for me here locally.' She loves it there. She has a big job at the mall. That's the way."

"I know," said Doreen, trying out for the chorus. "I was away at Harcum Junior College for a semester. I never thought I'd be back."

Various members of the group stared toward the street. The man in the green cap bowed his nodding head over his cup, the only one to acknowledge the girl's statement. Doreen observed that the top of the wool cap was worn to a fuzzy plain. The two women and their male companion placed their heads in a huddle and spoke among themselves, just loud enough so Milo and the green cap could still hear.

Two sisters dressed in identical stretch pants, one clad in a yellow sweatshirt, the other in red, both with the legend BECAUSE I'M THE DADDY, strode through the shop's front door. It was evident that the same hand had tortured their hair, beating it into stiff peaks.

"Here comes the news," said the third man, the one who'd said little until now. His dozen hairs had been stretched from ear to ear, a latticework of black thread decorating his scalp. The jacket he'd worn, two sizes too small, gave his arms the helpless look of a baby's. He kept the coat zipped throughout his meal.

"Coffee, light," the waitress whispered to Doreen, who was finding the company less than she'd expected. She'd entertained visions of college students downing coffee, preparing for an all-nighter. "And they each get three cinnamon doughnuts, served one after the other. Don't try bringing them all six at once."

The sisters commandeered the corner stools and said their good evenings. They poured a stream of sugar into the coffees. Their audience waited.

"They're converting the old Samters Clothing building into *state* offices," said one of them.

"State of chaos," said Milo.

The duo brushed off the remark, like an annoying piece of fuzz. "Three businesses filed for bankruptcy today," said the second sister. "Including you know who. Attorney Gillan got offered a job in Harrisburg. He turned it down. He hasn't told his wife yet— she's from there."

"That will be World War Three," said the redhead.

"Tammy Wynette is coming to the Masonic Temple. Her promoter called."

The siblings sipped at their beverages. They both worked at the city courthouse, the one making $1.87 more an hour than the other, which had almost caused a rift in the family. Even now, six months later, this gave the poorer sister the upper hand. No one could completely forgive that the richer sister had improved her lot. The poorer sister, in red, looked down and saw she had finished her doughnut, and another had not yet replaced it. The poorer sister harrumphed.

"She's green," said Milo, jerking his head toward Doreen. Then he rolled his eyes toward the brunette, who was gnawing a ragged nail, and said softly, "Nepotism stinks."

Outside, a husband and wife paused to stare at the scene in the shop. The woman wore a camel hair car coat and stockings so loose they pooled around her ankles and knees. The man was the first handsome person in the shop that night.

Finally, Doreen said to herself, some strangers.

She tightened the lid on a sugar sifter and gave the couple a warm smile. The others, she knew, were watching her, though they kept on with their conversation, which had the droning sound of a bee swarm.

"May I help you?" Doreen asked, her fingers gaily tapping the napkin holder. Immediately the balding man put a hand over his ear. The couple had left a seat between the rest of the group and themselves.

"Milo," the handsome man said, his right hand in a near salute. "Evening, Tom. Jimbo. And how are the girls tonight?"

The second waitress already had fixed the newcomers' order and silently set it before them, edging Doreen out. The wife peered into the cup of hot water.

"This isn't clean," she complained to her husband.

"What's that?" said Milo, having heard perfectly well.

"It's fine," Doreen whispered to the other waitress. "I saw it myself."

"What's that?" asked Milo, addressing Doreen.

"All the kids have mouths on them," said the redhead, and the man in the green cap corrected, "Not my Charlene."

"She's gone, isn't she?" said the man with the strings of hair. "You don't call that a mouth? You don't call that a mouth on her?"

Doreen shoved the chocolate vat into a corner, away from the window where she could be watched, and plugged the warming machine into the wall. She took a spatula and scraped the sides to hurry the warmth from the center. Then, reaching for a long-handled tablespoon, she filled its bowl with the hot syrup and lifted it to her mouth.

"I've got a mouth on me all right," she said, swallowing the sweet liquid.

The night-shift waitress was stationed out front, anticipating the needs of the regulars. Doreen couldn't believe it was just 7:15. This time of evening appeared to be interminable. The front of the shop seemed brighter than daylight, a bright glass bowl surrounded by a darkened street. A car drove past, a station wagon packed with family and wares, assuming the guise of the last train out. The urge to phone her mother shook Doreen. She helped herself to a second round of chocolate.

Baking wouldn't begin for another six hours, so the only other person to talk to was the janitor. He was in the men's room, scouring. The waitress rapped on the window—Doreen noticed that a tenth customer, a man in his twenties, had joined the party.

"Could you put up a new pot?" the waitress asked Doreen. "I'm busy with their doughnuts."

Now the topic was the former county commissioner, whom the daddy girls said was getting his own A.M. talk show, out of nearby Wilkes-Barre, Pennsylvania.

"The people here have talent," said the handsome man. "Look at that weatherman. He's bigger than Willard Scott."

"At least wider than Willard Scott," said Milo.

"But our guy knows birds," the brunette said with heart. "He spotted a cardinal in the hill section just the other day."

"What about your cousin?" said the latest arrival, the nephew of the man with the problem hair. He gestured to the sisters. "The one who plays McRuff the Crime Dog. I saw him in the parade. You got to act to get that," he added.

The poorer sister shook her hands in front of her. "You're not supposed to divulge his identity," she said. "It's supposed to be a secret."

"But he took his head off twice during the march," the nephew protested.

"It was hot," said the woman in defense. "The hottest Saint Patrick's Day in fifty years."

"Like damn Hawaii," said Milo. "The TV weatherman compared it to Hawaii."

"The students had a TV program at my college," said Doreen, unable to contain herself. "It was cable. I read the news once. My roommate did reviews of the films in the lecture hall."

The night-shift waitress shook her head apologetically.

"Is that a clean pot that girl has?" the handsome man's wife asked her husband.

Resentfully Doreen swished a scrubber in the coffee bowl a third time. It was 7:20. Maybe her watch had stopped. Maybe she was actually on the morning shift and she'd blacked out, her subconscious dreaming up these people as she waited for the paramedics. The clink of the spoons against the coffee cups was amplified. When the talkers grew quiet for a moment Doreen could even hear the scratch of the wife's fingers against her bagging stockings in her effort to pull the nylons tight around her legs.

"Some people don't know where their bread is buttered," said Milo.

The second waitress coughed a little into her hand. Then she went to the counter and scooped up the ashtrays, piled them in a soaking tub underneath the countertop, and put clean ones at every other place. Doreen rearranged a display of doughnuts in the showcase, counting them one by one to kill time. She made a show of touching the sweets with a piece of wax paper, to appease the wife.

"I copied the list of restaurant violations from the board of health," said the sister in red. "These places will get their notices in about seventy-two hours."

Doreen tried to engage the other waitress's eyes but the woman simply gazed into the night, her arms folded. The paper made its way down the counter.

"Three less than last month," said the man with the cap, running his finger down the page. "That shows an improvement. Some civic pride."

Milo glanced at the names and let out a laugh. "The Squeaky Clean Diner in Green Ridge," he said. "That's a good one." He continued to laugh and tears dripped from his eyes. "That was worth the trip," he added, the tears running the jagged course of his face. He pulled a thin white handkerchief from his pocket and blew, jabbing at his nostrils with the cloth.

"You got him," the sister in yellow said to her kin. "You got him this time," she nearly cheered. Her sibling bit into her cinnamon doughnut.

"So where's the real list?" asked the wife, who had taken a pen and notepad from her handbag. She retrieved a packet of tissues from the brown vinyl purse and used one to wipe the doughnut crumbs from her place.

"You think I'm Almighty God?" asked the woman who'd played the joke. "Almighty God couldn't get that list—there's somebody new in the office, the mayor's cousin. He had locks put on all the file cabinets. Almighty God couldn't find the keys."

The redhead twisted her stool to the side. "What, now they don't trust their own people? That's a shame. A real shame," she observed.

Pathetic. They're all pathetic, Doreen muttered to herself. Milo had seen her lips move and he glowered at her. She pulled her lips tight over her teeth and made a motion as though she were buttoning them shut. The janitor, Carl, rapped his knuckles on the glass partition, breaking the tension. He pointed to a yellow cone with the word *caution.*

"Watch your step if you come back here," he advised. "I'm doing the floor."

The nephew dipped his crueller into his coffee. He waited until Carl had the mop in hand.

"That's not very appetizing," he said, wiping the doughnut mush from his mouth.

"No regard for the customers," interjected Milo.

The brunette leaned her body forward so that her chin protruded beyond the counter. The waitress had been changing the register tape.

"I thought we agreed that we'd wait," she said sweetly but firmly.

The waitress spun around and, lifting her arm to the glass, placed a finger on her wristwatch. Carl popped his head out front.

"Sorry, folks. Sorry. I didn't see the time. I'll sweep the back steps first. No harm done. Thanks for your patience." He flashed a big, happy grin and whistled as he wandered off.

Slamming a tray of doughnuts into the case, Doreen ran after him. Her right knee caught the top of the cone, which tottered a bit. She found Carl sitting on a jelly container, flicking a handful of peanut crumbs, one at a time, into the garbage can eight feet away.

"Are you paid to do that?" she interrogated. "That's why you've been hired? That's some special skill."

She'd become so worked up that droplets of perspiration ringed her collar, glistening around her neck. The tiny beads of water broke at her temples.

"Take it easy, OK?" he said soothingly. "I'm on a break. I punched out. I was just going for the record."

Getting up, he moved the garbage can to the side and showed Doreen the writing on the wall: "W. Lowbar, 8/13, 92 peanuts from 8' (sitting). World record." Carl put the aluminum tub back into position and brushed the remaining crumbs from his palm.

They heard the waitress push open the swinging door, in search of Doreen. Seeing neither Doreen or Carl, she let the door go and shuffled back to her customers.

"Oh, God," said Doreen, her chin beginning to buckle. "Oh, God."

"What's it like to live someplace else?" Carl asked. "What's it look like other places? I've never been out of here except for one Phillies game. That was it."

"You're asking me?" Doreen said. "Is that your plan—work for my father and then leave?"

She stood close enough to see the downy facial hairs his razor had missed and she breathed in his slightly sweaty odor. Even with the sweet smell of fried dough all around her she could pick out Carl's scent. No one had come that close to Doreen since the food service director, the man she'd left school over.

They were nearly the same height, Doreen a little broader. She shut her eyes and threw herself against him. When she kissed Carl ferociously, he could taste the chocolate in her mouth, and he hung on to her sugary tongue for a moment. Carl went to hold her neck and she felt the coolness of his hand like a splash of cold water.

"Don't tell," she warned. "Do not tell. This never happened."

186

She was trembling and she wiped her face with her apron. The waitress called her name, asking for some help.

"It's no big deal," said Carl. "I was on my break."

"Nothing," said Doreen, her hand a shield for her mouth. Her mind flipped to Gail, the girl who'd just moved in with Carl and his sister.

It was 7:35. The regulars had shifted some, the redhead getting up a moment to stretch her back. The men were discussing the price of a haircut, how the city had the best barbers alive.

"We can't comment on the dead ones, now can we?" asked the green-capped man.

"And the best beauticians," said the ladies, providing their interpretation of women's rights.

"Absolutely true," the men conceded.

"I can sleep on my hair for a week and it never budges," said the richer of the daddy girls.

Doreen began picking up their litter, as instructed by the night-shift waitress, the wax papers and crumbled napkins moist from their coffee that had been shoved aside. Thankfully they ignored Doreen as the other waitress warmed their cups. People on the day shift never acted like this. Most customers were too busy, too hurried, to form this tight of a clique, and even the factory workers, spelled for their break, and the adolescent Buick boys stuck their waste inside the empty coffee mugs once they had finished.

Still shaken by her behavior with Carl, Doreen turned her back to the customers as quickly as possible, peering through the glass partition, her worse side toward the public. The husband and wife were telling about a bus trip to Amish country that everyone had hated. The group had voted to cut the day short by two hours, forfeiting a country dinner.

"But it makes you appreciate," said the handsome man. "It does make you appreciate."

"Some people would have known without making the trip," said Milo, which caused the thin-haired man to defend the handsome one.

A general grumbling was expressed, which swiftly was attributed to having overeaten.

"This always happens," said the poorer daddy girl, "when you have the filled kind." She wagged her head at Mr. Green Cap. "Stay away from the filled."

Doreen noticed for the first time that the flourescent lights in the back room were exactly the same as those in her school cafeteria. Away from home and not knowing anyone, she had eaten her first few meals there alone. By the third breakfast the food service director had spotted her.

Carl had dropped—or banged—a set of mixing bowls, and the ringing interrupted the regulars' speech and Doreen's reflections.

"You got a stallion back there? That kid's a stallion. Something's got him juiced," said Milo.

"Some little filly," said the redhead with a laugh.

The wife pulled her arms to her sides and lifted her eyes to her husband.

"Hey, hey, hey," said the handsome man. "That's enough of that."

The redhead flicked a piece of tobacco from the tip of her tongue. "We're all adults here, aren't we? Ain't nothing can be said that you don't already see on television."

Doreen had ten more minutes with these people. She didn't dare retreat to the back, for fear of stirring up Carl.

"I'm sure that noise was just an accident," Doreen said to the waitress, intending for them all to hear.

"I'll check," offered the waitress. "I need to run to the ladies' anyway."

Doreen's hand sprung up, determined to clamp the other woman's wrist, to hold her there, but the waitress was already through the swinging door. Doreen thought of other moments in her life when ten minutes had held such significance—her last night with the food service director, when he told her at the end of the evening, ten minutes before she was due back at the dorm, that theirs was a flirtation, nothing serious or lasting, and when she, crumpling, said he had pursued her, had made her interested, he dismissed the argument by saying she was a big girl, knew what she was getting into, and that he'd leave now so she wouldn't be late.

The customers had stopped their talk and Doreen hoped this was a sign that they were winding down, getting ready to part. As a kind of protection she began to chant in her head, This is my father's place. This is my father's place. She listened as the waitress and Carl exchanged some words that Doreen couldn't make out, and then she heard the waitress pull shut the bathroom door. This is my father's place, she repeated.

The nephew had lifted his water glass into the air, twirling it in his wrist arrogantly. The green-capped man pushed his glass forward with just a bit more sympathy. Snatching the tumbler from the younger man's hand, Doreen thrust it under the faucet.

"I'd like a new glass," he said, half-teasing, seeing if the others would follow.

She stood for a moment, casting about for a retort. The water overflowed onto her hand. Cupping her palm, she carried the water to his place.

"This is a new glass," she said, offering the handful of water. "And her hair is beautiful and Laurence Olivier couldn't play McRuff."

A drop of water leaked between her fingers, landing in the nephew's coffee cup.

"And we're all adults," she finished, letting the rest of the liquid drain into the mug.

Reaching under the counter for a cloth to dry her hands, she saw a small car pull into the shop's lot, the headlights reflecting in the store's windows. The man turned on his interior lights and, obviously lost, consulted a map.

The customer with the latticework scalp spoke. "Mouths on them. I told you. The kids have mouths on them."

"And I told you," said the man with the cap, his voice insistent, edgy, "not my Charlene."

"Ah, can it," said the redhead. "I've got to go. Some of us have work in the morning."

The nephew, put out that a larger stink hadn't been made, said he wasn't paying. He wasn't paying for shabby treatment. Doreen looked at him indifferently.

"What do you expect?" asked Milo. "This isn't the Ritz. It's a damn doughnut shop."

The night-shift waitress had finished in the bathroom and paused in the back to wash her hands a second time. She would total the regulars' bill. The lost man opened his car door, got out, and turned around, reading the street signs. Doreen found the movement familiar. He threw up his hands and, retrieving the map and then locking the car doors, placed his foot on the shop's first step.

He looked very much like the food service director. Doreen knew that it couldn't be, and even if it were, she told herself, he would not recognize her. He would not remember that her father had a doughnut shop. He would not recognize her out of context, away from the school.

The customers were standing up, one and two at a time, straightening their bodies and their clothes. The nephew was still grousing.

"Forget it," said Milo. "She's just temporary, I tell you."

The phone rang and the night-shift waitress picked it up. By the way the woman was speaking, Doreen could tell it was her father on the line.

"Your father wants to know," said the waitress, "if everything's all right. You didn't check in. You were going to check in with him."

The lost man yanked on the shop's front door, his only act of certainty thus far.

"Tell my father I'm a big girl," said Doreen.

190

Russell

For years, nearly forty years, the rumor persisted. An old timer, or an out-of-towner whose relatives hailed from the valley, would drop by and remind Adele that here, yes, here at Every Day, the mayor's men had concocted the story about the elephant being hauled away by truck in the deep of the night to a specialist in Washington, D.C. First His Honor's cohorts came up with a Philadelphia destination but abandoned this; Philly was close enough to check, so they sent the elephant farther south.

Several establishments made the same claim. Some said the setting had been Zummo's, the candy store, and others insisted on Ruddy's Roost, a bar in the flats. One historian cited Shookey's Shake Shoppe, pointing out its proximity to City Hall. The politico had access to all three. The only thing everyone agreed on: the meeting had not taken place in the mayor's office. Nothing, good or bad, ever came out of the mayor's office.

The mayor had to do something. The politician's campaign had been built on his promise to get the city's zoo a baby elephant. He raised all kinds of monies, won the election, and, six months later, Penny, so named because of the children's donations, paraded down Lackawanna Avenue, right behind the new mayor. A Republican mammoth purchased, through dubious methods and at half the price quoted, by a Democrat.

She never looked quite right. The people loved her, for the three weeks she was with them, because she was theirs, the citizens' own elephant, a symbol of the city's importance, its strength, a living relic that harkened back to the days when the earth was swamp, swamp that created coal, coal that created Scranton. Any outsider could see she was off, her color too blue, her skin too scratched, her eyes stunned. She preferred the indoor quarters to the yard area she shared with a donkey. She blew out the peanuts, refused her hay—"a finicky eater," the papers reported—and, twenty-one days after her grand entrance, lay down on the floor of the newly built "elephant house," a room the size of a one-car garage, and died.

The mayor got the call at 3:00 A.M. He was at the zoo by 3:15, had the head of sanitation there by 4:00, and met with his four closest aides at 5:30 in the doughnut shop. The waitress, half asleep, forced by the mayor to open early, served the wrong doughnuts and understood nothing. No one else witnessed the meeting. No one knew what went on that morning until months later, and even then there was still a good deal of speculation. No one heard anything. Except for Russell.

Russell, then a milkman, saw the group assembled, heard them say the name Penny and hush when he handed over his delivery to the somnambulant help. He thought it odd that the sanitation truck, parked in the alley, was headed in the direction of the McGuire Coal Mine. The men had decided to stuff the dead Penny into a shaft and tell the press she'd been rushed, a local veterinarian at her side, to a leading specialist in retirement out of state. The urgency of the matter, the mayor explained to the newspaper's city editor, demanded immediate action.

No press conferences were held, no investigations made, no calls to the so-called specialist or a check of the doctor's credentials. It was a time and a place where everyone took things on faith. Schools sent cards, posters, banners to the zoo. Children wept and prayed. The principals involved in the scam couldn't get a new elephant through legitimate means because they couldn't risk the inquiries that a legitimate organization would make. So they kept Penny alive, slowly recovering her health for months, and would have persisted with the lies even longer if the smell hadn't given them away. A smell in a place where the odor of sulphur, of burning coal waste, usually masked everything. When reelection came around the mayor made another promise, and he won again. Russell didn't vote that year.

Three years after Penny's untimely demise, one of the coal barons left the zoological society enough money to purchase two pachyderms. Instead they opted for one, Tiny, a pair of llamas, and fourteen tropical birds. With these additions the small zoo, already a popular spot, drew more and more visitors, from as far away as Hazelton, and the number of creatures on display rose to forty species. Dozens of people, mothers and fathers with toddlers, groups of teenagers, elderly couples, stood before the outdoor cages no bigger than the cars on a circus train and gawked, pointed, provoked, and imitated. A tour of the interior of the single, one-story building, white concrete with coal black trim, took about ten minutes if one dawdled. In summer the space grew so warm, and the crowds so dense, that the human smell competed with the stench of geriatric animals. Condensation formed on the windows of the two exhibits separated from the public by glass— the turtles and the flamingos. In June, July, and August Russell remembered watching those critters through a fog. The city fathers, having redeemed themselves, buried the history of the elephant house. Or tried to.

Russell, the only outsider to witness the historic meeting, came to work in the same doughnut shop thirty years, and many jobs, later. He had delivered milk, and when the local dairies shut down he tried pies, and when the pie man died he switched to the area's bread distributor, and when it was sold to a national company and his arthritic knees slowed his gait he moved inside to a local bakery, which burned to the ground (arson) in 1980. He thought about retiring, sat on his porch for two days and had enough of

feeling dead, and applied for the position of packer at the doughnut shop. It gave him a place to go in the middle of the night other
than the refrigerator. Since his wife's death ten years ago he slept
badly, so the hours, from three in the morning until around noon,
suited him well and justified his 8:00 P.M. bedtime.

The job was hard on the knees and feet—he stood as he filled
the boxes with doughnuts—cruellers, glazed, plain cake—for the
markets, the diners, the school cafeterias. But his work was easy on
the mind, monotonous as a rosary, and almost as meditative. He
always packed the exact number of orders, stacked them in piles
of ten for quick counting, and even pushed the racks to the back
door so that the salesmen could save a few steps between the shop
and their trucks.

The younger employees sometimes called him Pop, the only
part of the job he didn't like. He asked to be called Russell and they
complied, all except for Josh, the smart aleck who had worked in
New York City. It wasn't so much the word but the way the young
man spoke it, ignoring that Russell was a survivor, one who'd
endured life's slings and arrows. When the young man said Pop,
pronouncing it with a hiccup, he made Russell sound like a novelty,
some alien who'd just dropped into this period of history by
accident.

Funny enough, Josh had the smarts to ask Russell about the
elephant rumor. Russell was the only person, other than the mayor
and his men, four of them dead, one gone to live in Florida, who
could have verified the story. Josh wanted to know because he'd
just visited what remained of the zoo.

Russell told Josh what he felt comfortable with—that during his
time with the pie company Russell had brought bags of broken
crusts to the zoo, distributing his handouts right after his run. Tiny
could wend her trunk through the bars and shake a human hand,
he said. When she passed on seven years later, he fed Tammy, the
third and heartiest Asian elephant, the stale rolls from the bread
factory. The other animals got theirs, too, but Russell (feeling
remorse over the Penny incident), saved the best morsels for the
elephant.

He mentioned that a decade ago, when he'd finally joined the doughnut shop, he helped to spearhead a fund-raiser that benefited the zoo—grade-school children selling doughnuts door-to-door. By that time fewer than a dozen of the zoo's tenants were left, Tammy the elephant, the third in the line of pachyderms, chief among them. The money helped finance the zoo's heat for the following two winters. But Russell refused to go into the now-famous mayoral meeting.

"Man that Tammy looks old," Josh said to Russell the morning he asked about the former mayor's shenanigans. "Old and misera-ble. Butts her head against the cage walls for hours. Barely room to turn around. And not even a squirrel to keep her company, Pop."

For the past fifteen months Tammy had been the zoo's sole resident, the mountain lion having succumbed to its bad heart. Tammy occupied the same meager space she had when the zoo was full. Although there'd been offers from other zoos to take the mammoth, the citizens refused to give up their elephant. Russell had been asked to sign a petition, started by a group of out-of-towners, to send Tammy away. Though he wanted what was best for the beast, he couldn't put his name to the paper.

"Have you seen that thing, Pop? The way she looks up for a minute when a stranger passes, then goes back to banging her skull? Be better off plugging up some mine," said Josh. "Penny was the lucky one."

"It may not be much, but it's her home," said Russell, surpris-ingly defensive. "Lots of people round here still love her."

Mostly due to his arthritis, Russell hadn't been to the zoo all winter, so when Josh invited him to come along, he welcomed the chance. The March day, freakishly warm, had brought several people to the animal's house—a mother and her retarded son, about thirteen, two retired barbers, whom Russell recognized, and an eleven-year-old girl, a skinny little maid with rimless eyeglasses, a long braid, and a book. When Russell and Josh arrived she was holding court.

"Says here it can remove a thorn with its trunk and cries salt tears. It can walk up mountains on tiptoe, run up to forty miles an hour, and sense another elephant ten miles away," she read.

Tammy paused to eye her audience, turned carefully around, the cage too small for a stroll, and resumed beating her cranium on the opposite wall.

"That's our Tammy," said the retarded boy with pride.

"Social animals, they move about in groups of twelve to fifty, composed of mothers and grandmothers, sons, daughters, aunts, nephews, and nieces. The young give respect to the old; they help the old out of the pit when they have fallen in; they give them their place in feeding and drinking. If an older group member becomes lost—"

"That's enough," said Russell, a doughnut dangling from his index finger. "That's enough, little miss."

The child stamped off toward a maple tree and began reading a passage on its merits.

Josh looked down at the row of deserted cages and pointed to the single radiator, puffing its steam into the stale air. "This place is the worst," he said. "When things pick up in New York, I'm out of here."

"Penny was a gem," said Russell. "Good-natured, happy . . . this one, this one . . ."

"That's our Tammy," said the retarded boy.

Using his shirt sleeve, Josh rubbed the cage's legend to uncover Tammy age. "She's in her prime—thirty-four years old," said Josh. "She should be in the wilds rutting with some big bull. Ask the walking encyclopedia over there," he said, gesturing toward the zoo's child orator.

The others waved food now, carrots and celery and even a bag of pistachios. Tammy ignored them. They passed the pistachio nuts one to the other.

"Already had her fill," said a barber.

Before the visitors left, however, Tammy stopped her ritual long enough to take a doughnut from Russell's hand.

When Russell's feet and knees got really bad, the jaws of pain powerful enough to engage his spine and twist it sideways, he leaned up against the packing table and thought about all of the porches in town littered with the remains of old people. In fair weather, even on inclement days, they sat or were wheeled out, laps draped with the same blanket, spring, summer, fall, always a hat—made for someone else—balanced on their heads, their fingers curled and skin pearly, hands empty, frozen. Then he thought of the children in cafeterias, eating the morning's doughnuts, smiling, hands grabbing and pushing the sweets into their mouths, a simple act that only an old, old man (or a visitor from another planet) might find remarkable.

When he hurt the worst he would stop the morning manager, Marie Eden, hurrying to the storefront, and say, "If you need me, I'll stay an extra hour." This garnered him a score of new skills—he could empty, clean, and refill the soda machines out front, put up more coffee, even wait on customers if necessary. But Russell added the prices in his head and announced them before ringing up the amount on the register, which unnerved some folks. He was generally discouraged from working the front.

On the local news Russell watched the afternoon's media event, a demonstration by a busload of animal rights people. They said a busload, but the camera, panning the area, detected about ten.

"These people," said the group's spokeswoman, pointing to the three elderly men, one student nurse, the middle-aged mother, and her retarded son, "are incapable of understanding the victim's needs. We are taking legal action. This criminal behavior will not continue. There's a zoo in Baltimore waiting for her, a zoo where Tammy will be with her sisters."

Russell shook his head but hoped that the home team would at least make a showing. The interviewer placed a hand on an elderly gentleman's shoulder. "You've visited the zoo for the last sixty years, now, isn't that correct?" The man nodded slowly, cheeks sucked in, lips ready to form an answer. The reporter continued. "Should the city's elephant be sent to a more modern facility? Should Tammy have another chance?" The man considered the question long enough to feel the air go dead and then replied, "You're asking the elephant."

*   *   *

197

When Russell left by his back door at 2:45 A.M. the stars were plentiful, thousands of white flecks dusting the black sky and the air so brisk he didn't need a cup of coffee to rouse him. He pulled the collar of his jacket closer to his neck and wondered, for perhaps the thousandth time, at the lush foliage, small trees, dense bushes, even patches of forsythia and a bit of mountain laurel that fenced off his property from the city's culm dumps, the slack of abandoned mines. On the drive to work he remarked to his dead wife that the buildings downtown still held their shape, that at night they seemed solid and proud. At night it didn't matter that they were vacant. Turning into the parking lot he remembered Tammy, half a mile away, alone in the dark.

Josh was the one to tell Russell about Scranton High School. "Got to break it to the old man," Josh said, referring to Mr. Raymond. Josh had a nickname for everyone. "Shit. He'll have me soliciting all the way to Syracuse. I've got to quit before they close the place."

There'd been some talk about shutting down the town's oldest high school—not enough students—but no one thought it would happen. The administrator had canceled all cafeteria orders and services for the next fall—just in case—and the school board was said to be split over the decision, the vote running four to four with one abstention. Russell had attended Scranton High in 1928, leaving its halls and his top grades behind when his father dropped dead delivering six quarts of milk to the Muncie's. The dairy offered Russell a position the first day of his father's wake, and he started the next Monday.

"All goodness dwells within your halls, the light of truth burns bright," Russell sang quietly, and Josh said, "More deja voo-doo. Sing it, Pop."

Russell saw himself, for an instant, on the school auditorium's stage at an honor society induction, Alice Gilroy and Mary Grace Murphy and Hannah McDonough, whom he subsequently married, all in ivory-lace dresses, hair bobbed and flapperlike. There were fourteen female inductees and four males. His mother and father both attended. The stage, built by Italian immigrants in 1910, was as elaborate as a movie house.

"And youthful hearts are set afire when they behold your gold and white," he said musingly. He finished packing an order for the hospital tea room.

"How about this—they gut the building's insides, put on a glass roof, build an atrium, and stick the elephant there?" said Josh. "I'd even help."

"I guess, as you'd say, it's history. The school is history," acknowledged Russell.

"Lucky for you, Pop," said Josh, heading for his truck, "I like history."

On his way home from work Russell drove by Scranton High. Freed by the lunch bell, kids were sprawled on the steps, hanging on to the doors, cluttering the sidewalks. A poster advertised the juniors' Spring Fling, a dance at which there'd be plenty of doughnuts. He pulled up to the curb and rolled down his window. A teacher eyed him suspiciously.

"Something wrong, sir?" she asked curtly. "Having a problem driving?"

"I graduated—I mean attended here," he said, to which she groaned the reply, "Not another one.

"There's no decent science lab in that building, no computer room," added the teacher.

"I'm sure that's true," said Russell, and he started up the engine.

"How many shrines do you people need?" the teacher called after him.

Josh and the new waitress, the one majoring in nutrition at the college, were in the owner's office, trying to convince him to install a yogurt machine. Josh thought the yogurt profits would take some of the pressure off the salesmen, who had their own routes; the waitress felt guilty about selling "unhealthy food."

"If that's the way you feel," said Mr. Raymond, "you don't have to sell it." The waitress persisted, saying that selling yogurt would give the customers more options. She left with her last check in hand. Josh, being the son of the owner's second cousin, didn't get off as easily.

"Your sales are down," said Mr. Raymond. "I want you to check out Syracuse. See if you can sell that university. Those kids have got to eat."

Russell had been at the door, waiting for some health forms, half listening to the arguments that Josh had previously rehearsed with him. The young man nearly knocked Russell over as he shot from the office, kicking a thigh-high bag of stale doughnuts Russell had just packed up for the pig lady.

"Josh," he called.

"Later, Pop."

Waiting for the owner to calm himself, Russell went out front and checked the soda machine. Then he put on a fresh pot of coffee and took out a packet of instant decaf. He made a cup for Mr. Raymond, put fifty cents in the till, and carried the coffee to the office.

"Yes, Russ," said Mr. Raymond, sighing.

Russell handed him the cup, pointed toward the health forms, and thanked his boss. About to leave, he turned back and said, "They're right."

"Who's right?" asked Mr. Raymond.

"The kids. The kids are right. People's tastes change. They like something new," replied Russell, the pain in his knees causing him to bend just a bit.

Mr. Raymond walked to the window that separated the back from the front. The heat from the fryers had produced enough humidity to fog the glass.

"Come here," he said, gesturing to a clearing. "Look out there."

Dutifully Russell put his head to the partition.

"Out there, nothing's changing. Same people, same bad teeth, eating the same doughnuts. See her—the woman in the corner, Margaret? She's weighed the same for thirty years—went to school with the lady. Eats six sugar doughnuts every weekday morning on her way to the pocketbook factory. Across the street is the car lot. Same lot's been there since before I bought the business. Behind the lot, the AAA. Behind that, the power station. Behind that, the culm dumps," Mr. Raymond said, a hint of disgust in his voice.

Russell pulled the newspaper article about the high school from his breast pocket. The owner dismissed it immediately.

"They've been closing that place for the last five years. Don't see it. Just don't see it," his boss added. The two men backed away and, to drive the conversation home, Mr. Raymond asked Russell, in a tone nearly as arrogant as Josh's could be, "How are your knees?"

Russell refused to give in. "Much better, Mr. R. Much improved."

For a short time, a very short time in the sixties, the zoo had a bear. The governor of Pennsylvania's cousin, a native of Scranton (she was born, quite accidentally, in the city hospital while her parents were en route from Binghamton to Harrisburg), dipped into her considerable trust fund and bought the city a bear. She did this on the condition it be named Teddy and reside in a cage just downhill from the zoo, a separate quarters that visitors could observe from above as well as from the front. This was considered a "natural" setting for the animal. The pit cost more than the critter. A "den" was drilled into the rock, a small moat constructed around the cage's edge, and a twelve-foot-high fence of iron spears whose points turned inward was made, so that if the bear ever climbed to the top, a near impossibility, given the moat, it would impale itself. The design was considered so innovative that there was talk among the city's fathers of constructing a second tier for the zoo, one in which all of the animals could enjoy greater freedom.

But the zoo's addition didn't get much traffic—bears were common, likely as not to amble across Lake Scranton Road or to end up in the back of a pickup truck, their jaunts cut short during hunting season. Russell saw the bear just once. That day it seemed to constantly clutch an inner tube to its chest, a vestige from its past at the St. Louis Zoo, where Teddy had been conceived and raised. Russell thought about going back for a visit, the animal seeming particulary forlorn, but he didn't get a chance.

The sole witness who saw the teenage mother—age fourteen, it was discovered later—drop her infant into the pit watched, helpless, as the bear caught, and then hugged, the tiny being to his body, the baby's cry silenced by that warm embrace. By the time help arrived and the mother had escaped, Teddy had pulled off an arm. After the accident, and the bear's subsequent destruction by lethal injection, the cage became the second-most-visited spot at the zoo. The governor's cousin never made the trip to see what the generosity of an outsider had wrought.

Twice on his way into work Russell had fallen, his knees refusing to carry his torso, the joints absenting themselves, momentarily, from their duty. His body seemed to be forgetting its job. Holding on to the dumpster parked at the back of the shop, Russell raised himself up, took a breather, and put in his shift without anyone the wiser. Leaving one afternoon, he lurched forward, into the corner of a packing table, slicing his arm but making it appear as if he'd tripped on a shoelace. Russell altered his path in and out of the building slightly, so that he was always in grabbing distance of some kind of support. Only Josh noticed, and he said nothing.

Instead Josh placed a stool alongside the packing table, hoping Russell would take advantage of it, at least in the early hours. The first three days the packer moved the stool out of the way, but on the fourth, at 5:15 A.M., right after the salesmen left, Russell used it. He found himself sitting at the table and reaching for a doughnut—a rare occurrence. Still warm from the fryer, the doughnut massaged his tastebuds and slid effortlessly down his throat, leaving a stream of sugar behind. Even on a bad day a doughnut tasted good.

During the past week he had found himself thinking about Tammy—was it Tammy, or Penny? Unable to sleep one night, he drove to the zoo at 12:30 A.M., parked his car in a lot one hundred feet from the main building, and walked in the dark toward the elephant. Russell drew close enough to hear Tammy banging away at the wall of her cage. Apparently she couldn't sleep, either. The words of the little girl who'd extolled the elephant's virtues came to him, "They can sense another elephant ten miles away." Sonar. Or radar, perhaps. That being the case, then certainly she knew that an old man stood outside her home. When she ceased the banging—it took him a few minutes to realize that she'd done so, the noise being so much a part of the dark—he put his hand flat against the door and bid her a good night.

The pictures, circa early 1950s, came from a flea market where Josh had just dropped a delivery. Black and white, the products of one of the early self-developing Polaroids, their edges were serrated and the background faded to a soft gray. He'd paid a dollar for six, all taken at the zoo. There was a crowd shot, and a photo of the monkeys clinging to the bars, a mother and baby looking on; two pictures of a lion at feeding time, its mate lying on a raised platform; one picture of six boys, all arms and legs, smirking at the camera, a hyena in the cage behind them; and a photograph of a group of kids lined up for an elephant ride, the compact pachyderm sporting a saddle and a headdress. Josh spread the photos on the packing table and asked Russell about the elephant. The man recognized Penny immediately and felt his stomach, not his knees, twist as his eye traveled over the young riders; in the middle of the group stood Russell's six-year-old son, neck crained toward the camera, his eyes half closed against the brightness of the day, the rest of his body hidden by the torsos of the children around him. His son Stephen, who died of polio not long after the town discovered Penny's body. Russell culled that photo from the rest and told Josh he would pay him for it.

"Was that Penny?" Josh asked. "Or Tiny—the second elephant? Can you tell?"

Russell placed the picture in his breast pocket and said, "Yes, I can tell."

When Josh left, his question unanswered, Russell took a paper napkin from the counter out front, folded it carefully around the picture, and then slid the small, soft package back into his pocket.

Josh was at Russell's house, leaning into the porch, when Russell pulled up. Sometimes youth seemed to just about ooze from Josh—his wavy hair damp, skin taut over those long bones, mouth in a permanent sneer, leg or hand going, keeping time with some inner rhythm. Russell and Josh were taking a ride to the zoo. A caller to the local radio talk show had described "A human chain, yes, a human chain," in front of Tammy's cage.

"Bet they got this idea from something on the TV," said Russell.

"It's like they're ecoguerrillas," said Josh. "In California they hug the trees that the loggers want to pull down."

The small entranceway was blocked with a dozen cars, horns blaring. Josh bounced in his seat with excitement, which was cut short by Russell's comment about the streamers on the hoods.

"It's a *wedding* party," Russell explained. "They come here to the park to take pictures."

The twosome backed up, parked the car, and sauntered along a neglected utility road that snaked around to the zoo, Josh pulling at the brush that grew in the path. He stuck a leafy branch in his shirt sleeves, contorted another into a crown, and formed a wreath for Russell, saying, "Camouflage, Pop." They made it to Tammy's in less than five minutes.

One of the two barbers present waved to Russell. Eight people stood before the cage, arms linked. From the erectness of their spines, an observer could see that most were unsettled by having to touch one another.

"Come," the barber said, "we're practicing for next week's demonstration. We have fifty people already signed up, and fourteen children from Mrs. Van Wee's preschool."

A reporter from the paper stood to the side, taking notes. Josh removed his leaves. "Just fooling around," he explained to the journalist.

Russell placed a hand on the bars and watched as Tammy stopped hitting her head and ambled toward him. He offered her the bag of doughnuts, which she plucked out one by one. When the bag was empty, she pushed it toward Russell.

"She doesn't look good," he said to the first barber. "She's favoring that one foot."

"She's perfect," said one of the human chains. "Our Tammy's perfect."

Josh was talking to the student nurse at the end of the chain, filling her in on the demonstration tactics of the tree people. "It

204

probably would be best," he said wryly, "if one of you would tie yourself to the elephant."

Russell, who heard the remark, called to him, the brusqueness of his tone betraying his anger.

"Work," he called. "You and I have work." They left together, but Josh declined the ride home and walked to the shop instead.

Nearly a block beyond the high school (whose closing had been delayed for a year due to "logistical problems" in getting the students bussed elsewhere), Russell spied the cardboard fort with tiny sneakered feet and rimless glasses making its way to the dirt playground. Skinny arms lifted the structure over its head, pushed it to a spot marked with stones, and picked up the book *How to Build Your Own Playground Using Recycled Materials*. Russell struggled out of the truck and asked the little girl if she needed help. A half dozen other children, all older and larger, were gathered around her.

"We're creating a pro-to-type," announced the same little miss whom he'd recognized from the zoo. She began reading aloud chapter three of the book.

"She's relentless," said the child's father, who was resting behind a pile of scrap lumber. "Thanks for the offer. The other parents will be here soon. She got the idea from a newspaper article and the kids in the neighborhood signed us up."

Russell waited for the girl to stop reading, then pulled on her long brown braid. "Young lady," he said. "Keep it up. Someday, when you're older, you'll go far."

"I'm not going anywhere," she said, her head poking at the sky. "I'm going to stay right here."

The demonstration slated for the following week was canceled due to rain, although Mrs. Van Wee's preschoolers did show up and sing a medley of elephant songs. The animal rights people had backed off, abandoning Tammy for a cause in upstate New York involving lab animals. Russell was in the hospital, recovering from surgery on his right knee. He and Josh hadn't spoken in ten days.

Two days before he was due to return to work, Russell had a

visit from Josh. Josh walked into Russell's apartment along with the visiting nurse, Josh claiming to be Russell's nephew. In a shopping bag he carried a machine that turned your tub into a miniwhirlpool and two dozen doughnuts, one of which he handed to the nurse. Alongside the bed sat a large and ugly palm plant, stuck in a straw hat with a card from the waitresses at the shop. The nurse went into the kitchen to have a doughnut.

Russell was in an overstuffed chair, doing some exercise where he bent and lifted his knee fifty times. He threw a pillow at Josh, who caught it.

"Mr. Raymond said you were on vacation. I got the real story out of Doreen and Marie," Josh explained.

"I *am* on vacation," said Russell. "Thank God it's nearly over."

The young man hugged Russell's shoulders and rubbed his knuckles over Russell's head. Josh pulled out the water machine, read the directions in the voice of a game host, livening up the room, and offered to set it up. Russell said he'd leave that to the nurse.

"I've got a plan," said Josh, pulling two rubber elephant noses from his pants pocket, and Russell replied, "Me too."

They met at 2:00 A.M., as planned, at the shop. Josh had a sack of tools and two pairs of gloves, a cake of Valium he'd made by crushing a bottleful of pills and stirring the powder into a cupcake mix, which he later baked—and a portable camp light. He also had a pair of ski masks, which Russell snatched from the sack and left behind.

They parked on a side street, two blocks from the park's back entrance. Josh marveled at the constellations and spotted two shooting stars in the August night.

"Awesome," he whispered. "Never saw any of those in New York."

Russell led the way. He had wrapped his knees ahead of time and the bandages swished against his pants as he walked. But this made less noise than Josh stumbling behind him.

"Walk in my path," said Russell, kicking a stone.

Five hundred feet from the utility road Russell plucked a branch of mountain laurel, which still grew in abundance. The two men paused long enough to identify, with the help of a penlight, some rustling in the brush—a possum scurrying down the embankment.

Josh had the zoo's double doors opened immediately. The frames were so worn that they parted easily when he pressed the crowbar between them. There was a ceiling light with a dirty string that illuminated the twenty paces to Tammy's cage—Josh wanted to use a flashlight but Russell insisted that Tammy would find the overhead light more familiar. The two argued briefly over the Valium.

"They told me it was for her own good, to keep her calm," pleaded Josh. "She'll think it's a doughnut."

"No, she won't," said Russell. "She'll know."

A second door, leading to the corridor behind the cages, also had a lock, which Josh picked at while Russell went to speak with Tammy.

"It's OK now, it's OK," he soothed, a doughnut at the end of his hand, the cake pushed to the side. "Here you are. You up to a walk?"

"Bingo," said Josh. "I got it." Flipping on his flashlight, he hurried down the corridor toward Tammy's quarters. The backs of the cages, some kind of metal sheets, had individual bolts and locks. He could hear Russell speaking gently to the elephant and Tammy breathing heavily. Throwing his weight into the motion, Josh slid one of the locks open. The two bolts at the bottom gave way easily. A steel bar was stretched across the back of the cage. A set of keys hung from a hook on the opposite wall, right beside a metal prodder. Josh could feel the vibrations from the head bashing, which Tammy had begun once again.

The idea was to get her into the yard (seldom used now) and from there, using a leash, lead her out of the park.

"Tammy, please," Russell was saying. "Tammy."

Josh ran around to the front to join him, the keys to the yard gates in his hand. It was already 3:15 and he was beginning to panic. "Plenty of time," said Russell. "We've got plenty of time."

Russell took Josh outside to suck in the night air and watched as his partner climbed to the zoo's one-story roof and then jumped down into the yard. Josh swung the outer doors wide open—and returned to the corridor to unlock the door that kept Tammy from the outside world.

"You ready, Pop?" he asked, and Russell took his post inside.

Looking down at the row of vacant cells, Russell found himself wishing they were filled. Yes, it was an old, deserted, stink-infested zoo, obsolete before it was built, but it had been theirs. Josh shuffled about in the corridor, listening for a response. Russell could not move. Russell wanted to believe that this zoo was better than nothing.

"Pop," Josh cried, "Pop—you there? What's happening?"

The words came to Russell, as did the picture of his son, Stephen, and the scene at the doughnut shop with the mayor's men, the moment when he had been younger and afraid. Tammy turned toward the packer and rubbed her skin on the wall. She blew some waste from her trunk.

"It's still nice," he said to the elephant. "Isn't it? It's still home."

Leaving the building, Russell headed back toward the car. Josh yelled for Russell to get moving, his voice high and frightened and arrogant. He had scrambled into the yard and had opened the doors himself.

"You should see her in the open, Pop, under the stars," Josh was saying, calm now. "She's beautiful. She's waiting here for you."

The three took the route past the abandoned bear cage, down to the bottom of the hill where the truck was waiting. Russell had secured the leash to a worn collar, though he didn't need it— Tammy was just behind him, tame as a family retriever. Josh, who'd run ahead to speak with the animal rights people, handed over the Valium cake in case Tammy grew anxious during her journey. Stroking her great head, the skin nearly as calloused and gray as his own, Russell pulled the sprig of mountain laurel from his pocket and, wondering what the elephant would remember of this time and place, laced the flower around her collar.

Epilogue

A just-baked yeast doughnut is good eating on its own, but most customers prefer a honey dipping, or a sugary glaze that melts in the mouth, leaving a sweet aftertaste. The folks who prefer plain tend to be rare; you'll remember Audrey Voxe had affection for these, as did Russell Myles. If the doughnut's to be iced or filled the waitress—Terri Kudja's probably the one doing the processing—the waitress needs to take care; too much jelly and the shell will burst, leaving the customers with sticky fingers and the strong desire to wash their hands.

Icing can be applied quickly and carefully, a coat of vanilla, chocolate, lemon, or apple cinnamon. Not so much that it kills the flavor of the doughnut—just enough to enhance the experience. The effect should be satisfying, like you've finished up something worth the effort. Enough said.